By SARIA BRYANT

ELEMENTAL THRONES
Shadow's Wound

UNDERWORLD MAGES
Mage's Marines

TOUCH OF LEATHER
If You Let Me

Published by DREAMSPINNER PRESS
www.dreamspinnerpress.com

SARIA BRYANT

MAGE'S MARINES

Published by
DREAMSPINNER PRESS

8219 Woodville Hwy #1245
Woodville, FL 32362 USA
www.dreamspinnerpress.com

Mage's Marines
© 2025 Saria Bryant

Cover Art
© 2025 Andrei Bat
https://99designs.com/profiles/bandrei
Cover content is for illustrative purposes only and any person depicted on the cover is a model.

Trade Paperback ISBN: 978-1-64108-810-7
Digital ISBN: 978-1-64108-809-1
Trade Paperback published April 2025
v. 1.0

To those with terrible sperm donors.

CHAPTER 1

MAX CRASHED to the floor, his vision swimming from the pistol cracking against his temple. The boot to his ribs was completely unnecessary; he was already caught. As he choked on air and the taste of blood, he forced himself upright. It wouldn't keep more punishment from raining down on him, but he'd be damned if he gave his father the satisfaction of seeing him writhe on the floor.

He swayed to the side, swallowing against the twisting of his stomach as the room spun out and away from him. He was intimately familiar with the signs of a potential concussion, but that was the least of his problems right now.

When he could finally focus, he recognized the dining room. Not the small one the family used. This was the big one, meant to impress and intimidate, which meant when he'd been dragged in here, he'd interrupted a business meeting.

A borderline hysterical laugh bubbled up in his chest, and he pressed his hand to his mouth to keep silent, focusing on the pain of his broken fingers to steady himself.

Blood trickled into his eye as he blinked at his father, who was staring at Max with familiar disappointment and loathing from the head of the table. He knew better than to look away, but he couldn't help it as his gaze slipped sideways, black and bright spots fighting for territory in his vision.

When he focused again, he was staring at a strange man sitting near his father, a bodyguard standing behind him. Handsome enough that even through the fog and muffled panic filling his mind, Max noticed the storm-cloud-gray eyes, strong, scruff-covered jaw, and black, silver-touched hair long enough to run his fingers through.

That was all the confirmation he needed. He was delirious.

The laughter tried to escape again, but when Jake stalked into the room from behind him and bowed to his father, Max's blood went cold.

"Your son, as promised," Jake said, his lips twisting into a sneer as he glanced at Max.

"No," Max whispered, refusing to believe it. But how else had they caught him so quickly? He'd planned for *months* to ensure he got away clean. He'd learned plenty of lessons from his previous attempts. Everything had been perfect. He just had to get to the airport and he could disappear into Asia, where his father had no power and no contacts.

Jake was the one person he trusted enough to tell his plans to, who had promised to drive Max's car as a decoy while Max took his motorcycle for the extra speed and maneuverability.

Max had even paid him a few thousand dollars for the trouble.

His father gestured to one of his men, and Jake turned, obviously expecting some reward. "Your services are appreciated. Your betrayal to my blood is not."

Jake realized too late his mistake. "Wait," he said, but that was all he got out. He wasn't nearly fast enough to dodge the bullet.

Max flinched from the sharp, muffled sound of the silenced gun, unable to look away as Jake's body slumped towards the floor, before it was dragged away by his father's men. He should have felt remorse or revulsion, but that was hardly the first corpse he'd seen, and even the sting of betrayal barely registered against the dozen stabbing and pulsing pains in his body.

His father sighed, an exaggerated sound Max knew was meant for him. "I warned you last time I would not tolerate this nonsense again, Max."

Nonsense. Like him wanting his own life, away from the violence and blood his father traded in, away from the suffocating control that took away his choices of when and what to eat, when to sleep, when to piss, was nonsense.

"I'm sorry, Father," he said, the words slipping out before he could stop them, much less control the thick sarcasm that came with them. "I really thought this would be the last time."

Fury and disgust twisted the man's face before he straightened. "You are no longer my son. I should have disowned you the moment I learned you were a *twink*."

Max couldn't help it. The hysterical laughter escaped. Never in his life did he ever think he would hear that word from the homophobic asshole's mouth. The man had made no secret of despising Max's *proclivities*. Not since the day Max made the mistake of telling his mother that he found a boy cute when he was five.

His life had been a waking nightmare ever since.

The punch to the back of his head to shut him up wasn't at all surprising. He nearly went to the floor again, but somehow stayed on his knees. "Dis'n me then," he slurred, spitting blood and hoping it stained the flawless wooden floor. "Or fuc'n kill me. I don't... care anymore." Death would be preferable to one more day in this hellhole.

He listed to the side as his vision wavered and went black.

CHAPTER 2

CAIUS WATCHED the young man slump to the floor with a mix of shock and dismay. Instincts shouted at him to get a medic as the scent of blood filled his nose, but common sense stayed his hand. He was no longer an acting colonel. Technically, he was a civilian now, and sitting in a mafia boss' home wasn't exactly the best place to reveal that he had connections to the armed forces.

He didn't even want to be here, but as he intended to permanently move to Denver, and under shifter law he was technically alpha of a pack of three, he was required to make his presence known to any powers in play, including the underworld.

The last thing he'd expected walking into this meeting was to see Savino order his own son beaten and then murder someone.

He could smell Quinn's anxiety and rage behind him, but he trusted Quinn not to interfere. As much as they both might loathe the situation, they didn't have any power here, much less authority.

Still, when Savino motioned for one of his men, who pulled out a gun and aimed it at the unconscious man, Caius couldn't stop himself from clearing his throat.

"If I may," he drawled, sipping the tea he'd been given as Savino eyed him. "If you intend to kill him, perhaps you'll let me take him off your hands instead." He felt Quinn's eyes boring into the back of his head, but he knew he didn't need to explain. They'd both seen far too many innocents die at the hands of those in power, and if he could finally save one, he'd do it. Not that he could prove the young man was innocent, but he'd put money on him being more upstanding than his father.

Savino made no effort to hide his distaste when he eyed Caius. "You ask me for my own son?"

Caius smiled faintly and set his tea down. "As you've just disowned him, I believe he belongs to no one, yes?"

He considered pressing further, but the sudden Spark of magic in the room made his breath catch. There was a mage here? Not just any

"I'd like to ensure the Order doesn't force his hand."

With a soft swear and a wince, the healer shook her head. "He wouldn't survive them," she murmured. "But it'll cost extra."

"That's fine. Just get him back on his feet."

Convinced Max would make a full recovery, he left her to it and stepped out of the room, finding Quinn slouched in a chair with his phone. Caius stretched his senses past the doors, confirming no other mages were in the vicinity, before sinking into a chair next to Quinn. Since they'd rushed from Savino's place, he hadn't had the chance to confirm if Quinn had managed his part of the job.

He might have been required to make his pack's presence known, but he wouldn't pass up an opportunity to keep an eye on a criminal. "Did you get in?"

Quinn tipped his head back with a grin. "Of course," he said. "Their security was a joke. Whatever plans they make, we'll be able to see."

Caius nodded, some of his tension easing. He may have gone in with the vague intention of keeping an eye on Savino's operation for when and if Caius built a pack strong enough to challenge him, but for now, he was only interested in making sure Savino didn't have regrets about selling his son. Or at least not acting on them if he did.

"What are you going to tell Lukas?"

Caius let his head fall back with a groan, tempted to bash it into the wall. Lukas had served with him almost as long as Quinn, but he doubted the sniper would be happy to hear he'd swindled a mafia boss' son from him. Though he hoped the fact that the son was also a mage would be enough to appease him. He doubted it, but he could hope. "The truth, obviously," he said on a sigh.

Quinn laughed. "Good luck. Put him on speaker when you do. I wanna hear."

That wasn't going to happen. Considering Lukas was still dark from whatever mission he'd been sent on, Caius likely wouldn't get a chance to speak with him until he returned home. For now, he was more concerned with getting Max healed and settled so they could bind him before anyone else realized what he was.

CHAPTER 3

MAX FOUGHT the familiar haze of drugs in his system until he could open his eyes. The room was bright with light, so he hoped he hadn't lost too much time, but the lack of pain beneath the cottony fog wrapped around his body shattered that hope. With a groan, he rolled his head to the side, blinking at the unfamiliar nightstand and clock telling him it was late afternoon.

There was a glass of water there, and he immediately fumbled for it. His fingers wrapped around it, sliding in the condensation. When he tried to lift it, the glass slipped free, clattering to the nightstand before toppling to the floor. *No.* He rolled over, trying to catch it even though he knew it was too late, a sob of frustration threatening to make him hyperventilate.

"Hey, hey, whoa."

Max flinched from the unfamiliar voice, flopping on the bed and nearly following the glass to the floor before hands caught him and eased him back.

"Hey, easy, you're safe. I'll get you a fresh glass."

He squinted blearily at the stranger, at the deep red hair he was sure was dyed and the bright hazel eyes beneath. The grin was strange. He couldn't remember the last time someone had directed anything more than a leer at him.

Before he could ask where he was, the man was gone, disappearing out a door and thundering down a set of stairs.

Max stared at the door a moment before sitting up, grunting as he collapsed against the headboard to catch his breath. His body ached, but he was sure he didn't have a concussion despite the lingering tenderness on the side of his head, and his ribs didn't feel cracked. When he looked at his hand, his last two fingers were taped together, but he could move them, and they definitely weren't broken anymore. He knew he hadn't imagined the sharp pain of them breaking beneath a bootheel or three, and he highly doubted any doctor would put him in a medical coma for some broken bones. The only way he could have healed this quickly was with magic, but that was as unlikely as a coma for the same reason. Mage healers tended to be expensive.

What the hell happened? And where was he?

He'd fully expected his father to kill him. That's what the bastard had wanted ever since Max failed the year of conversion therapy he'd been forced through. Most likely even before then. He knew he should have at least pretended, but he couldn't give up the sick twist of satisfaction every time he pissed his father off by the simple act of existing.

He knew how fucked-up that was, but he blamed it one-hundred-percent on his family.

Footsteps on the stairs drew his attention back to the door, but instead of the redhead, the man with salt-and-pepper hair he'd glimpsed at his father's table stepped into the room. And damn, he was even more attractive without the concussion muddling everything.

"Am I your hostage?" he asked, because that was the only sensible conclusion. This man had kidnapped him right from under his father. Or bought him. Honestly, that sounded more likely, all things considered.

The man paused, studying him with a frown before offering a glass of water. "Not exactly."

"Shame," he said, blaming the drugs for his absolute lack of a filter. And the fact he wasn't freaking out. Maybe he did have a concussion. Or he'd reached the limit of fucks he could give. Either way, he took the glass and sipped the cool water, hiding his smug amusement at the perturbed expression on the man's face. If there was one thing he'd learned well, it was to make everyone else more uneasy than he was. Especially kidnappers.

The man cleared his throat, retrieved a chair from a desk across the room, placed it beside the bed, and sat. "My name is Caius Ward. I bought you from your father when he was going to kill you."

"Gee, thanks," he said, not bothering to tone down the sarcasm. "I'd *so* much rather be a sex slave than dead." Nice fantasy, maybe, but not so much something he wanted to *actually* experience.

"You're not a sex slave." Caius eyed him like he wasn't sure whether Max was joking.

Which was fair; Max wasn't quite sure himself. His head was a little fuzzy, and his entire body felt hot and tight like he was feverish. "Then why did you bring me here?"

"Why don't you tell me why you were running?"

Max returned the narrow-eyed look and sipped more water, wishing it had ice and lemon in it, but he knew how useful wishing was. Caius didn't strike him as a mob boss. He'd met plenty of goons and crime lords, and most had a sleazy edge to them. Maybe it was the jeans and sweater rather than an expensive, ill-fitting suit, but Caius looked like someone respectable.

Not that Max could trust his instincts. He'd trusted Jake, after all. The fact that Jake was one of the few people he'd fooled around with made that lapse of judgment *so* much worse.

But if Caius had really bought him, and even spent the money on an actual mage healer, he probably wouldn't kill Max. He still wasn't convinced this wasn't some kind of sex slave thing, but at least he had one advantage here when he finally made his escape: Caius knew absolutely nothing about him or where he'd go when he made a run for it.

"I overheard my father planning an arranged marriage," he finally said. He expected some kind of ridicule, but Caius tilted his head and kept silent. "To Dr. Rena Schurz. She's the head scientist at *Magierseele*." Magesoul, the largest entity dedicated to all things magical aside from the Order itself. Despite the fact few mages actually worked there, they offered new products several times a year.

"I looked her up, thinking maybe I could convince her to help me get away from here." Max slid his thumb through the condensation on his glass. "All the rumors I found made her sound like some mad scientist from Nazi Germany. Human experiments, genetics and shit. Her grandmother was supposedly doing it too, during the war. Helga something. There's no proof, but I'm pretty sure she's on the government payroll."

"Wouldn't be surprised," Caius murmured.

Max jerked his head up. "You don't think I'm crazy?"

"I'm undecided. But the government has always been interested in enhancing humans, even before the forties. There's rumors the military managed to make their own mages, but all the documents are sealed."

"And you know this how?"

"Up until a few months ago, I was a colonel in the Marines."

At least his instincts were right about the respectable thing. Unless Caius had been court-martialed or something. "Uh-huh. And what could a colonel possibly want with a mob boss' son?"

Caius tilted his head, tapping his thumb against his knee as if choosing his words. Max was about to tell him to spit it out when Caius said, "You're a mage."

Max laughed. "Okay, Hagrid." When Caius looked at him in confusion, Max rolled his eyes. "Too old for Harry Potter, got it," he muttered. "Look, I don't know who told you I was a mage, but I'm not. I certainly never Sparked as a kid." He would have burned down his father's house before making his first escape attempt if he had.

"You Sparked after you passed out."

Max shook his head. No way in hell had he Sparked. He'd know if he was a mage. He sipped his water again, grimacing at the too warm temperature. Seriously, would it have killed them to give him some ice? He set the glass on the nightstand and tossed back part of the blanket, sighing in relief at the cool air.

"Sorry you wasted your money, but I'm not a mage. But you can make the kidnapping up to me by getting me a one-way ticket to Japan." He paused as he realized he was dressed in only a pair of boxers and a loose T-shirt that wasn't his. "Where the fuck are my clothes?"

"They were filthy and covered in blood."

Max looked up in time to see Caius give him a slow once-over, which should have been a red flag, but there was no leer that usually followed. He started to pull the covers back over himself, but it was too hot for that. "Why is it a hundred degrees in here?" He threw the covers off completely and swung his legs over the edge of the bed. Dizziness swept over him, and the next thing he knew, he was pressed against Caius' chest and floating through the air, only to land in a bathtub with cold water raining down on him.

He slumped with a soft groan of relief, but it was short-lived. The scent of smoke caught his attention enough he looked at his hands and froze. Tiny bright orange flames danced around his fingers, sizzling and hissing as the water hit them before flickering back to life. "What the fuck." This wasn't real. He shook his hands out, but the flames clung to him as if glued there.

No. No, no, nonono. This couldn't be real. He was twenty-two years old. Mages always Sparked by fifteen at the latest. There was no way in hell he was a mage.

Before Max could start hyperventilating, Caius gripped the back of his neck and shoved him forward until his head was between his knees.

"Fuck," Max gasped, coughing as he forced a deep breath into his lungs. "*Fuck*."

"Believe it now?"

"No." If he closed his eyes and pretended really hard, he could wake up from this, right? Because if his father found out he was a mage, even running to Japan wouldn't save him. "This can't be happening to me." As if his life wasn't enough of a nightmare.

"You need to come to terms with this soon. I can only hide you from the Order for so long."

Max groaned and squeezed his eyes shut until he saw sparks of color. He had to run before the Order found him. They tracked down every mage within days of their Spark and whisked them off to be trained in their magical army. "Bet you'll make your money back when they get here."

Caius removed his hand from Max's neck and shut off the water. "I don't intend to let the Order take you. I'd rather bind you to me and my pack."

Max blinked water out of his eyes and flexed his fingers; the flames had died out for the moment. "Of course you would," he muttered. That was the biggest pitfall of being a mage. Everyone wanted to bind them.

It took a moment for the rest of that to sink in. "Wait. Your pack?" Fuck. Caius was a shifter? He should have known. How else would Caius have known he'd Sparked? That wasn't something normal humans could sense unless the magic went out of control. He pressed his hands against his face with a hysterical laugh. This day was a shit sundae, and the ice cream machine had diarrhea.

"Max," Caius said, "look at me."

Max ignored him and hunched over his knees again. He couldn't do this. He might not know much about mages or shifters aside from what he'd seen in the media and the news, but even he knew all mages were wary of shifters. It was a popular trope in movies. A shifter coerced a mage to accept a binding, which forced them to do the shifter's bidding, and used them until either the mage grew powerful enough to break the bond or the shifter fell in love and released them.

Considering his shit luck in life so far, he doubted either of those were in his future.

"Max." This time, Caius' voice was sharp.

Max flinched, bracing himself for a blow as he was pulled to his feet. "Quinn!"

Panic clawed up his throat, but he knew better than to fight. He was already caught. That had never stopped him before, but he knew at least his father's men would never kill him without a direct order. He had no idea what Caius intended to do with him, other than bind him. And likely turn him into a sex slave.

He had to escape before that happened, but he had to get through the damn panic attack first, and whatever punishment they intended to deal out. He squeezed his eyes shut again, focusing on the chill from the water clinging to him and on not hyperventilating.

"The fuck did you do?"

"Nothing," Caius said, sounding defensive.

"The hell you didn't, he smells terrified. Get out."

A pathetic whimper escaped Max when arms wrapped around him. A warm scent of cinnamon filled his nose, and he carefully blinked his eyes open when no attack came.

"You're okay, Max. You're safe."

That wasn't Caius. It sounded like the redhead. Max raised his arms to push away, but they found their way around the stranger instead.

"I'm Quinn, by the way. Kinda wish we were meeting under better circumstances. But I have a brilliant idea, if you wanna hear." There was a hint of a lilting accent to his voice, but Max couldn't focus enough to place it.

Max fought for two controlled breaths before he got his voice to work. "Sure."

Quinn propped his chin on top of Max's head. "Why don't you take a shower and clean up any blood we missed while I find you some clean clothes, and then when you're ready, I can make you some food? Be warned, I can only make eggs and bacon or a killer grilled cheese sandwich."

His stomach rumbled and let them both know what it thought of that idea. "Okay."

"Great," Quinn said brightly.

Max expected Quinn to release him, but he didn't, and it felt too nice for Max to move first. Several long moments ticked by before the awkwardness finally won out and he forced himself to let go.

Quinn smiled and stepped back. "You can toss your wet clothes in the sink. I'll be in the kitchen when you're done." He closed the door behind him, leaving Max standing alone in the bathtub like a drowned rat.

What the fuck was his life? This had to be a lucid dream, but pinching himself didn't accomplish anything but a bruise.

With a sigh, he peeled off the wet shirt and boxers and tossed them in the sink. He really wanted a hot shower, but the thought of his entire body catching fire was enough he set the water to lukewarm instead. Then he stood there, fighting the haze of shock and post-panic as he wondered what he was supposed to do.

He couldn't possibly believe he was safe here, but… they'd healed his injuries. Even his father had never wasted the money for a mage to heal him before. If Caius intended to bind Max for his powers, he'd at least want Max alive. Which was more than his father apparently wanted.

It wasn't much, but he could work with that.

The water went cold before he felt like himself again, but losing time was familiar enough to ignore. He found the clothes waiting for him and dressed in another too-large shirt and sweats, pulling the drawstrings tight.

He'd left his phone behind in the hopes he wouldn't be tracked on his way to the airport, but his keys and wallet were on the nightstand. He shoved them in his pocket before he stopped near the bedroom door.

He could do this. He could figure out how to deal with being a mage. How to keep these shifters from binding him. How to keep the Order from getting hold of him.

He was so utterly fucked.

He let out a slow breath and descended the stairs, then lingered at the bottom as he breathed in the scent of cooking garlic. His stomach rumbled again, reminding him he hadn't eaten in over a day.

"In here," Quinn called.

With another breath, he forced one foot in front of the other as he followed the voice to the kitchen. There were no walls dividing the kitchen from the rest of the floor, and he could see out of the floor-to-ceiling windows. A rare, unobstructed view of the foothills stretched beyond the backyard, so different from his view of city buildings and the claustrophobic feeling of his own home. His feet itched to run into the forest and disappear despite the dusting of snow on the ground.

"Hungry?" Quinn patted the spot at the island counter next to Caius.

Max carefully sank into the chair, eyeing the half-eaten sandwich on Caius' plate. It oozed melted cheese with what looked like avocado, tomato, and bacon.

Quinn grabbed a can of Dr Pepper from the fridge and set it in front of Max.

He hesitated a moment before nudging it away with his fingertips. "Can I have a water?"

Quinn gasped and snatched the can, cradling it to his chest. "You decline the nectar of the gods?" he asked, shooting Caius a dirty look when he snickered. "Neither of you are worthy," he sniffed.

Max tensed as he waited for Caius' reaction to that lack of respect, but Caius ignored them both in favor of checking his phone.

Quinn traded the can for a glass of ice water. "So, grilled cheese or breakfast? Or we have, like, fifty takeout menus you can browse through."

Max grimaced, his stomach twisting at the thought of greasy food. "Eggs and toast?"

"No bacon?" Quinn turned back to the fridge for the carton of eggs.

"I don't eat pork."

"Aren't you Italian?"

Max rolled his eyes, ready for any number of jokes or derogatory comments, but Quinn only chuckled.

"Cheese and avocado for your eggs?"

"Yes, please." He sipped his water and watched as Quinn cracked eight eggs into a bowl and popped four slices of bread into the toaster. "I can't eat all that."

Quinn waved a hand at him. "Eat what you can. One of us will finish the rest."

Max sipped his water rather than argue. "Sorry for freaking out earlier." He was still freaking out a little, but the last several years had been one constant low-grade panic attack, so that was nothing new.

Caius glanced up from his phone and set it aside. "Freaking out is understandable. Your entire life has been upended."

"Yeah, you've basically gone from one shit existence to another," Quinn said dryly.

Caius shot a dark look at his back. "He means being a mage, not being brought here."

Quinn glanced over his shoulder with a frown. "Obviously," he said, sounding offended.

Max eyed them both, unable to figure out the dynamic between them. Caius spoke like he was the head of the pack, but Quinn didn't seem overly concerned about pissing him off. His father had disposed of people for any lack of respect. He'd always wondered how his father retained any loyalty. Fear could only control people for so long. He'd imagined killing his father so many times that sometimes they felt like real memories instead of only dreams.

Only now that he'd finally gotten free, he was at the mercy of a pack of shifters.

"I don't really have a choice in any of this, do I?" He sat back as Quinn set a plate in front of him, piled high with scrambled eggs, cheese, and avocado, surrounded by buttered toast. "I had a ticket to Japan. I could change it for the next flight out." Even as he said it, his brief flare of hope fizzled out. He was a *mage* now, and if there was one thing he knew was true of mages, it was that they always ended up bound to someone one way or another.

"Even if we wanted to put you on a plane, you wouldn't get far," Quinn said, and Max almost believed his apologetic tone was genuine. "The Order has to know you exist by now, and they'll narrow down where to find you soon."

"How? Denver is huge."

"They put nets over the bigger cities. Like a magical sonar. A new mage Sparks and they know when and where almost instantly." Quinn pulled a jar of strawberry jam from the fridge and set it beside Max's plate. "Even if the plane took off before they get here, they'd be waiting for you when you landed."

Max stared at the pile of food, silently seething and blinking the burn from his eyes, breathing through the tight knot of helpless frustration in his chest. He might have been used to it, but it was worse now. He'd technically escaped his father, but he was still trapped.

He picked up a fork and scooped some jam onto a piece of toast even though he'd lost his appetite. "So either the Order takes me, or I let you bind me." He didn't miss the quick look Quinn and Caius shared, but he pretended not to notice. Feigning ignorance was one of his best honed skills.

"How old are you?" Quinn asked.

"Twenty-two."

Max made a face and shrugged. "Technically they could."

"But?"

"But they usually prefer getting their hands on mages as young as possible."

"The new laws prevent them from taking anyone younger than ten," Caius added. "Mages are usually required to train until sixteen, then serve eight years in the field. Most are supposed to be free by twenty-four."

Quinn nodded. "There's a chance they won't want to deal with training an adult."

"But," Caius interjected, "it would be easier to convince them to let you be if we bound you first."

And having the power of a mage behind them wouldn't hurt Caius' pack either, but Max kept that thought to himself. At least if they needed him, they might be more willing to let him have some kind of a life. Not that he planned on sticking around unless he had to.

Caius picked up his phone when it chimed. "Lukas landed and is already on the way," he said. "He should be here in a few minutes."

Quinn snorted. "And you still haven't told him, have you." He rolled his eyes at whatever look Caius gave him. "Awesome," he added with enough sarcasm to season Max's eggs. A man after Max's own heart. "This'll be *so* fun." He pushed away from the counter, turned back to the fridge, and pulled out stuff for another grilled cheese. The brief glimpse Max got of the inside was almost depressing—beer bottles, bacon, and cheese. Other than some avocados, there were no fresh fruits or veggies as far as he could see.

Just how big was this pack? Max poked at his eggs before taking a bite, forcing himself to eat and not freak out at the idea of another shifter showing up.

He couldn't trust them, could he? They'd probably say anything to keep him here. Surely the Order wasn't *that* prepared or determined that they'd follow him all the way to Japan. As far as he knew, Japan wasn't under the Order's thumb. At least, not as much as the Americas and Europe. Japan had their own government magic institute, though he knew next to nothing about it, other than it served as a loophole for them to have their own standing army without violating their treaty with the US, since mages technically weren't considered a militaristic power.

He ate slowly as he weighed his options. If he was going to risk running, he had to do it before they bound him. He was in borrowed clothes, didn't have much money on him, and he had no idea where his bike or car were. He doubted he had enough cash for a taxi to the airport, but he could run until he was far enough away to find a ride.

Not much of a plan, but it would have to do. He might be able to slip away later if he only had to get past Quinn and Caius, but every new shifter who showed up decreased his chances of getting away.

He shoved the last bite of a piece of toast in his mouth and pushed the plate to the side, half the eggs and toast still on it. "Thanks for the food," he said, getting to his feet and heading towards the stairs. He spotted what had to be the front door on his way and didn't think twice about racing for it.

He heard Quinn's surprised shout from the kitchen and cursed, adrenaline forcing him to move faster. He was a few steps from the door when it swung open. He barely got a glimpse of a tall, dark-haired man in fatigues with a large duffel before he was face down on the ground, a knee in his lower back and a gun pressed between his shoulders.

He snarled and thrashed against the pinning hold, but he was lacking at least a hundred pounds of muscle to be able to budge the man.

"Who the fuck are you?"

"Let him go," Caius ordered.

There was only a moment of hesitation before the weight and gun vanished; then Caius offered Max a hand and pulled him to his feet.

Max eyed the open door with a yearning so sharp it hurt.

"Max," Caius said, turning him with a hand on his shoulder. "You are not a prisoner here."

"Sure," Max scoffed, tearing his eyes away from the door.

Caius sighed but kept his hand on Max's shoulder. "Lukas, this is Max, a mage who Sparked yesterday. Max, this is the third member of my pack, Lukas."

Max looked up and found amber eyes focused on him with an unsettling intensity. It was similar enough to how Maurice would watch him when his father wasn't around that he took a step back, bristling when he hit Caius' chest.

Lukas blinked and holstered his gun, his expression blanking as he grabbed his dropped duffel. "Nice to meet you," he said, before nodding to Caius and stepping past them, disappearing down the hall.

Caius squeezed Max's shoulder before closing the door. "If you run and the Order finds you, we won't be able to protect you. Whether they'd train you or force you to serve, I don't know, but I'm certain they would bind your magic to them." He grasped Max's shoulder again. "I won't lie. Having a mage bound to us would help solidify our standing in the city, but you wouldn't be trapped in a prison. You would be pack." With that, he released Max and headed down the hall after Lukas.

Max watched him go before looking at Quinn where he'd propped his shoulder against the wall with his arms crossed.

"Can't blame you for trying to run," Quinn said after a moment. "If you really want to leave, I'm sure Cap will help, but as soon as word gets out about you, you'll be on the run forever. Even if you got out of the country, you'd have to be a citizen for any guarantee of protection."

Max scrubbed at his face, masking his sob of frustration with a snarl. "This isn't fair." What the fuck had he done to deserve this? If he was a mage, why hadn't he Sparked as a kid?

He startled when Quinn pulled him into a hug but gratefully let the other man take his weight.

"It's not," Quinn agreed. "And I know you can't trust us, but Cap will protect you if you give him the chance. We all will." Quinn shifted his hold and tugged Max to the couch, pulling him down to sit. "For now, why don't you give me a list of things you need? I don't mind sharing my clothes, but they're a little too big, and they don't suit you at all."

Max let out a watery laugh and slumped into his side. Quinn seemed nice. Nice enough that Max wouldn't mind getting to know him better. Of all the people his father could have sold him to, Max could certainly have ended up somewhere far worse. Like in a lab being experimented on.

"I could use access to a computer," he murmured. If he was going to be stuck here for more than a few weeks, he should at least finish his semester. "I have online courses to finish for my graphic design degree." He'd scheduled all his finals on the same day, which would suck, but he hadn't been planning on taking them. He'd been ready to walk away from it all in order to get free.

Fat chance of that now.

When Quinn squeezed his shoulders, he sank further into the couch and Quinn's side. "And some fruit would be nice."

CHAPTER 4

FAR, FAR too tired to deal with whatever the fuck was going on, Lukas reached his room and dumped his bag in the corner, then sank into his chair to pull his boots off. He'd been gone over two weeks, which was common enough that he was used to things changing when he returned, but finding a mage in his home was something he deserved a heads-up about.

He glanced up when Caius stopped in his doorway and knocked, bracing his elbows on his thighs and narrowing his eyes at his alpha. "Is the mage what you wanted to talk about?"

"Yes." Caius glanced down the hall before stepping into Lukas' room and closing the door. "He's Savino's son."

"The mafia boss?" Oh, things just kept getting better and better. "And you took him why?"

"His father was going to execute him for trying to run away. He Sparked, I bought him, got him healed, and brought him home."

"And now you're going to bind him," Lukas guessed, turning back to his boots. He could see the logic in that and might have even agreed it was a good idea. Denver might be a big city, but they were shifters, and they were the first ones to try to claim territory here since the shifter massacre over fifty years ago.

He didn't care about having a large pack, he was fine with it being the three of them, but he knew Quinn would prefer at least a few more members. And if Caius truly intended to hold territory here, they'd need more than a few. A mage would certainly help, depending on how good Max was in a fight.

"We all are."

"Come again?" Lukas looked up at Caius, sure he was joking.

"What's mine is yours," Caius replied, echoing the words he'd sworn when he first accepted Lukas and Quinn as pack.

He squinted at Caius as his exhausted brain tried to pinpoint why that sounded wrong. "That doesn't include people."

Caius sighed and leaned back against Lukas' dresser, resting his hands on the edge. "We need him. Maybe as much as he needs us. He's a fire mage, or at least has a strong affinity for fire. You know the Order will want him for his sheer destructive power alone."

"Fuck the Order," he muttered. Of all the corrupt organizations, he was convinced they were at the top. "He didn't look too keen on sticking around, much less letting you bind him," he said, finally getting his boots off and slumping in his chair with a yawn. He'd napped on the plane, but he'd been running on catnaps, fumes, and caffeine for over a week. He needed a shower, a hot meal that didn't come out of a tiny pouch, and sleep, and he didn't care about the order of the last two.

"He'll come around," Caius said with the air of someone used to getting his way.

Lukas didn't even have the energy to roll his eyes.

"How'd the mission go?"

"Other than a new boot nearly getting us all killed, it was a success." Lukas forced himself to sit up before he fell asleep where he was. He pulled his shirt off and threw it in the general direction of the hamper. "I need a shower and sleep."

Caius nodded and pushed off the dresser. "I'll wake you for dinner. Steak?"

"Gods yes. Two. And all the sides." With a groan, he pushed to his feet. Just a few more minutes and he could pass out.

He locked his gun in the safe and stripped the rest of his clothes off on the way into his en suite, lingering a few minutes longer than he usually would to ensure he got all the grime and sweat off. Then he pulled on a pair of clean boxers and face-planted into his bed, sinking into sweet oblivion a moment later.

LUKAS WOKE to the scent of food. Not the permeating scent of someone cooking, since that would be hoping for too much in this house, but hot food that wasn't dehydrated or freeze-dried nonetheless. Stomach growling, he rolled out of bed and found a clean shirt in the dark before following his nose to the kitchen.

It was nice having familiar walls around him again, even if the scent of a strange mage tickled his nose.

Caius, Quinn, and Max were at the dining table, setting out the last containers of food.

Quinn glanced at him, his gaze dropping with a quirk of his eyebrows. "Too good for pants now?"

"You like the view," he quipped without thinking, sinking into his seat and popping the lids off his containers. He inhaled deeply, mouth watering as he cut into the rare steak and shoved a large bite into his mouth. Fucking heaven. Two weeks without a decent meal was far too long.

He devoured all of one steak before his hunger was sated enough to notice the awkward silence around the table. He glanced over each of them, noting Quinn's disappointed pout and Caius' pinched expression before focusing on the mage. Max had barely touched his food and smelled like anxiety and fear.

Still not wanting to stick around or be bound then, not that Lukas could blame him. If he'd recently Sparked, Max likely knew only what most people assumed about mages and shifters, which was generally skewed at best or, more often, horrendously wrong.

Max glanced up, meeting Lukas' eyes a moment before quickly looking away again, the thread of fear spiking in his scent despite the flush in his cheeks.

Strange. And interesting. The hint of arousal, not the panic.

Lukas focused on Caius and raised an eyebrow, silently asking what he'd missed.

Caius' tight smile wasn't much of an answer, but Quinn, never able to sit in silence for long, cleared his throat. "Max agreed to stay for a few weeks to finish his semester, but only if he's not bound."

"Well that's stupid," he said, cutting into his second steak. "You know you can be bound by force, right?"

"Lukas," Quinn hissed.

"What?" he snapped. "You expect him to trust you if you don't tell him the truth?"

"You're lying." Max glared at him, his hand clenched around his fork like he would use it to stab someone.

"Why do you think the Order is so adamant about getting their hands on a mage as soon as they Spark? They want the first binding. All that's needed is a bit of your blood and they own you."

"Bonds can be broken," Max said, but Lukas could hear the doubt in his voice.

"Sure," he agreed. That was technically true enough. "If you know how to break them. Or by another mage. How many of those do you think would be willing to break a binding held by the Order?"

Max turned his glare on Quinn and Caius before eyeing Lukas again. "If that's true, then the Order could break your binding on me anyway."

Lukas nodded, glad to see Max was quick on the uptake. "Except consensual bonds can't be broken by force." Not if the bound mage wanted to keep them, at least. Enough pain or torment could change anyone's mind eventually, but there was no sense in scaring Max further.

Max's expression remained dubious, but he fell silent and looked like he was considering Lukas' words.

Taking that as a good sign, Lukas focused on eating. He could eat cold food when he had to, but he much preferred when a hot meal was still hot when it hit his stomach.

Eventually, Max stabbed his fork into his salmon and sat back with his arms crossed. "I'm not stupid enough to think you wouldn't bind me by force if the Order couldn't break it," he said, though he sounded more resigned than angry. "What's in this for me?"

"Other than being pack?" Quinn asked, because of course he did. He thought pack was everything.

Lukas knew better.

Caius ignored that. "What do you want?"

Max straightened, looking like he hadn't expected a negotiation. He glanced around the open floor space, at the house that was big enough for a much larger pack than the three of them.

Lukas expected Max to ask for something expensive or for money outright. He didn't really expect an actual answer.

"Freedom."

"I meant it when I said you weren't a prisoner," Caius said.

Max scoffed, flexing his fingers against his arms as he chewed on his bottom lip. His scent was a mess of emotions ranging from fear to hope to despair and resignation. "And I'm not going to be a sex slave."

Lukas choked as he inhaled a chunk of steak. What the hell?

"Who the fuck said anything about being a sex slave?" Quinn demanded, staring at Max in shock.

Lukas drained his glass of tea and finally got the steak down properly. He eyed Max when he caught the subtle change in his scent; beneath the muddle of negative emotions, he almost smelled like mischief.

Max tilted his head, hesitating before flicking his fingers at Caius. "That's not what he bought me for?"

"Fenrir help me," Caius muttered under his breath, scrubbing a hand over his face.

"Cap? The fuck?" Quinn demanded.

Caius leveled a glare at each of them, Lukas included, which was completely uncalled for. "Of course you're not a slave. Sexual or otherwise," he said tightly.

Lukas gave him props for managing that with a straight face. Especially since the mirth coming off Max was strong enough to make his nose itch.

Max crossed his arms again and stared Caius down, which was quite a feat; Lukas had seen his alpha stand unflinching in the face of irate generals and entitled suburban housewives. After a moment, Caius' shoulders released some of their tension, his expression turned sympathetic, and his scent shifted to protective alpha.

Lukas mentally rearranged their pack hierarchy, with Max firmly in the category of *Do Not Fuck With*.

"Max, I promise you, you will be protected here. And far happier than you ever were with your family."

Max's breaths hitched, but his expression didn't change. His fingers turned white where he gripped his arms, and he swallowed hard before letting his head dip forward. "Fine," he said quietly. "Bind me."

Lukas shared a quick look with Quinn, seeing his own surprise mirrored on his face. Apparently, even overly optimistic Quinn expected more of a fight than that.

He finished eating and dumped his containers in the trash. He personally didn't care much about expanding their pack, but he knew Caius needed more than his bottomless bank account if they were going to successfully hold territory here.

"Do we have everything we need?" Lukas asked. Better to get this taken care of before Max changed his mind.

"Yes." Caius pushed his barely touched plate of food aside and stood.

Lukas snagged a beer from the fridge and propped against the counter to sip it as Caius disappeared upstairs. He focused on Quinn and Max now that the need for sleep and sustenance was taken care of.

Even though Quinn was short for a shifter, Max was a few inches shorter, and thin enough to look frail, though Lukas couldn't decide if that was more genetics or lack of proper nutrition. The few mages he'd worked with always looked like they would break in a strong breeze.

Max poked at his salmon, glancing at Lukas from beneath his messy tawny brown fringe.

Yeah, binding this mage to them was going to go *so* well. He could already taste the chaos it was sure to cause.

CHAPTER 5

CAIUS GATHERED the needed ingredients from his office, along with three small bowls and brushes. He'd never intended to need them, but an unspoken rule for a pack alpha was to always have the necessary components for a binding spell on hand. Even though the Order claimed most mages, there was the occasional mage like Max, or those who Sparked but weren't powerful enough for the Order to deem them worth the trouble.

He took everything to the living room and set the three bowls out on the live-edge coffee table.

The ingredients were simple enough: crushed mage ivy, blood anise, and wolf knot blossom. He mixed a batch in each bowl, then added a small bottle of black tattoo ink to each.

"Okay," Caius said, sitting back and glancing towards the dining room, where the others were watching him. "All that's left is a few drops of blood from each of you."

Lukas tossed his empty beer bottle into the trash before joining him in the living room. He picked up one of the bowls before sitting and flexing a finger, his nail shifting into a sharp claw. He cut his finger and squeezed some blood into his bowl, watching it expectantly. "Isn't it supposed to do something?"

"It needs mage blood."

"Can't believe I'm doing this," Max muttered under his breath, almost quiet enough that Caius' shifter hearing didn't pick it up.

Caius waited until Max stopped on the other side of the table before offering his knife.

Max couldn't hide all of his flinch, staring at the knife like someone familiar with the sharp edge of a blade. He flexed his fingers, and Caius pretended not to notice the tremble in them as Max took the knife and cut his own finger to bleed into the bowls.

Lukas' lit up with a soft fiery orange glow.

"Holy fuck," Max breathed, staring at it as if he still couldn't believe he was a mage with power.

Quinn gently pried the knife from Max's slack grip to add his blood to his own bowl and watched with a grin as it lit up.

Caius took the knife back, wiped the blade on his pants, and added his own blood to the last bowl.

"Now what?" Max asked, pressing his thumb against the cut on his finger.

"I was thinking of using your back, unless you have a preference," Caius said. He picked up one of the small brushes and stirred the mixture in his bowl.

When Max shrugged, Quinn grabbed one of the chairs from the dining table. Max hesitated, gripping the hem of his shirt before letting out a loud breath. He pulled it over his head and turned to straddle the chair, wrapping his arms around the solid wood back.

Caius barely contained his growl as he looked over Max's back. The entire expanse of it was littered with old scars—cuts and tiny circles and the familiar pucker of a bullet wound in his shoulder. That solidified his plan. As much as he hesitated to expand his pack, he'd need more than the four of them to take out Savino.

It might take years, but Max's father was as good as dead.

But that was a problem for later.

For now, he took a few calming breaths and stood behind Max as he dipped the brush into the bowl. When he brushed a streak of black across the center of Max's back, Max twitched with a soft yelp of surprise.

"Fuck, that's cold."

"Sorry," Caius said, watching as the ink shifted and rearranged itself in response to the image in his head. Binding marks were as close as a shifter would ever get to touching magic for themselves. As he added more ink, the mark expanded into that of a wolf, its head tipped back and mouth open on a silent howl. The black ink on Max's skin lit up with the same orange glow, until the wolf image was completed. When the glow faded, the ink turned white like Caius' own wolf, shades of black and gray adding texture and shadows.

Lukas snorted softly when he leaned in for a look. "Bit on the nose, don't you think?"

Caius ignored him and stepped aside, letting Quinn take his place. He sat on the arm of the sofa as Quinn and Lukas made their own marks. When they'd finished, Max's back had three wolf tattoos. A white wolf howling at a crescent moon. A red one curled up beneath a blooming hawthorn, pink and white blossoms littering the ground. And a black one standing on top of a cliff, eyes and ears forward, keeping watch.

As Lukas made the final brush stroke, the weight of power charged the air. Their marks rearranged and resized in a smear of ink and magic until they were connected into a single scene. It covered the entirety of Max's back and hid most of the scars. The glow faded from the tattoo and the bowls, the sharp ozone scent of magic dissipating.

Max's fingers were bloodless where he gripped the back of the chair, his breaths short and quick.

Caius crouched beside him, recognizing the wide-eyed look of panic from years of serving. It was the same look new recruits wore during their first mission. "Max," he said firmly, gripping the back of Max's neck. His skin was hot, nearly feverish, when Caius flexed his wrist to brush against his pulse point, scent marking him and claiming him as pack. "Max, look at me."

Only when Max's eyes snapped to his did he realize he'd tapped into the binding. He cursed silently. The one fear all mages shared was being bound to a shifter. Mages could bind other mages, like the Order did, but a powerful or stubborn mage could resist the compulsions of another mage.

But the magic of shifters and the magic of mages were fundamentally different. Mages were elemental, drawing their powers from the natural forces that made up the universe. Shifters were the remnants of divine magic granted to their ancestors millennia ago, and divine magic always outweighed the natural. At least enough for shifters to dominate a mage when bound.

There was nothing to do about that now.

"You need to breathe," Caius said, drawing in a deep breath, holding, and slowly breathing it back out. He did it again, then a third time, before Max was able to draw a shuddering breath.

Max coughed and latched on to Caius' wrist with a bruising grip as he struggled to steady his breathing.

"You're safe. What's wrong?"

"Hot," Max choked out, the scent of smoke coming from him a moment before tiny flames sparked along his arms and hands. "Burning."

Fuck. Caius glanced at Quinn, but he didn't need to say anything; Quinn was already rushing up the stairs. He straightened and scooped Max up with his right arm to follow. Max felt far too light, but that was another thing to worry about later.

He went upstairs and directly into the cold shower without bothering with either of their clothes. After the incident that morning, he should have expected this. A binding increased the abilities of both sides, sharing power between them. Now that he saw that sharing in action, maybe three bindings was a bit more dangerous than he expected.

Max gasped as cold water rained down on them. It took a few moments for his death grip on Caius' shirt to loosen and his labored breathing to ease.

Caius waited until the feverish heat faded before setting Max on his feet. "Better?" he asked, keeping one arm around the mage as he turned off the water.

With a nod, Max slumped into Caius.

Quinn hovered near the door with a fresh set of dry clothes. "You okay?"

"Yeah," Max said, though his voice was faint and he was starting to shiver.

Caius snagged the towel hanging over the curtain rod and wrapped it around Max's shoulders before nudging him out of the tub. He bit his tongue against saying anything; giving orders was second nature to him at this point, but he wasn't sure if the bond would turn everything he said into a compulsion. He settled on asking, "Need any help?"

Max shook his head and let go of Caius to lean against the counter instead, pulling the towel over his head and scrubbing at his face.

Caius pretended he couldn't smell the salt of frustrated tears and stepped out of the bathroom behind Quinn, pulling the door shut behind him. He glanced down at himself with a sigh, his clothes already forming a puddle. "Can you grab me some clothes?"

He ignored Quinn's snicker and looked at Lukas, who had a shoulder propped against the open bedroom door. "Do we have ice packs?"

Lukas peeled away from the door, and Caius took a moment to breathe once he was alone. He didn't regret binding Max since it needed to be done, but he hadn't realized how difficult it could make controlling his magic. The sooner they found someone who could train Max in the basics the better, but he didn't know where to start. There weren't many mages not controlled by the Order, and he doubted any would want to put themselves in the Order's crosshairs.

He turned when the bathroom door cracked open. Max's hair was still wet, dripping down his neck, but at least he didn't smell like terror, and his heartbeat was steady. He opened his mouth to tell Max he should rest before snapping his mouth shut. He'd have to figure out where the line between suggestion and compulsion was with the binding eventually, but for now he'd have to censor his words.

"You can rest if you want. We'll leave you be as soon as I change," he said, waiting for Max to step towards the bed before taking his place in the bathroom. He tossed a towel out to soak up the puddle he'd left, then stripped his clothes and tossed them into the sink. When he heard Quinn return, he stuck his right arm out for the dry clothes, keeping his back to the mirror as he dressed.

Bad enough that he could see the hint of silver on the left of his chest; he didn't need to see the full spiderweb around the bullet wound. A mess of scar tissue and silvery blue veins covered most of his left shoulder where the aconite bullet had exploded. He still couldn't lift his left arm more than a few inches, and since he was lucky to be alive at all, he considered it a fair trade.

Healing might have been possible by a high-level mage with the talent and patience to deal with aconite poisoning, but the one he'd been referred to was so expensive, he would have had to give up any plans of forming his own pack, even one as small as this one.

He scrubbed a towel over his hair and finished changing before stepping out of the bathroom.

Max was slumped on the bed, a gel ice pack clutched to his chest like a teddy bear.

"You good?" Caius asked, stopping at the foot of the bed to look him over.

"Yeah."

"Yell if you need anything," he said, feeling the weight in the words that made them a compulsion, but he couldn't regret it if it meant Max asked for help when he needed it. He left the door cracked a bit and headed downstairs.

Quinn and Lukas followed, sinking into their usual seats on the large sofa.

"We'll need to be careful of the binding," Caius said, sinking into his overstuffed armchair and rubbing his forehead. "I didn't think it would be so easy to tap into it."

"Probably because he agreed to it," Lukas said, slouching into the cushions before propping a foot on the edge of the table. He motioned to the discarded bowls with his chin. "What about those?"

Caius sighed and stacked them, leaning over to set them on the bottom of the TV stand and covering them with some junk mail that hadn't been thrown away yet. "They need burned with mage fire."

"Whenever he's able to control it enough not to burn the house down," Quinn said.

Lukas snorted. "That'll be a while. He smelled like a campfire before you got him in the shower."

Caius groaned as he slumped in his chair. "He needs help. And we need spellwork laid down." He might have been willing to risk Savino or his rivals attacking without the benefit of protective wards, but that was before Max. As soon as word of a mage not claimed by the Order spread, they'd be facing a far wider range of potential enemies.

"I might know someone," Lukas said after a long moment.

Caius rolled his head against the back of the chair until he could look at Lukas directly. "Someone you trust?"

Lukas shrugged. "He saved my life a couple times. I saved his. He hates the Order, and I'm pretty sure he's one of the few not directly bound to them."

Caius raised an eyebrow. There weren't many mages who fit that last. "Rían?" he guessed. When the brass needed to call in a mage who could get the job done, Rían was one of the few who even the generals spoke highly of, despite working for the Order.

If Lukas had a way to contact him, Caius certainly wouldn't complain.

"Yeah. Not sure I can get hold of him or not."

"Try," he said, before turning his attention to Quinn.

Quinn met his eyes and shrugged. "Well, now that he's bound, we should probably take him shopping. He needs clothes and his own laptop. Apparently, he's only two semesters from getting his degree."

"Okay. We'll head out after breakfast."

When neither of them brought up any other issues, he bid them good night and headed upstairs. His room was on the third floor, over the guest room Max was in. If he was still and listened, he could pick up the steady breaths of Max's light sleep. Hopefully, he'd remain that calm for the night and until they could get another mage to help him.

With a groan, he sank into his bed. Civilian life was supposed to have been easier, but at this point, he would have preferred the endless paperwork and interpersonal responsibilities of his regiments. At least they were familiar.

He had no idea what he was supposed to do with a mage now that he had one.

CHAPTER 6

SETTING HIS toothbrush on fire was Max's first clue that his control was slipping.

He dropped the plastic stick into the sink and drowned the flames in water, gripping the counter as he breathed.

In, hold, out. In, hold, out.

He closed his eyes, focusing on the cool marble under his fingers and the sound of running water and the lingering scent of smoke.

A few minutes passed before the panic eased its grip, but he was relieved when he didn't lose himself to it like he sometimes did. He'd never been allowed a real therapist, because that was a sign of weakness, so he'd had to research how to get through panic attacks on his own in a desperate bid for any control over his own life.

He shut off the water and collapsed onto the bed, pressing the fresh ice pack Quinn had dropped off to his chest, intending to stay there all day. If he couldn't even brush his teeth without catching fire, he definitely didn't want to be near others. Even if part of him wanted to be.

He wasn't sure if it was the binding or what, but something had changed. He still knew deep down that he should have run. Gotten on a plane and disappeared to the other side of the world. But Quinn and Caius had healed him. Called him pack. Promised to protect him. And if staying meant the Order couldn't take him, maybe he should find a way to deal with that.

He couldn't deny he was curious about shifters, and all three of them were gorgeous. Even Caius' salt-and-pepper hair didn't detract from the warm butterflies in his gut. He was pretty certain Quinn had a thing for Lukas, if the few hooded looks he'd caught the redhead throwing last night were any indication.

Not that he should care. Except he did, because Lukas seemed completely oblivious, which was either a tragedy or a blessing, and he hadn't decided which.

With a groan, he rolled back and forth on the bed. His entire body felt like tiny flames were licking along his nerves. It didn't exactly hurt, but it wasn't the most pleasant sensation either. He needed to set something on fire, but there was nothing in the room. No trash or anything. Except for the toothbrush.

He rolled out of bed and stalked back to the bathroom, eyeing the partially charred plastic in the sink. Well, it was already ruined. Not like he could make it any less usable. He bit his bottom lip and stared at it, willing it to burst into flames again.

It remained stubbornly fire-free.

With a sigh, he picked it up, turning the melted plastic between his fingers. Almost immediately, he felt warmth crawl from his hand to the toothbrush and watched with fascination and unease as flames erupted from his fingertips.

The toothbrush warped and crackled as it melted further, but the flames didn't hurt him. His skin didn't blister or even turn pink. He maintained the flames until he held an unrecognizable clump of blackened plastic that he tossed in the trash. He shook his fingers to put out the flames, but they didn't go out. They clung to his fingers like living superglue.

"Fuck," he hissed, shoving his hand under running water.

The flames sputtered and hissed, slowly dwindling before they finally snuffed out.

Max slumped against the sink, keeping his hand under the water until he couldn't stand the cold any longer. Seriously, how was this his life? He pressed his palms against his face and breathed. In and in and in until his lungs refused to hold any more. Held until his chest ached and gray shifted at the edges of his vision. Then out and out and out.

It didn't do anything for the certainty that he'd burn this house down in his sleep, but at least his fingers stopped shaking.

He flinched as someone knocked on the bedroom door.

"Max," Quinn called.

With a sigh, he pushed himself out of the bathroom and found Quinn leaning into his room without stepping inside.

"Hungry? Cap brought back some pastries and egg croissants." The question was followed by a change of clothes being tossed at his face.

Max caught them by reflex, then hesitated despite the rumble in his stomach. He didn't trust his control of his magic, and he was used to lurking in his own room most days. As much as he'd liked pissing his father off, he'd never been actively suicidal. He opened his mouth to decline, but Quinn held out a hand and wiggled his fingers.

"You'll want a full stomach."

He eyed Quinn with a suspicious, "Why?"

"You'll see," Quinn said with a grin, then turned and galloped down the stairs.

Unable to resist his curiosity, he changed into the jeans and sweater before following. When he found Quinn alone in the kitchen, he relaxed. Of the three of them, Quinn seemed the most harmless.

He settled at the counter and accepted the plate of food Quinn set in front of him, tearing off small pieces of croissant without eating most of them. He tried to keep focused on his plate, but his eyes kept getting drawn to Quinn. To the shift of lean muscles beneath his thin shirt, the flex of his shoulders and back as he moved, the trim waist and very nice ass.

A different heat from the flames crept up his neck, and there was a strange tug inside him. A shivery force of gravity beneath his skin, pulling him towards Quinn.

Was that the binding? He found all three of them attractive, gorgeous beyond even what he was used to seeing in movies, but now he had the mistaken impression he might actually have a chance of being with any of them. Not that he cared to fall into bed with his captors. He wasn't *that* desperate to get laid.

Besides, if he wasn't a mage, there was no way in hell they'd even be interested in him. No one needed a useless bony guy who could set them on fire by sneezing.

"Hey," Quinn said, coming around the counter with a frown. "Whatever you're thinking about, stop." He leaned in, hooking his arm around Max's shoulders and squeezing.

Max tensed at the unexpected touch, but he couldn't resist pushing into Quinn's solid warmth. "Are you a telepath or something?"

Quinn snorted, brushing his wrist against Max's neck and mussing his hair. "No, but my nose is excellent, and you smell like bad thoughts."

"Not all bad," he muttered before he could stop himself, heat creeping up his neck again.

Quinn pulled back enough to look at him, his lips slowly pulling into a grin. "Oh yeah? Tell me what else you were thinking."

"That you're unbelievably hot." Max blinked and snapped his mouth shut before groaning, covering his face with his hands. Fuck, why had he said that? He slumped against the counter as Quinn's delighted laughter sank into his head and stuck there like an earworm. When he finally peeked through his fingers, Quinn was propped against the counter beside him and waggled his eyebrows.

"You're pretty hot yourself."

Max's ears burned as he scrubbed at his face. "Are all shifters unnaturally gorgeous assholes?"

Quinn snickered. "Don't let Lukas hear you say that. He already thinks he's Fenrir's gift to shifters."

He raised an eyebrow, about to ask if Quinn thought that too, but Quinn straightened and bumped their shoulders together.

"We're leaving as soon as Cap is ready," Quinn said, tapping Max's plate. "You have maybe five minutes to finish eating."

Max shoved a bite of croissant into his mouth. "Where are we going?"

Caius answered from the stairs behind them. "Quinn said you were in college."

"Yeah. Online, since I wasn't allowed on campus and all."

Caius sat on Max's other side with a confused frown. "Not allowed?"

Max shrugged and ripped apart more of his croissant. "After the umpteenth time I ran, I was homeschooled. Haven't been to a school since eighth grade. Pretty sure that was just an excuse, though. Daddy dearest didn't want me bringing shame or attention to the family with my *predilections*."

"I see. Would you rather attend classes in person?"

That was a trick question. It had to be. Max didn't respond immediately, watching Caius from the corner of his eye. He knew better than to voice his desires; that was the quickest way to have to fight to keep what he did have. But the thought of going from one cage to another was unbearable, even if this one was gilded.

He dropped his croissant and dusted his fingers off before turning to face Caius directly. "Yeah, I would."

"Okay." Caius nodded as if he really had no qualms about letting Max out of his sight. "We'll get you what you need to finish this semester. By the time the next one starts, you should be able to protect yourself on campus."

"Seriously?"

Caius raised an eyebrow, reaching for the cup of coffee Quinn set in front of him. "What?"

"You're just... gonna let me go off on my own?" Even as a kid, before he'd started his escape attempts, he'd always had bodyguards hovering around him.

Caius glanced at Quinn, obviously confused. "Isn't that what you wanted?"

"You're the one who said the Order was going to jump me!"

"That was before we bound you. I expect they'll show up soon regardless, but things should be resolved well before the New Year."

Quinn drummed his fingers against the counter. "We should get going if we don't wanna be out all day."

Caius glanced at his watch. "Is Lukas not coming?"

"He's out on a run."

Max glanced between them, still unable to comprehend their relationship. Caius was obviously the boss, but unlike Max's father, he wasn't punishing Quinn for stepping out of place. "You all are, like, military or something, right?"

Quinn beamed at him. "Marines, yeah. We're both out," he said, flicking a finger from himself to Caius, "but Lukas has a few years left on his contract."

"Why'd you leave?"

Caius grimaced, but instead of snapping at Max to mind his own business, he sighed and set his coffee down. "Medically retired."

"I served my eight years and didn't reenlist." Quinn tipped his head towards Caius. "He offered me a pack, so I joined him instead."

"It's just the three of you?" Weren't packs supposed to have dozens of shifters?

"Four of us," Quinn said firmly, poking Max in the shoulder. "You're pack now."

Max made a face, ignoring the fresh burst of warmth in his chest as he shoved another bite in his mouth. He doubted pack meant family like the movies liked to portray, but it was still more than he'd ever found at home.

"Ready?" Caius asked.

"You don't actually need me to go, do you?"

Caius raised an eyebrow and stood. "You don't want me picking out your things for you."

"You really don't," Quinn agreed. "Everything will be beige and scream 'old man.'" He returned Caius' dark look with an unrepentant grin and headed for the door.

With a groan, Max followed and hoped he didn't set the car on fire. Especially when he saw the sleek cobalt-blue sports car in the driveway. He let out a low whistle as he dragged his fingertips along the side before getting in the back seat.

Quinn settled in the driver's seat and slid his sunglasses on, popping a piece of gum in his mouth before backing out. "So, other than a phone, laptop, and clothes, what else do you need?"

"Nothing." Max winced when Caius shot him a glare over his shoulder, his mouth dropping open when Quinn smacked the back of his hand into Caius' chest.

"Stop with the scary face, O captain, my captain."

Caius turned his glare on Quinn. "It's colonel."

"O colonel, my colonel doesn't have the same ring to it."

Caius sighed, muttering under his breath about corporal punishment.

Ignoring him, Quinn continued. "Seriously, Max, whatever you need. Or want. Might as well take advantage of the colonel's platinum card. Any hobbies you need supplies for?"

Were they testing him? "No?"

Quinn let out an exaggerated sigh. "We'll figure it out along the way." He braked at a red light and turned on the wipers when the snow flurries started. "How about a gaming laptop? Lukas and I play some online games sometimes if you wanna join in."

"Really?" he asked before he could help himself.

Quinn glanced at him in the rearview mirror and grinned. "Yup. We'll get you set up."

BY THE time Max was "set up," they'd fought their way through an insane holiday shopping crowd to get him a new laptop worth a few grand that he was frankly terrified to touch, an art tablet and one of the newest phones on the market, several bags of winter clothes, two pairs of shoes, and a pair of combat boots almost as expensive as the laptop. And that was only the "necessities."

He also had a bag of nail polishes, eyeliner, and skincare products Quinn had insisted on when he'd caught Max staring at someone's stunning makeup. The shifter had even waved down an employee for a quick tutorial, since Max had never dared touch the stuff before, no matter how much he'd wanted to. His father would have skinned him alive, literally, to remove it.

Caius hadn't said a word, which wasn't as surprising as the fact Max had caught him watching more than once with a look of interest.

After that, Quinn had dragged them past every hobby shop in the strip mall until he found Max's kryptonite: an art store.

Max spent almost half an hour drooling over the wide selection of sketchbooks, paint pens, felt-tip pens, alcohol markers, acrylic markers—every type of pen and pencil he'd ever wanted to get his hands on.

Quinn, having finished programming Max's new phone and adding their contacts, grew tired of waiting and started grabbing one of everything despite Max's weak protests.

Honestly, he couldn't find the will to protest much more when said protests had been summarily ignored for hours. And he wanted the art supplies. He clutched the bag to his chest as they headed back to the car, only to nearly run into Caius when he stopped, a low, feral growl rumbling out of him. Max backpedaled into Quinn, who caught him and nudged him to the side.

Max risked leaning around Caius to see what was going on, expecting to see his father or his men, but all he saw was a guy in torn jeans and a loose black hoodie. He couldn't have been older than Max, but he was a mage. Max could feel it. A strange pressure in the air, like a storm about to break. The fact that the falling snow swirled away from the guy as if blown by a wind might have been another clue.

"Who's that?"

Quinn growled, shifting to put himself partially in front of Max. "Someone from the Order."

Fuck.

"You're not taking him," Caius snarled.

The man held his hands up as he strolled closer. "Just here for a look, wolf." He flicked two fingers in a clear order for Caius to step aside.

Caius tensed, his growl deepening as he adjusted his stance as if to fight.

Max took an involuntary step back as he realized that's exactly what Caius intended to do. Something rippled along the edge of his senses, a twist of energy gathering around Caius, though he couldn't tell if it came from the shifter or the mage. No, it was definitely from the mage.

"Stop it!" he yelled, silently cursing himself even as he waved a hand, like that would do anything to dispel the strange energy. He was not prepared for the surge of heat that rushed through him, unleashing itself in a wave of flames.

They ripped through the air, tearing apart the energy pressing around Caius before swirling over their heads and diving for the mage.

With a shocked curse, the man threw his hands up. Fire wrapped around him in a tunnel of blinding orange flames that circled higher like a tiny tornado. A moment later, it dispersed with a sharp crack like thunder, the snow around them turning to freezing rain that reached all the way to the edge of the parking lot.

The man glowered at them, his clothes smoking and a small lick of fire still flickering in his hair, but otherwise unharmed. "You," he snarled, fresh flames of his own cascading around his hands as he stepped towards Max.

Caius stalked forward to stop him. "Attacking us would be a violation of Article 29, section 4B."

The man stopped, flicking a frustrated, wary glance at Caius. "You're military?"

"The mage is bound to me and my pack. Tell the Order to fuck off."

He sneered, lifting his chin but snuffing his flames. "You won't be able to keep him."

"Try me." Whatever face Caius made, the man paled in response and stepped back with his hands splayed.

With a last considering look at Max, the man turned. A translucent doorway appeared in the air in front of him and he stepped through before both vanished.

Quinn let out a gusty breath and sagged against Max.

"Car. Now," Caius ordered.

Max was all too happy to oblige, hurrying to the car with Quinn still holding on to him. Once on the road, he glanced behind them, expecting to see another doorway appear or a black SUV following them. "That was bad, right?"

Caius growled. "We should have had another day or two. Either the shield the healer put on you wore off, or she sold us out."

"No way is our place gonna be safe now if they found him already," Quinn murmured.

Caius hissed before swearing and pulling out his phone. When the line connected, he said, "The Order found Max. Did you ever get in contact with Rían?"

CHAPTER 7

LUKAS SAT on the sofa with a cup of coffee early the next morning. He'd texted Rían two days ago, then again yesterday after the attack, but he still hadn't gotten a response. He knew the mage wasn't dead only because his messages were marked read, but he must have been neck-deep in a job if he hadn't responded by now.

He only knew two other mages well enough to have their contact information, but he didn't trust them half as much as he did Rían.

His phone vibrated with an incoming call, and he smirked. Speak of the devil. "Hey, squirrel."

"Wolf," came the immediate response with an audible eye roll. "Why are you contacting me?"

"Need to call in a favor."

"For?"

Lukas hesitated, tapping his thumb against the rim of his cup. "My alpha found a newly Sparked mage. The Order is after him. He's in desperate need of a magic crash course, and some better wards on our home would be nice." They only had the basics that would protect against natural disasters.

A long silence followed, which wasn't surprising. He knew this might blow up in his face. Being a mage, Rían didn't trust shifters, but even he had to admit a mage would be better off with Lukas and his pack than with the Order.

Rían let out an explosive sigh. "I'll be there tomorrow. And I'm still going to charge you out the ass if your place is a pain to shield."

"So glad you're not dead," Lukas said dryly.

"Feck off and give me the address." As soon as Rían had what he needed, he disconnected.

Lukas didn't take it personally, especially as he hadn't really expected Rían to call or help in the first place, despite Lukas saving his life a few months ago. He set the phone aside and turned his attention out the large bay windows, sipping his coffee and watching the sky darken before gray crept in. He probably should have been trying to sleep, but he didn't feel like dealing with the nightmares. It was easier to inhale caffeine and wait for his body to reach its limit.

He tilted his head as he heard someone upstairs. It was still too early to be Caius, and Quinn was in his lair downstairs. When he glanced over, he saw a sleep-tousled Max. The sharp scent of woodsmoke and citrus was stronger since he'd apparently lost control of his magic yesterday. Lukas was about to offer a greeting when Max spotted him and froze, his eyes widening as fear soured his scent.

Lukas didn't flinch only because he'd had years to train himself not to flinch from anything. Hard to be a decent sniper if every little thing got a reaction from him. Instead, he looked away from Max, turning his attention back to the window, where the sun was peeking over the horizon. "Good morning."

Max murmured something that might have been a "Morning," before inching into the kitchen. With the open floor plan and no walls for him to hide behind, there was nothing to dampen the stench of wariness.

This was one of the reasons he'd been leery of binding a mage. As a shifter, living with someone who feared you was a nightmare. He was lucky enough that most of the men in his squad had no problem with shifters, and the one who did wasn't part of his team.

He listened to Max making breakfast as he watched the sunlight slink its way across the neighborhood, glistening on the fresh snow. They'd gotten at least a foot overnight. Hopefully the sidewalks were clear enough for a run.

Lukas stilled completely when Max moved towards him, pretending not to notice even though the tang of nerves in his scent made Lukas' nose burn. He could hear Max's heart threatening to burst out of his chest.

"C-coffee?"

He tilted his head slowly as he turned his attention to Max and the coffeepot. "Sure," he said, holding his cup out to let Max refill it. "Thanks."

Max hurried back to the kitchen like he expected Lukas to pounce and eat his heart out.

When Quinn finally stumbled around downstairs, Lukas breathed a sigh of relief. If anyone could break the tension in a room, it was Quinn.

Sure enough, as soon as the redhead shuffled up the stairs, he moved straight for Max and draped himself against his back. "Bacon?"

Max's lips twitched, and his scent cleared almost immediately.

Lukas tried not to take it personally, letting the quiet banter in the kitchen go in one ear and out the other as he picked up his phone. He was usually guaranteed a week minimum between missions, but he still marked himself unavailable for the next few days due to pack business, just in case. Considering the size of the house, it would take Rían at least that long to put proper protections in place.

And Lukas doubted anything would stop the Order from trying to get their hands on Max, even with their three bindings on him. It was rare for a mage to Spark past eighteen. Rarer still to have as much literal firepower as Max had shown. Even if he was technically too old to be forced to serve eight years, he was powerful enough the Order wouldn't want him running around without their leash.

Caius would have to find a dedicated trainer for Max. There was no way he'd learn even a fraction of what he needed in a few days. The problem was, most trainers worked for the Order. Few mages ever escaped their grasp, even after their mandatory eight years.

He texted Rían again, asking if he knew any.

The response was a *Yeah, me* with a kissy face.

Lukas snorted and balanced his cup on his knee. *You still work for Order*

Only for another 2 months

He considered that with a soft hum, wondering if Rían would actually manage to finish his service. *Not sure we could afford you*

I'll give you the Special Fucker discount

Lukas couldn't help the laugh that escaped. *Do you want my ass that badly?*

It's a pity discount

Fuck you

You think too highly of yourself, wolf

Lukas rolled his eyes and stubbornly ignored the sharp pang in his chest. It was harmless flirting and banter; Rían didn't mean anything by it.

"What the fuck's got you in such a good mood?" Quinn asked, sprawling on the sofa with his head in Lukas' lap.

"Nothing," he replied, locking his phone and tucking it under his thigh. He pretended not to see Quinn's smirk as he sipped his coffee, ignoring the fact Quinn likely hacked into all of their phones on a regular basis to snoop through their shit.

He resisted the urge to adjust his pants to hide the growing problem Quinn's head in his lap was causing. Instead, he motioned towards Max, who was scooping what smelled like scorched eggs onto plates. "You still think this was a good idea?"

Quinn followed his gaze and sighed. "You weren't there. His father's men beat the shit out of him, and I'm pretty sure it wasn't the first time. His own father was going to kill him." He shook his head, his scent twisting with anger and heartache. "Besides, he's cute."

"You think everyone is cute," Lukas muttered. That was one of the first things he learned about Quinn. The second was that Lukas wasn't Quinn's type.

"Not true," Quinn said. The devious twitch of his lips gave him away, but his next words weren't for Lukas, they were pitched louder for Max as Caius came down the stairs. "I would never call Cap cute."

Not one to ruin a good prank, he raised his own voice so that Max could hear him. "Caius is definitely a smokin' hot Daddy."

Max nodded his agreement without looking up. "Damn right he is."

The look on Caius' face was priceless, before he shot Lukas an accusing glare.

Lukas raised his free hand in a *WTF do you expect?* gesture as Quinn cackled like a madman.

Max finally looked up, saw Caius, and turned red all the way to his ears. "I uh…. Breakfast is ready."

Between Caius and Max smelling like mortification and embarrassment, and Quinn's manic delight, breakfast alternated between excruciatingly painful and endlessly entertaining.

Lukas let them stew until he finished his third cup of coffee. "Rían will be here tomorrow."

Caius latched on to that like a drowning man. "Good. Does he need us to get anything?"

He shrugged and pulled out his phone to ask. "If he does, I'll go grab it later." He took his dishes to the sink and rinsed them. "Going for my run," he said, heading to his room.

Caffeine hardly had an effect on him anymore, but he was still buzzing with a restless energy he was used to after coming off a long mission. He could, and had, waited days for a target before, but the longer he had to wait, the more he had to move once he was back home.

He changed into his running pants and windbreaker, found his cordless headphones, and scrolled to the bilateral stimulation music that helped him relax on his way out the door. He didn't much care where he went, so he picked a direction and took off, his feet keeping to the pace of the stim beats.

The scents of the city were still new enough that he paid attention to his surroundings, but even that wasn't enough to distract him from mulling over Max's wariness towards him. Max didn't seem to have a problem with Quinn or Caius, even after the attack yesterday. If Max grew up in an abusive environment, Lukas could only assume he reminded Max of someone.

As much as that grated on him, there was nothing to be done about it except to wait for Max to realize Lukas wasn't a threat. Unlike the guy following Lukas from twenty paces back. He wasn't sure if it was the Order or the mob or a petty thief, but they were about to have a very bad day.

He turned into a park, still deserted this early, and headed for the small tunnel where one of the jogging paths looped over itself. There, he stopped and turned off his music, waiting in the middle of the dim tunnel. He didn't have long to wait, and the guy stalking him proved he wasn't alone. While the one who'd been following him came up from behind, two others stepped into the tunnel in front of him.

None of them smelled like a mage. Only stupidity and arrogance.

He tilted his head as he breathed in their scents. They were clean, so not desperate or homeless. There was a tang of metal and gunpowder on each of them. Regular bullets, no aconite. Not too surprising, considering most shifters avoided this city as much as possible. He still wasn't decided whether Caius was a genius or absolutely mad to be trying to establish pack territory here.

Regardless, the men either had to be with the mob or hired hit men. They obviously thought he was the weakest member of the pack. There was a slim chance they were one of his own enemies, here for revenge for someone he'd taken down on a mission, but he was always careful to cover his tracks.

Not that it mattered. A fight was a fight, and when they rushed him instead of pulling their weapons, his adrenaline spiked. Always a fun time when they underestimated him. He knew he looked young, but he couldn't be too annoyed when it gave him an advantage. He was even feeling charitable enough to let the first guy get a couple of hits in, before grabbing his face and ramming the back of his head into the cement wall.

The man immediately crumpled, and Lukas turned to the next. This one had a large, ugly scar on his cheek like someone had taken a knife to it. Definite gangster vibes.

Lukas tilted his head with a taunting smile when the man eyed his fallen comrade. When it looked like the man was having second thoughts, he bawked like a chicken, snickering when it had the desired effect.

Scarface turned red and swung at him. The third guy was still lingering near the exit behind them, so Lukas focused on dodging and weaving, letting Scarface get a few glancing blows before jabbing him in the ribs.

He wasn't too concerned about letting the fight drag on. He was still restless and antsy, and a fight was better than a run any day, even against a human. Surely they knew he was a shifter and that they stood no chance.

"Gonna tell me what you're after?" he finally asked when Scarface started slowing with exhaustion. "Are you Savino's men?"

Surprise flickered through Scarface's scent. "You know Savino?"

"I wouldn't say *know*—" His body moved before he fully registered the sharp tang of metal in the air, grabbing Scarface and yanking him around to use as a shield as the asshole at the entrance finally made his move and opened fire. Even if regular bullets wouldn't likely kill him, he hated being shot.

Scarface jerked as several bullets hit him in the chest, before groaning and turning into literal dead weight.

Lukas snarled and tossed him aside as the gunner took off. "No you don't," he growled, racing after him. Shifter speed meant he caught up within moments, and he launched himself at the man's back, driving him hard to the ground. He winced at the resulting earsplitting screech. "Shut the fuck up," he snarled, shoving the man's face into the sidewalk. "If you're not Savino's, who are you working for?"

When the man remained stubbornly silent, Lukas shifted, digging a knee into one of the pressure points in his lower back until the man screamed.

"Tell me!"

"You'll kill me!"

"Tempting, but no. What're you after?"

The man struggled beneath him, as if he really thought he could get away, before slumping with a pathetic whimper. "He wants the mage. Figured you'd be the easiest way to lure him out."

"And who's he?"

"Mr. Wright."

"He got a first name?"

"Timothy."

Lukas dug his knee in again as he pulled out his phone to do a quick search. He could already hear sirens in the distance, but he wasn't worried. A few seconds later, he was staring at a picture of an old, balding white man who owned a construction company off Cherry Creek and was listed as a co-owner on a dozen others. "This the guy?" he asked, shoving his phone in the man's face, and was rewarded with a nod.

"Can see why he'd have to get a mage by force," he muttered, sending the information to Quinn as he ignored the man's pleas to be let go. He sent a quick text to his CO so no one was caught with their pants down if the police flagged his name for something. Then he slipped his phone into his pocket and pulled out his ID as the cops finally arrived.

He held his hands up, offering his ID as he stood. "Corporal Hunt. I was assaulted by these three men," he said, motioning to the tunnel. He contained his smirk at the man's outraged snarl and resigned himself to a long morning of dealing with police.

CHAPTER 8

WATCHING MAX shoot Caius discreet glances full of confusion, awe, and longing was physically painful. The cautious ones Caius returned when Max wasn't looking were almost as bad.

Quinn was saved by a text from Lukas. It was nothing more than a name, but he quickly escaped the resurgence of teenage hormones and awkwardness to his lair.

His multicomputer rig hummed to life as he sank into his chair and started his search. It didn't take long to pull up some basic info on a Timothy Wright, one CEO of a mediocre construction company with his hand in several others.

He was digging into the numerous lawsuits and charges filed against him, ranging from discrimination to sexual assault to racketeering, when his phone dinged with an alert. "This is like some wannabe mob boss," he muttered, pulling out his phone. Like they needed another one of those to deal with.

He stared at the message on his phone for a moment, sure it was a joke, because no way would the police have any reason to pull Lukas' information. He'd hidden a couple of passive controls in the government databases while still enlisted to ensure he received a notification any time their names or files were pulled.

"What the fuck?" he hissed, switching to another computer and pulling up the security footage from Lukas leaving the house. He flipped through several feeds before he found the corresponding cameras on the path Lukas had taken, and then he was watching Lukas jogging through the park, the same guy tailing him since a block from their house.

He swore when Lukas disappeared into the tunnel and was out of his seat when three men followed him in. His heart nearly stopped when the man near the entrance fired his gun and took off, only breathing again when Lukas raced after him and drove him to the ground.

"Fucking hell," he hissed, watching until the police arrived. Only when Lukas went with them without being handcuffed did he turn back to his original task, trusting Lukas could handle the police without Quinn interfering.

He grabbed a few mug shots on the three attackers to run through his facial recognition program, then put on some music to lower his blood pressure as he tore into the past thirty years of Mr. Sleazeball's life.

His wife was dead from a car accident, though there were rumors that she'd been about to hand over hard evidence of crimes that could have put him away for good. Said evidence had obviously never been recovered.

A twenty-seven-year-old daughter, married to a surgeon, ran one of Daddy's smaller companies, though from what he could find, she was clean, with a three-year-old daughter of her own. Some recent pictures on social media included Wright, so not estranged, despite the rumors of her mother's death.

Quinn's search on the three who'd attacked Lukas came back, marking two as loyal men to Wright, and one hired goon who'd been a core suspect in several hits and kidnappings, but never charged. Why they'd gone after Lukas was the real question, but he was sure it had to do with Max.

He wasn't aware that he'd lost several hours until the smell of cooking meat made his stomach growl. He winced as he sat back, rubbing a kink in his neck and turning to head upstairs. Max was at the stove, and Quinn was glad to finally have someone besides him in the house who could cook. He was getting sick of fast food and takeout.

"Hey," he said, slinging an arm over Max's shoulders. "Where's Cap?"

"Right here," Caius said, apparently following his own nose down from his office.

No sense in wasting more time. "So we might have a problem." As if to prove his point, his phone chimed with a new alert. When he pulled it up, he found a news article with footage of Max's fire tornado. With a groan, he slid it across the counter for Caius to see. "Looks like the mage is outta the bag."

Caius frowned as he stared at the phone. "I thought you erased all the footage."

"Well yeah. From the security feeds. That looks like a phone recording. Even I'm not that good, sorry to say."

Caius sighed and scrubbed at his face.

"Sorry," Max murmured.

"Hey, no. This isn't your fault." Quinn hooked his arm around Max's shoulders again, giving him a squeeze. "I'd put money on the Order being behind this. If they can't take you from us on their own, they're gonna pit the city against us."

Max leaned into Quinn, misery oozing out of him. "Can they really do that?"

"The Order generally gets away with whatever they want," Caius said with a dark scowl.

"They can do what they want," Quinn said, "but we're not gonna let anyone take you from us. Also, I'm pretty sure this is why Lukas was attacked this morning." When both Max and Caius looked at him in alarm, he realized he probably should have led with that. "He's fine," he hastily added. "He's with the police, but the assholes who went after him work for this guy."

He grabbed his phone and switched screens, pulling up Wright's info. "Luckily, they were sloppy. Doesn't look like any of them've realized what they're dealing with yet." He hoped it would take a while longer for the general public to notice a shifter pack had claimed the area as their territory, and bound a mage to boot.

Caius growled, his nails threatening to gouge the granite counter where they were changing to claws.

Max squeaked and started to back away, but Quinn tightened his hold and snapped the fingers of his free hand in Caius' face. "You're freaking out our mage."

With a wince, Caius tore his eyes away from the phone, focusing on Max as he leashed his wolf. "My apologies," he said, flexing his fingers as he stood. "Send me Mr. Wright's address and the info you have on him," he added to Quinn, before grabbing his keys and heading out.

Well, that wasn't good. Caius rarely drove himself anywhere since his injury. Either he was pissed over the attack on Lukas or the possibility of them being after Max. Probably both. Quinn could only hope he didn't do something stupid, like Lukas taking on three attackers. They really couldn't afford one pack member held up with the authorities, let alone two.

He waited until he heard Caius' car start before grabbing his phone and sending over the address for the construction company where Mr. Sleazeball usually was this time of day.

"This is all my fault, isn't it?" Max asked.

Quinn turned Max towards him and grabbed both his shoulders. "This is *not* your fault. We knew this was likely to happen the moment Caius took you from your father." Granted, they really should have had more than a few days before anyone started making moves against them. It didn't bode well for them if the Order was able to work this fast.

"Why? Why would you risk anything for me? I'm not even a real mage."

"*A mhuirnín*, you Sparked. You're a real mage." He slid his hands up to cup Max's face. "The fact you haven't been bound by the Order means anyone and everyone who wants power in this city might be stupid enough to come after you, but you are pack. You're bound to not one but three shifters. None of us are going to let anything happen to you."

Max let out a shuddering breath, his fingers twisting in the hem of Quinn's shirt. "My father is going to be *so* pissed when he finds out."

"Your father can go deep throat a twelve-inch cactus. And take another up the ass for good measure," Quinn muttered, grinning when Max spluttered a laugh. "Also, you're burning something."

Max spun away with a curse, shoving a pan of something that used to be edible aside before it caught fire.

Quinn let out a slow breath and prayed to all the old gods that they survived this war.

CHAPTER 9

CAIUS PUT the address into the GPS and took off. The fact Lukas had been attacked was bad enough, but if Wright really was after Max, he wouldn't be the last. It was only a matter of time before people far more dangerous than a corrupt CEO came for them.

He had to send his own message before that happened and make it clear that Max wasn't going anywhere.

When he reached the construction company, he parked and surveyed the area. Decent-sized buildings with clean streets, with several cars parked out front. He scrolled through everything Quinn had sent him as he watched the office through the large windows.

He cracked his car window and breathed deep. The nearby river blanketed the area with the smell of water. Thankfully, with winter setting in, any lingering smell of trash or waste there may have been was diminished. Beneath the usual scents of a big city, he caught two different perfumes and a horrible cologne, all of which seemed to permeate the building in front of him. As far as he could tell, there were only three people inside, and it was early enough that he hoped the staff hadn't taken lunch yet.

Sure enough, at half past, two women stood from the receptionist desk and flocked out of the building.

Once they were gone, Caius pulled on a pair of black gloves and his sunglasses before striding up to the door and inside with all the authority of a ranked officer. He hardly paused as he quickly scanned for the most likely spot for an office and continued towards the back. He was inside the corner office and closing the door behind him before Wright realized he was there, and by then it was too late.

The lock sliding into place was loud.

Wright pushed up from his desk with an indignant scowl. "I don't know who the fuck you think you are—"

"Sit down," Caius ordered, staring at the man like he was a new recruit who'd pissed on the floor.

The man blustered for a moment before sinking into his chair. "Who are you?"

Caius raised an eyebrow. "You attacked one of my men without knowing who I am?" He might have found that hard to believe, but old white men could be appallingly arrogant. The current president was a prime example.

"I haven't attacked anyone," Wright scoffed. "Now please get out of my office."

Caius stepped closer to the desk, towering over the man. His nose twitched when he caught the sickly smell in his scent. It was almost masked by the terrible cologne and too much deodorant making his nose burn. That wasn't the smell of a cold or flu. Whatever it was smelled terminal. That would explain why he was after Max. Apparently mage equated to healer in his mind.

He set his phone on the desk and hit Play on the park footage.

Wright watched it in confusion for a moment before he paled considerably. He rallied quickly enough and shoved the phone away. "Obviously that's not me. I've been at my desk all morning," he snapped, but fear soured his scent even further.

Caius tucked his phone into his pocket. "You should be more concerned about how those men led us to you. The police may be slowed by red tape, but I'm not." He stepped around the desk and looked out the large window with a nice view of the river.

"The mage is bound to me." He tilted his head when Wright's scent spiked with adrenaline. It might have been over a year since he'd stepped onto a battlefield, but his instincts were as sharp as ever. The moment Wright put his hand on the gun, Caius was on him, slamming his head into the desk with his left hand. With his other, he twisted the gun from the man's grip with enough force to dislocate his finger, then pressed the muzzle to Wright's temple.

He grimaced as the stink of urine filled the office. "Pathetic," he muttered as he removed the clip and tossed it across the room with a flick of his wrist. The bullet in the chamber followed, before he dismantled the gun entirely. He doubted Wright even knew how to put it back together, but pocketing the mainspring would ensure he never did.

"Come after me or mine again, and I'll rip your intestines to pieces while you watch."

When he reached his car, he flicked the spring into the grass before driving off. He doubted Wright would come for them again, but this was only the beginning. They'd need every alert and preventative program Quinn had available, but even that wouldn't keep them safe.

He never thought he'd be in a position to need a large pack, but for the first time since his father died, he wished his uncle hadn't usurped his authority. A pack of four wasn't much against an entire city's underworld, but he hoped their skills would be enough until they figured out a plan.

CHAPTER 10

HELP FINALLY arrived that evening, in the form of a tall, lanky man who Lukas introduced as Rían.

Rían was nothing like what Max expected, and not just because of his striking crimson eyes with flecks of gold. He tried not to stare, but it was hard not to. He'd never seen eyes like that outside of movies and wondered what kind of genetics had created them. Or maybe it was a direct result of power. The scent and pressure of magic around the other mage was thick enough that Max was sure he would have felt it even before he Sparked.

"You're lucky I got my freelance license last year," Rían said, the lilt of an Irish accent wrapped tight around his words. "And your wards are shite. I could sense a mage here from two miles out," he added, shedding a coat that looked like it was for a far colder climate than even a Colorado winter. Beneath he wore a simple T-shirt, but Max's attention caught on the dozens of pieces of jewelry. Necklaces and bracelets in silver and thin leather, a simple strip of red cloth, silver rings on almost every finger. Max might not know how to tell what spells were set in them, but every one of them practically vibrated with power.

Then Rían turned to Max and froze.

A complicated play of emotions passed over his face before he spun on Lukas. "Three of you bound him? Are you feckin' insane or a gobshite? No, don't answer. I forget you have a death wish." He threw his large bag onto the sofa, where it landed with a muffled clatter of glass and metal. When Lukas didn't move, Rían looked at him as if considering turning him into a bug. "Out."

Lukas shot Max an apologetic look as he beat a hasty retreat. "So glad you're not dead, squirrel," he muttered, closing the door to the small library-slash-sitting room.

Rían grumbled softly in what Max assumed was Irish as he opened his bag. He pulled out a large jar filled with rocks, metal strings, and something that moved like liquid but shone like a star in the night sky. He started to open it before eyeing Max and reaching into the bag again instead. He pulled out a strange device and tossed it over. It was a solid circle of dark, thick metal, a cylinder in the center with a silver ball inside. Two red lines marked a small area in the center of the cylinder.

The moment Max caught it, the strain of holding back his magic eased, as if the restless surge of flames inside him were sucked into the metal circle. "Oh fuck," he groaned, nearly sobbing with relief. He hadn't realized how hard he'd been fighting against setting things on fire until it felt like all those muscles released and left him shaky.

"Thought so," Rían murmured. "Just hold that for now while I ward the room. I'd walk you through how to do this yourself, but I can only stay for two days, and I can't even teach the basics in that time."

He opened a pouch hanging against his chest, and a tiny furry creature climbed out with a soft bark. "Yes, yes, I know you hate the pouch," he said dryly, holding his hand out for the creature to climb into. "Niamh, this is Max. Max, this is Niamh, my sugar glider familiar."

"Adorable. Hello," Max said, laughing when Niamh preened. He desperately wanted to ask if he could pet it, but he didn't dare.

"Don't encourage her," Rían muttered, but he smiled as he said it. "Let's get this room warded, you slacker." He tossed his hand up, and Niamh took to the air with a series of chitters and barks as she glided around the perimeter.

Max slumped into the sofa without letting go of the device, feeling helpless as Rían set to work. It was clear he knew what he was doing, and Max could only dream of ever being that confident in anything.

Rían opened the jar and placed smooth white stones along each wall. Next came the metal strings, which he tossed into the air and caught with a web of magic, stretching, twisting, and tying them with flicks of his fingers until they formed the skeleton of a canopy around the room. Another flick of his wrist and the strings flew to the walls and ceiling, each end of one connecting with a stone.

Niamh barked and spiraled up to touch the center, and Rían flung the jar as if slinging paint off a paintbrush. The glowing liquid inside rushed up and out as if drawn to the metal. The two elements sang as they touched, a high-pitched whine rising beneath the otherworldly harmony. The pressure and weight of magic grew oppressive, threatening to squeeze Max's lungs to pulp before Rían brought his hands together with a resounding clap, shouting something Max couldn't understand.

The magic burst like a popped water balloon, a cascade of sparkling bits of raw magic raining down around them. When they hit the floor, they faded with a pulsing glow that seemed to be absorbed by the boundary of the room itself.

Rían let out a heavy sigh and sank onto the other couch. "That should be enough to keep you from destroying anything," he said, rummaging in his pack for a small vial of dark blue liquid. He drank it with a grimace, but the pale complexion that had set in improved a moment later. "Don't practice your magic anywhere but in here. I don't have the time, power, or supplies right now to ward the entire house like this."

Max nodded, not about to complain. Simply knowing he had a place he could relax his hold on his magic was enough to reduce his stress levels.

"Now. I take it you don't want the bonds gone?" he asked, sounding resigned. When Max shook his head, he muttered what was an obvious curse under his breath and reached into his bag again. This time he pulled out a velvet pouch and poured a small crystal globe onto the table between them. "This'll show us what we're working with. Put the trainer down and pick up the crystal."

Max reluctantly set the metal device aside, flames swelling inside him as soon as he let go, but he was ready and held them back. Barely. When he picked up the crystal, it glowed a bright, warm orange with specks of silver. "Fire, right? Is that bad?"

"No affinity is bad, but fire is notorious for being harder to control." Rían held his hand out, and Max dropped the crystal into it, where it lit up with a brilliant swirl of colors. "If you recently Sparked, I'm surprised you haven't set everything on fire yet."

Max winced. His pile of charred toothbrushes was growing every day.

Rían raised an eyebrow, amusement tugging at his lips. "Or have you?"

"My toothbrushes."

He laughed. "Could be worse. You'll want to keep an eye out for your familiar," he started, pausing when the pouch against his chest stirred. He raised an eyebrow and tugged it open as another sugar glider poked its head out and crawled into Rían's hand.

Max inhaled sharply at the immediate pull. It was one of the cutest things he'd ever seen, but more than that, he felt like it belonged to him.

"Wondered why I had three of them," Rían said, holding the sugar glider out to Max with a faint smile. "I think this one belongs to you."

The sugar glider leapt across the table, gliding onto Max's arm.

"Don't fight the bond."

Max wasn't sure what that even meant until he felt the connection burrow into him, deeper than the bonds from Caius and the others. The presence of a quiet mind bloomed inside him, and the heat that had been roiling beneath his skin since his flames first appeared cooled considerably. He closed his eyes with a sigh of relief, the tidal pressure against his control easing even without him holding the metal device.

The sugar glider chirped and climbed its way to Max's shoulder before rubbing against his cheek and tucking in against his neck. Its fur was the softest thing he'd ever felt, and he couldn't resist stroking it from head to tail.

"That's better," Rían said, sinking back against the sofa. He jumped as Niamh glided down and dropped the mess of metal strings in his lap before sailing around the room. "Niamh! One of these days I'm going to skin you for your pelt," he muttered, setting the mess aside before pointing to the metal device beside Max.

"That's a beginner's tool for focusing magic and learning precision. You need to hold it with a hand on either side and let your magic flow into the metal. The force and amount of magic will move the silver ball. Too much or too fast and it will rise higher. Too little or slow and it will sink. Your end goal is to keep the ball inside the red lines for as long as possible.

"For now, focus on how it absorbs all your excess magical energy. I'll make a shield for you later so you don't need to worry about catching shite on fire. Or exploding yourself."

"What?" Max nearly dropped the device as alarm slammed into his chest, his heart racing.

Rían raised an eyebrow. "Fire mage," he said, as if spontaneous combustion was a matter of course. "And you're bound to three feckin' shifters. Frankly, I'm amazed you're still alive."

Max groaned and slumped into the cushions, holding the trainer in a death grip. He really didn't need that extra nightmare. Bad enough he was afraid to touch anything flammable. What if he blew up Caius?

"Max," Rían said, far more amused than he had any right to be. "Relax. By the time I'm done here, you won't have to worry about destroying anything unless you really try."

He wasn't sure how much he could trust Rían, but Lukas trusted him enough to bring him here, and Caius and Quinn trusted Lukas. "Promise?"

"Absolutely." Rían gathered up the strings, shoved them back into the jar, and set it on the floor as Niamh swooped past and dropped a couple of stones into it. "You get a feel for your magic. I need to put at least basic warding on the rest of the house."

"Sure." Max stretched out on the sofa, holding the device over his head as his sugar glider settled below his throat. The soft vibrations of purring soothed an ache inside him. He'd always wanted a pet, but this was so much better. For the first time in his life, he felt something close to safe.

For the next couple of hours, he was content to play with the training device. Once he was convinced he couldn't blow it up or lose control of his flames while holding it, he concentrated on pouring more of his magic into it. The silver ball shot to the top of the cylinder and stayed there as he pushed more and more. His hands warmed and the metal brightened with a hint of a glow, and still there was an inferno inside him that seemed inexhaustible.

It was terrifying.

Even in the movies, the hero always hit a limit. Rían had seemed tired after warding one room.

Max hadn't felt drained even after his fire tornado. How the hell was he supposed to keep an endless sea of flames in check for the rest of his life?

The metal absorbed more and more heat, the entire circle growing warm. When it turned bright and hot enough to threaten to bend beneath his fingers, he *finally* felt the flames sputter inside him. The silver ball dipped lower with the fluctuation, and he pulled back, grinning as the ball responded and slid to the bottom.

He lost track of time as he moved the ball up and down. Even with magical exhaustion setting in, it was still too easy to send the ball all the way to the top, but he could finally feel the edges of his limits. And he could see which mental muscles were needed for control of power and shape and size. It wasn't much, but having something to work with was more than he'd had before.

By the time Quinn called him down for lunch, he'd managed to hold the ball between the lines for a full minute. He rolled off the couch with a hum, cradling his familiar to his chest as he headed to the kitchen, feeling lighter than he had in years.

He slid into a chair at the table, not surprised in the least when Quinn set a plate with a grilled cheese sandwich in front of him, sans bacon. Rían sat across from him, eyeing his own sandwich like it was the strangest thing he'd ever seen.

Quinn dropped into the seat next to Max. "So, Lukas says you're Irish."

Rían glanced up with an expression of wary amusement. "Yeah."

"Yeah? What clan? I'm Quinn Faoil."

He shook his head with a soft laugh. "Of course you are." He picked a piece of avocado off his sandwich and offered it to Niamh before answering. "Rían Fáidh."

Max picked out some avocado and tomato for his sugar glider, stifling his laughter over Quinn's thickening accent. When Quinn didn't respond, he glanced over to find him gaping at Rían, rolling his eyes as he reached over and pushed Quinn's open mouth closed.

Quinn snapped out of it and sat up straight. "Feck off! You're not a descendant of the Tuatha Dé Danann!"

Rían shrugged and took a large bite of his sandwich.

"What's the tooth de den?" Max asked with a wince as he butchered the pronunciation.

"Legendary gods of Ireland, and the source of the fae myths," Quinn said, still staring at the other mage like he was one of those gods himself.

"Sorry, what?" It was Max's turn to stare at Rían, waiting for him to roll his eyes or tell them that of course gods and myths weren't real, but he remained silent as he continued eating.

Max dropped his sandwich, feeling dizzy at the thought that he was about to have another world-changing revelation. "Please tell me mythical creatures aren't real."

"Hey," Quinn said, more than a little offended.

Max waved him off. "You don't count. We've known shifters existed as long as mages have," he said. "I mean, unicorns and shit aren't real. Right?" He shot Rían a pleading look.

Rían sighed, licking a smear of avocado off his fingers. "Not anymore. Mostly."

He let out a strangled sound and pressed his face into his hands. "Mostly?"

"I've run into some strange things in the deep, untouched parts of the wilderness, but most of the shite I clean up is made by humans, shifters, or mages. Or some combination of the three. Never seen a unicorn, and as far as I know, I've never met a fae. But I haven't been back home since I was ten."

Rían shoved the last bit of sandwich in his mouth and chewed as he studied Max. "You shouldn't have to worry about any of that anyway. You're too old for the Order to brainwash, and you're bound to three shifters," he said with a quick, disapproving slant to his lips and glance at Quinn. "Which, by the way, is not helping with your control over your magic. One shifter bond is bad enough. Three and you're literally playing with fire.

"I'll have to make some charms and amulets for you. Be sure to wear them, especially whenever you leave the house."

Max nodded, more than willing to do anything to keep his magic under control.

"And you need to name your familiar. You'll need a pouch like mine to keep her in when you're not at home, and always keep her by your side. I'll give you a list of supplies. You can set up a cage if you want, but don't lock her in. She might be an animal, but she's a familiar. Their sense of danger is far more acute than ours, so listen to her."

"Got it," Max said, even though he most certainly did not. He didn't know the first thing about animals or familiars. He was one step away from a meltdown, though thankfully it would only be the mental kind. If anyone gave him a new piece of information to process, like that vampires were real, he was going to lose it.

"Eat up," Quinn said, bumping their shoulders together. "Don't you need to get back to practicing?"

"And I need to finish your wards," Rían said, annoyed. "How you survived here this long is beyond me," he muttered, getting to his feet before pointing at Max. "Practice with the trainer or bond with your familiar. Either of those will help you the most right now. I'm going to finish the property line and work my way back in."

Max resisted the urge to salute and snagged his sandwich, feeding more to his sugar glider before tearing off pieces for himself. "What should I name you, hmm?"

"How about Stripes?" Quinn suggested.

The sugar glider stopped eating and barked at him in clear disapproval.

Max laughed. "That's a no. Don't worry, I won't let anyone else name you," he cooed, rubbing a finger against the top of her head. That earned a soft purring sound before she climbed up his arm and tucked in against his neck.

"Cute," Quinn said, gathering up the empty plates. "You want company or quiet while you practice?"

Max snorted. "Why don't you go flirt with Rían?" he suggested, finishing his sandwich and sliding his plate over.

Quinn gasped. "I was not flirting."

"Uh-huh. Your accent naturally exploded all over us by itself, then?"

He glared and pinched Max's leg. "You're a little shite."

"Thank you. And point made. Now get lost."

Quinn grumbled as he stood. "You are not nearly as scared of us as you should be."

That wasn't entirely true, but Max bit his tongue before he could say he was still plenty wary, especially of Lukas. Not that it was the shifter's fault that he was too quiet and intense.

He headed back upstairs and stretched out on the sofa again, resigning himself to an afternoon of staring at a little ball and willing it to hover between the lines.

CHAPTER 11

"So HERE'S Rían, sitting up in the tent in the middle of the night, dead asleep, and he goes, 'Wolf. You don't have magical powers. *I'm* the mage. I'll turn you into a neeeewt.'"

Caius chuckled as Lukas and Rían regaled them with stories from their missions, Quinn even adding a few of his own. He was content to sip his tea and listen, glad to see Max relaxing enough to laugh.

Dinner wasn't nearly as rowdy as a mess hall, but it had the same kind of comfort, being surrounded by people who belonged to him. For a moment, he was keenly aware of what his uncle had stolen from him.

His father had been alpha of a large pack and expected Caius to take over. Instead, Caius had joined the Marines when he turned eighteen, needing to get away from the empty wilderness of Wyoming. His father had been disappointed, but they'd kept in contact, up until his death four years ago. It wasn't until he finally returned home for the first time in nearly twenty years that he realized how deep his uncle had sunk his teeth into the pack.

In their eyes, Caius had abandoned them all for humans and their wars. The pack named Kostas their new alpha, and Caius was exiled.

A pack of four could hardly be considered a pack by most standards, but it was his. And thanks to his father's refusal to become obsolete in the modern age, and his expectation of Caius taking over the pack, the majority of his wealth was legally transferred to Caius, despite his uncle's betrayal.

When the war stories turned to talk of gaming, Caius grabbed a beer and slipped outside to the patio. The temperature had dropped again, and more snow was in the forecast, but the cold didn't bother him. As much as he'd resented growing up away from a proper city, he preferred the deep snows found in the wilderness. His wolf shifted restlessly inside him as he sat on the swing bench, staring out at the edge of the national park on the other side of their backyard.

He hadn't shifted since he'd been shot with aconite. The doctors might have assured him it was safe enough, but his arm had limited range as a human. He wouldn't be able to run as a wolf.

The door slid open, and Quinn sprawled with boneless grace in the chair next to him. "So, you gonna make a move or what?"

"Excuse me?"

Quinn snorted, running his fingers through his hair as he scanned what little they could see of the neighborhood. "C'mon, Cap. The way you two have been pining over each other is painful to watch."

Caius frowned. "What?"

"What do you mean what?" he demanded with a wide-eyed stare. "Don't lie to me. I can smell it on you!"

Fuck. With a huff, Caius looked away. He couldn't deny his attraction for Max, but he was sure he'd hidden it better than that. Besides, Max got along with Quinn far better than he did anyone else. "He likes you."

"Mmm, yeah," Quinn said, drawing out the words. "Pretty sure he'd fall into bed with any of us. Even Lukas, eventually. But we're not gonna make a move until you do. You bound him first, and you're our alpha. So suck it up and bed him, yeah? I want my turn."

He braced a hand on Caius' shoulder and pushed to his feet. "And hurry up. The house smells like UST so bad, I'm surprised Rían hasn't commented on it," he added, patting Caius on the head before dancing back inside.

Caius growled and wondered if he could get a court-martial backdated. He lingered where he was, draining his beer as true night sank in. He waited until the sound of chatter faded as the others moved to Quinn's lair for gaming before heading inside.

He intended to head straight for bed and instead found Max sitting on the sofa, watching him like a deer in headlights.

"Quinn said I should wait for you?"

Caius swallowed a sigh, unable to help the way his gaze drifted over Max. The clothes he'd picked out suited him. Form-fitting jeans and an overlarge sweater that gave a teasing glimpse of a shoulder. He was even experimenting with the eyeliner they'd picked up, adding an enticing smudge of darkness around his eyes to contrast with the electric blue of his nail polish.

He stepped closer, intending to shoo Max off to bed, but his fingers found their way into silky brown hair instead. "How are you settling in?"

Max blinked, his eyes owl-wide even as he leaned into the touch. "Fine," he said, his breath hitching when Caius' fingers ghosted against his cheek. His lips parted on his exhale, his scent changing almost immediately. There was no denying the sharp, thick tang of arousal.

He couldn't resist stroking his thumb across Max's lips, a quiet growl escaping him when a hot, wet tongue flicked out and tugged his finger in. "Come to bed with me," he murmured, heat blooming in his gut when teeth scraped against his thumb.

His finger slid free when Max stood and slipped his arms around Caius' neck with a grin before hopping and wrapping his legs around his waist. "Thought you'd never ask."

Caius grunted at the unexpected weight, settling his hands on Max's ass. He buried his face in Max's neck, breathing in his scent, full of the warmth of a campfire and a hint of orange blossoms.

He turned for the stairs, ignoring the warning twinges in his left arm as he carried Max up to his bedroom. He may not have much mobility left in it, but he could damn well handle carrying Max for a few minutes. He kicked the door shut behind them and set Max on his feet, sliding his hands up Max's back and around to cup his face. "Tell me if you want me to stop," he murmured, making sure the bond enforced his words before brushing their lips together.

Max melted into him, his hands still buried in Caius' hair. "Don't stop," he breathed, tugging him closer for another kiss.

Caius groaned as Max opened for his tongue, tasting the lingering remnants of the peach ice cream he'd had for dessert. He backed Max towards the bed and hooked his fingers under Max's sweater.

He broke the kiss long enough to pull the sweater over Max's head, dropping it to the floor and diving back in for another.

Max shivered beneath Caius' hands as they explored bare skin. The binding marks may have hidden most of the scars from view, but they were still there. Small bumps and uneven lines detailing a nightmare of a life.

Caius was no stranger to abuse or the malice that lived in some men, but it was something he would never comprehend. When his hands moved to Max's front, he found similar scars there. He pulled back when his finger dragged across the other end of the bullet wound he'd seen the other night, glancing down as he circled it with his thumb.

"Sorry," Max whispered, ducking his head, his scent taking on an acrid stench like he was ashamed.

"Don't," Caius said, grasping Max's chin and gently forcing his head up until their eyes met. "Don't ever apologize for someone else's cruelty."

Max's eyes were suddenly too bright in the darkness, and he blinked repeatedly, struggling through several shallow breaths before nodding.

Caius kissed his forehead, his nose, lingering on his lips. He slid his hands down Max's chest, his stomach, hooking two fingers in the front of his jeans.

Max's grip on Caius' arms tightened. His scent changed again, turning thick and heady with the spike of his arousal.

He popped the button with his thumb before dragging the zipper down, swallowing Max's soft moan as he pushed both jeans and boxers until gravity did the rest. Once Max was bare, Caius chased the goose bumps rippling across exposed flesh with his fingertips.

He settled a hand on Max's lower back before reaching for the lamp, turning it to its lowest setting, then grabbed the lube from the drawer. Then he turned and tossed the bottle onto a pillow. Once he was settled on the edge of the bed, he pulled Max down to straddle his lap.

"Caius," Max murmured, voice pleading. He dragged his fingers down Caius' chest, reaching the bottom of his shirt and unbuttoning it on his way back up.

Caius focused on keeping his breathing steady as Max reached the last buttons and pushed his shirt off his shoulders. He knew Max could see the mess of his arm. The silvery blue remnants of the aconite bullet fused with his skin glinted in the corner of his eye. He expected questions, maybe revulsion, but Max barely slowed in his mission to remove the shirt, then bent closer to press his lips over the worst of the wound, two inches above Caius' heart.

When Max sat up, Caius tangled a hand in his hair and dragged him in for another kiss, sliding his other hand along Max's thigh until he could grip his ass.

Max pressed closer with a moan, rocking forward, grinding himself against Caius' stomach. His hands roamed from arms to chest to shoulders as if unsure where to focus, leaving shivers of pleasure in their wake.

Caius pulled his hand out of Max's hair and fumbled blindly for the lube. When he found it, he thumbed it open and squeezed too much into his palm. It took a moment to warm as he spread it over his fingers, breaking the kiss enough to watch Max's face as he slid a finger along his cleft.

Max pushed closer with a gasp, lifting onto his knees and burying his face in Caius' hair. "Please."

Taking advantage of the new position, he fastened his lips to Max's chest, trailing wet kisses from one nipple to the other as he slowly pressed a finger inside. Fingers twisted in his hair as Max keened, bordering on the point of pain as nails left shallow scratches across his shoulders. He growled as Max's scent sharpened further as he alternated between pushing onto Caius' finger and grinding into his stomach.

He needed more of that scent. Needed to bury his nose in the musk and smoke and citrus until it filled his lungs. He urged Max to lift up higher until he could take the mage into his mouth.

"Fuck! Fuck, Caius," Max gasped, curling over Caius' head, his hips jerking with short, aborted thrusts like he was fighting to hold still.

That wouldn't do. Caius gripped Max's ass with his free hand, working another finger in and swallowing until Max hit the back of his throat.

"Yes," Max hissed, his gasps and sharp cries of pleasure growing louder until even Rían could likely hear.

Precum coated his tongue, the taste matching Max's scent with bitter and salt beneath it, and the musk of sex filled his nose, but it wasn't enough. With a twist of his wrist, he pushed his fingers deeper and found the spot that ensured Max came apart.

With a broken off cry, Max spasmed and shuddered with release, spilling down Caius' throat. His grip went slack once he was spent, his body turning boneless as he panted against Caius' hair. He sank back down to sit and slumped into Caius' chest with a long, satiated moan.

Caius held him with a soft, pleased growl, languishing in the scent and taste of Max while the mage caught his breath. Then he shifted his fingers, curling them enough that Max arched and gasped his name.

There was no rush to get Max worked up again, so Caius took his time, dragging his tongue along Max's neck as he added more lube and another finger.

By the time Caius neared his own limit, Max was hard again and apparently running out of patience. He fisted both hands in Caius' hair and dragged him in for a searing kiss. "Fuck me."

With a growl, Caius toppled Max to the bed and stood. He stripped with military efficiency and grabbed the lube, raking his eyes over Max as he sank to a knee between his thighs. Max's breathing sped up as Caius poured lube into his hand and coated himself. With his other hand, he snagged Max's leg and pulled him to the edge of the bed, then leaned over him. He captured both wrists and pinned them over Max's head with his good arm, gripping his hip with the left and lifting Max enough to press against his entrance.

Max tipped his head back with a long, pleading moan and wrapped his legs around Caius, digging his heels into Caius' ass to pull him closer. "Please, please, hurry the fuck up." It sounded more like a demand than a plea, even as he flexed his wrists against Caius' hold.

Intent on savoring the moment, Caius pressed his nose into Max's neck and breathed deep before sinking into his heat.

Max thrashed and arched beneath him with a hissed, "Fuck!" He tilted his head to the side, baring more of his neck, his legs shaking as they squeezed tighter around Caius. "More."

Caius obliged, inching deeper and deeper until he was buried completely in the too warm heat. He dragged his teeth against the rabbit-quick pulse at Max's throat before sealing his lips against it, leaving a mark as he rocked his hips in slow, shallow thrusts, ignoring the ache and burn starting in his left shoulder.

Maybe it was the bond at work, maybe it was something else, but he doubted he'd ever get enough of Max. Of the scent or smell of him, as addictive as his moans and sharp cries of pleasure. They were overwhelming, filling Caius' senses with the burning need for *more.*

He pulled back and out, gripping Max's thighs and flipping him to his stomach. The surprised yelp drew a soft rumble of a chuckle from him, before he sank back into Max with a groan, gripping his hips tight enough to move in earnest.

Max was a sweetly begging mess beneath him, stretched out on his hands and knees, flushed with pleasure and the heat of flames beneath his skin.

It still wasn't enough. In all his forty-two years, the need to claim had never been this strong before. Binding Max, marking him as pack, neither satisfied the primal need to put a far more visible mark on him. "Tell me you're mine," he growled, giving up the fight against his wolf. The lighting suddenly changed as his eyes turned gold and his breath caught.

In human form, he could smell magic, but the wolf could see the echo of it. A mage always looked brighter than a normal human because of the swirl of raw energy coalesced around them.

Max was lit up like a sunset. Thick threads of oranges and reds and purples, and a bright blue edging to white at his core, with sparks of silver scattered throughout. The outlines of the tattoo were a darker blur of magic against the brightness, a tangible mark, but it barely scratched the possessive itch of his wolf.

"Y-yours," Max whimpered, tossing his head back with a sharp whine.

He would have howled if he'd let his wolf out any further. Instead, he dragged Max closer, lifting his hips higher before rutting into him. With one hand, he found Max's leaking cock and began stroking, planting his other hand between Max's shoulder blades to pin his chest to the bed.

With a curse, Max bucked into Caius' hand, pleas falling from his lips like prayers one moment and commands the next.

Unable to hold back any longer, Caius sank his teeth into the juncture of Max's neck, biting down hard enough to break skin and taste blood.

Max screamed and jerked beneath him, spilling over Caius' hand as he shuddered through a second orgasm a moment later.

Keeping his teeth locked in place, he gave a few more deep thrusts before his own release ripped through him. His wolf finally satisfied, Caius carefully released Max's neck, licking away the smear of blood as he continued to lazily grind into him, riding out the last tremors of pleasure.

Eyes closed and body completely limp, Max groaned and gasped for air, barely even twitching as Caius pressed a lingering kiss to the claiming mark.

When his shoulder threatened to give out, he eased back, snatching the discarded towel from his earlier shower to wipe them down. Then he pulled the covers back and nudged Max to the other side of the bed, flicking the lamp off before stretching out next to him. When Max remained quiet, he reached over, smoothing sweat-damp hair back from his face. "All right?"

Max hummed and leaned into the touch, grasping Caius' wrist and rolling into him. "Yeah…. That was amazing."

"It was," he agreed, sliding his hand down Max's side and over his ass with a deep sigh of content.

"We can do it again?" Max asked, keeping hold of Caius' wrist as he rolled to put his back to Caius, then wiggled until he was tucked against his chest.

"Mmhmm."

"Good." Max sighed and nuzzled against Caius' palm before trapping it between his cheek and the pillow.

Caius buried his nose in Max's hair before hooking his other arm around him, pulling until they were flush against each other. "Quinn will likely want a turn next," he murmured, closing his eyes as lethargy settled into his limbs.

Max's heartbeat spiked, and he tilted his head back as Caius nuzzled along his neck. "Is that okay?"

"If it's okay with you. Wouldn't have let them bind you if I wasn't willing to share."

"No shit," Max breathed, sounding dazed. Which wasn't too surprising.

He wasn't sure how much Max actually knew about shifters, but an alpha willing to share a binding or a mate with anyone was practically unheard of. But Quinn and Lukas were more than just pack. They trusted each other with their lives. Had survived some of the worst missions together. Their pack was forged through fire and blood, and he fully meant it when he said anything of his was theirs.

Including Max.

CHAPTER 12

WHEN LUKAS saw Rían had made omelets and hash browns the next morning, he was overjoyed at having a home-cooked meal, even if it was breakfast. If he hadn't known Rían would refuse outright, he would have suggested that Caius offer him a place in their pack.

He couldn't exactly blame Rían for not wanting anything to do with shifters, especially as he was nearly done with his required service to the Order and was one of the few mages not bound to them. If anyone could walk away at the end of their service, it would be him.

The three of them were nearly done eating by the time Caius and Max deigned to join them, and Lukas snorted quietly at the way their scents were thoroughly mixed. Not that he expected anything less, considering how loud Max had been last night.

Rían retrieved two plates from the oven and set them on the table, his eyes flicking to Max's neck and the new claiming mark there with a brief frown, but he didn't comment. He picked up his own plate and set it in the sink. "I should be finished with your wards in about an hour, but you'll have to get someone else to add anything other than protection from basic magic attacks and trespassers." He didn't wait for a response before slipping outside, leaving the four of them alone with a silent, smitten Caius and an endearingly embarrassed Max.

Quinn was, unsurprisingly, the first to break the silence. "Finally," he said, exasperation in every letter. "So, good?" He glanced between them with a grin and waggle of his eyebrows.

Max flushed and shoveled food into his mouth, refusing to look at any of them.

Lukas finished his coffee and left them to Quinn's probing in favor of his morning run.

Even though Caius said he took care of the man who'd sent thugs after him, he still kept his guard up and his senses tuned into his surroundings. The longer Max was with them, the higher the chance of someone getting an idea of trying to take him. And anyone smart would try to pick them off one by one.

He didn't believe in fate or luck, and he certainty didn't think he could see the future, but he trusted his instincts. In the patterns picked up by his subconscious. That had saved his ass more times than he could count on a mission, when something felt off, enough to set his teeth on edge, and he'd gotten his men out before a building exploded around them.

He had that same feeling now. Like something dark hovered just past the horizon, too close to ignore but too far away to see or prepare for. Waiting games might be the worst, but he was a sniper. Waiting was what he was best at.

LUKAS FOUND himself in the sitting room later that afternoon, watching Rían make charms and amulets while coaching Max. He didn't understand a word of it, but he was fascinated by the charms and gentle working of magic. Rían's magic always felt different from others, more refined and precise, and he'd certainly proven to be far more talented and reliable than other mages Lukas had worked with.

"Here," Rían said, finishing with a necklace and holding it out to Max. "Wear this all the time, even at home. It's enchanted pure silver, and I've put a dozen protective wards into the triquetra itself."

Max took the necklace like he was afraid it would shatter with his touch. "Isn't silver toxic to wolves?"

Lukas shook his head. "That's a myth. The only thing that really hurts us is aconite. Or a very lucky head shot."

He didn't look entirely convinced, but he put the necklace on. Once it was in place, Rían nodded and slumped against the couch where he was sitting on the floor.

"Get some rest, squirrel."

Rían shot him an annoyed glare, which was ruined by his yawn. "I need to make a few more charms."

"You don't," Max said. "You've done plenty. I can feel the power in this thing. It should be more than enough by itself."

Rían frowned at him. "If you were a trained mage, maybe. But you pissed off the Order, and you've got the attention of the entire city now, too, if not the state. That charm is only going to protect you a handful of times before it goes out, and any mage worth anything will know how to override it fast. Once I leave here, I won't be able to get another one to you for a few weeks, at least. I already have another two assignments." He muttered a familiar curse in Irish under his breath.

"Do they not give you time to recover?" Lukas asked with a soft growl.

Rían shrugged. "I only have two months left. They're determined to work me to the very end."

"Get some rest," Max said. "Then maybe show me how to recharge this thing without blowing it up?"

Rían looked like he wanted to argue, but he must have been more exhausted than he was letting on, because he nodded. "Only need a few hours."

"Yeah right." Lukas suspected he needed more like a solid ten and had no intention of waking him before then.

"And name your familiar!" Rían added over his shoulder.

"I already named her Aradia!" Max called back with a roll of his eyes.

Once Rían was out of earshot, he turned his attention to Max, who was holding the amulet up and flicking it so it spun. The magic infused in it was visible, making it look like a tiny ball of molten silver. The small smile on his lips wasn't something Lukas had seen except when Caius or Quinn was fawning over him.

"Can you tell me why you don't like me?" The words escaped before he could think better of it, but Max was supposed to be pack now. A bigger pack might have members who didn't get along, but it was just the four of them. Any issue with one was an issue for them all.

Max sighed and dropped the necklace. "It's not that.... You remind me of one of my father's men. He was quiet and would always watch me, laugh when he would sneak up and scare the shit out of me. I know it's stupid—"

"It's not stupid," he said firmly. "I'll try not to sneak up on you, but I can't help being quiet."

"That's okay." Max bit his lip, glancing at Lukas before standing and carefully stepping around Rían's mess of supplies to sit on the other end of the couch, drawing a leg up so he could face Lukas. "Can I ask something?"

"Sure." Lukas shifted to mirror him so they faced each other, his curiosity piqued.

"You all can really turn into wolves?"

"Yes."

Max narrowed his eyes at him. "Don't laugh at me."

"I wasn't."

"You were on the inside."

Lukas snorted but didn't try to deny it. "Is that really what you wanted to ask?"

"No…." He squirmed, and his scent shifted with an interesting mix of embarrassment and arousal. "Wolves, when they have sex, they… you know…."

Lukas raised an eyebrow as he certainly did not know. Maybe he had an idea, but he definitely wanted to hear Max say it. "They what?"

Max glared even as his ears turned red. "They pop a knot!"

"Yeah, and?" Lukas tilted his head and nearly choked holding back a laugh. He lost it when Max flung a pillow at his face, using it to smother his laughter.

"You're a dick."

"So I've been told." Lukas dropped the pillow to his lap. "What are you trying to ask?"

Max shrugged, picking at a piece of lint on his sleeve. "The movies always imply that happens in your human form too."

"And by movies you mean porn?" He snickered as the other pillow hit him and tossed it back. "That's a Hollywood myth. We're not a hybrid." He tilted his head with a smirk. "Why? Disappointed you didn't get some hot alpha knot?"

"Don't make me set you on fire."

"Oh, feisty," he purred, enjoying the way Max flushed. "Do you want to see?"

"Your knot? No thanks."

Lukas laughed. "My wolf, you little shit."

Max shivered, hugging the pillow to his chest. "Yeah, okay."

"Sure you won't freak out?"

"Can't be any worse than in the movies, right?"

"The movies never get anything right," Lukas muttered. He considered dropping it, but he hadn't shifted in a while. He'd been away on missions the last couple of months, and Caius hadn't shifted since his injury, so they never had a proper pack run.

He stood and moved to the far side of the room, pretending not to notice the sudden spike in Max's heartbeat. He ran his fingers through his hair as he took a slow, deep breath, before pulling his shirt off and shoving his jeans and boxers down as he unleashed his wolf.

Maybe there used to be a time when the movies were right, with the shift being an agonizing tearing of flesh and reshaping of bones as a human body bent and twisted into a shape it shouldn't be able to take. But mages had mingled with wolves for centuries, and their legends said a powerful mage had gifted wolves with a painless shift centuries ago.

Between one breath and the next, Lukas shed his human skin and the world tilted as he landed on four large paws. He gave a vigorous shake of his body, settling his thick black fur into place before promptly sitting on his hind legs and focusing on Max.

The mage sat frozen on the couch, hardly breathing as he stared. "Holy fuck," he whispered. "Oh my fucking God. The movies are *so* wrong." He leaned forward as if to stand and ended up on his knees on the floor, though he didn't seem to notice. "You're really a wolf. Holy crap."

Lukas tilted his head as he watched, his tail tip thumping against the floor in amusement. It'd been a while since he'd seen someone's first reaction to a shift. Watching a human's brain break in real time was never a disappointment.

"Can I pet you?"

He lowered his head and stood, then took a step forward when Max didn't flinch. He slowly crossed the room and pressed his nose into Max's cheek, breathing in the smoke-and-citrus mixed with Caius' winter storm scent. The fingers burrowing into his fur felt amazing, and he closed his eyes, leaning into the scritches and squirming to guide them to the back of his neck, then to his chest.

"You're really just an overgrown puppy, aren't you?"

Lukas growled, cracking his eyes open when Max froze, wariness curling through his scent. If he could have rolled his eyes he would have. Instead, he settled for licking Max's face, his tongue hanging out when Max spluttered and wiped his mouth.

"Augh, gross. Dog breath. In my mouth," he whined, gagging.

Lukas jumped forward, ignoring Max's indignant squawk as he sprawled his considerable weight over the mage and pinned him to the floor.

"Fuck, you're heavy," Max groaned, squirming beneath him. His arms flopped like a beached whale before giving up. "I take it back. You're not a puppy, you're a big, scary wolf, now get offff."

Lukas ignored him and licked his face again, pleased when the lingering fear in Max's scent cleared, though the smell of burning fur was far more concerning.

CHAPTER 13

RÍAN LEFT that evening, after showing Max how to channel magic into his amulet and the wards, though the wards should last far longer than the amulet despite both being hastily put together. Max was absolutely certain he would cause the amulet to explode if he tried to pour magic into it without Rían there to help, but that was a problem for Future Max.

Rían left the training device and promised to send some tutorials when he had the chance, but for now, Max locked himself in his room to work on his assignments. Now that he wasn't constantly focused on not burning everything to ashes, he could get caught up. With finals in less than two weeks, he needed to cram in some serious study time.

Days passed without incident, though Max fell into old habits and didn't leave the house unless he had to. Lukas was called away on another mission, which was disappointing when Max had just started to feel comfortable around him. He spent his days studying or exploring his magic and his nights with Caius. He'd expected Quinn to make a move, but he seemed content to let Caius have priority.

Max was putting the finishing touches on his last assignment when Caius called him for dinner. Before he could say he'd be down in a few minutes, his body was already halfway to the door, tablet and pen still in hand. He tried to stop, to turn around and at least put the tablet down, but he had zero control over his own body.

Aradia landed on his shoulder with a soft bark, rubbing against his cheek, but it was a small comfort.

Magic coiled in his hands, responding to the fear and anger thumping in his chest, but thanks to Rían's spells, he didn't feel on the verge of losing control of the flames.

Caius and Quinn both froze when he stepped into the room, turning to look at him.

"What's wrong?" Quinn asked, glancing past Max as if expecting a threat behind him.

"What's *wrong*?" he spat, stalking past Quinn on his way to Caius to shove him hard in the chest. "You used the bond on me! I couldn't even fight it before I was up and walking down here!"

Caius lifted his hands with a wince. "I'm sorry. It seems to take any statement as a command."

"Well fix it," Max hissed. "You promised I wouldn't be your prisoner." He'd felt the bond before, as a shiver of suggestion in the back of his mind, but it had always been something he was willing to do. His body moving without his will controlling it was an experience he never wanted to go through again.

Quinn cleared his throat, throwing his own hands up when Max spun around to glare at him. "Why don't you dial back the pyromania, and then after we eat, we can experiment with the bond and see how to control it better?"

Max blinked and looked down at his hands to see bright white and blue flames surrounding them. With a yelp, he tossed his tablet on the table before shaking his hands out, which did nothing but make a whooshing sound as the flames sailed through the air. He closed his eyes with a groan, forcing his breathing to steady before he could panic.

He was safe here. He didn't *really* want to burn the house down, or Caius or Quinn.

Reaching inside himself, he found the spigot on his magic and imagined turning it from full blast to a trickle. The swell of flames in his hands flickered and lessened, and when he opened his eyes, the flames had turned from blue to orange, until they fizzled out with the faint scent of smoke.

"Your tablet looks fine," Quinn said, offering it to him.

True enough, there was no melted plastic or any sign of heat damage at all. Max sighed and set it aside before sinking into a chair at the dining table. He glanced at Caius to make sure he hadn't caught fire, relieved when there was no sign of damage on him either.

Caius sat beside him at the head of the table. "We'll figure something out. Unless you're in danger, the bond shouldn't be needed."

Max sat back and crossed his arms. "There has to be some kind of guide on how it works. People have been binding mages for centuries."

"Yeah, and most of those were done with every intention of keeping the mage under someone's control," Quinn said dryly.

Max made a face, but that was easy enough to believe. He didn't even want to think what would happen if his father managed to put a binding on him. He picked at his salad, feeding pieces of lettuce to Aradia between bites.

They ate in a tense silence, before Quinn bumped their shoulders together. "Come on, let's figure this out." He slung an arm around Max and tugged him towards one of the overstuffed chairs in the living room. "Sit."

Max sat without thinking, only realizing afterwards that he'd felt the bond at work. He tipped his head back with a glare, a faint curl of satisfaction in his gut when Quinn backed away with his hands up. Maybe being a mage wouldn't be so bad, once he learned to control it properly. Once the people who were after him were dealt with and everyone else learned he wasn't worth the risk of messing with.

Caius sat on the sofa across from him. "Lift your right hand."

He grabbed his right hand with his left to keep it in place, but it still lifted of its own accord. "I don't like this," he hissed, managing a deep breath only after he dropped both hands again.

What followed was a long, strange session of Simon Says. The silver lining was that, after about twenty minutes, his limbs moving on their own was more an annoyance than panic-inducing. Eventually, he grabbed his tablet to finish his assignment and tried to ignore his left arm's acrobatics.

It was late in the evening when Quinn told him to pat his head and Max stopped with his arm in midair.

"Fucking finally." Max sat up and leaned forward. "Do it again."

"Stick your tongue out."

Nothing. Not even a twitch of magic.

"What'd you do?" Caius asked.

"Honestly, I just thought, 'I don't care if he does that or not.'"

"Seriously?" Max eyed him in disbelief. "All this time and that's all it took?"

Quinn shrugged. "I've been trying not to put intention into the words, or pretending I'm talking to no one."

"Stand up," Caius said.

There was a brief pulse of magic, and Max's muscles tensed as if to push to his feet, but then it fizzled out. He jumped to his feet anyway, not missing the frustrated pinch of Caius' eyebrows before Max threw his arms around Quinn. "Thank you," he said, pressing a kiss to his cheek before dropping into Caius' lap. "Bed. Now."

Quinn snickered. "You've turned him into a nympho."

"Excuse you," he said, as Caius stood and carried him to the stairs, "it's satyromaniac for men."

"How do you even know that?"

"I get bored easily." Max grinned as Quinn's laughter followed them up the stairs. "Just so you know, I don't mind if you keep using the bond a little in the bedroom," he drawled, yelping with a startled laugh when Caius tripped up the last steps.

"Noted."

IT SNOWED again overnight, dropping another few inches.

Max braved the elements enough to sit on the swing bench on the porch, breathing in the crisp fresh air. He learned within minutes that the cold no longer bothered him. The moment he started to feel chilled, the flames rose up beneath his skin to keep him warm. As nice as that was, he didn't want to think about how nightmarish summer would be.

He tipped his head back to watch Aradia climb up the post at one end of the porch and sail to the other side, a burst of wind magic keeping her in the air. Naming her seemed to have unlocked some familiar ability that let her access her own magic, though she seemed to still be learning how to control it.

He pushed the bench back and let it swing forward, the metal training device forgotten beside him. The day was far too nice to bother with studying or training. There was a restless itch building inside him, but he wasn't sure what to do to relieve it.

The door slid open, and Quinn poked his head out. "Hungry?"

"Starving," he groaned, getting to his feet. He wasn't sure if it was because he had free access to the kitchen or because magic drained so much energy, but he was hungry all the time now. He settled at the counter as Quinn set a plate with a grilled cheese sandwich in front of him. He eyed it with a wrinkle of his nose. "Not that I'm complaining, but we really need to learn to make something new." Aradia swooped in to land beside him with a bark of agreement.

"Believe me, I've tried. Nothing else I've made is edible."

"Nothing?"

"I made mac 'n' cheese once. It was lumpy and crunchy." Quinn pointed at Max's face of horrified disgust. "Yeah, that's what Cap and Lukas looked like when they ate it."

Max shuddered and bit into the sandwich, thankful it tasted normal. "Are they still out?" Lukas had returned late last night, and he and Caius had left earlier for supplies.

"Yeah, they said they'd be a while." Quinn sat with his own sandwich and bumped his knee against Max's. "So I was thinking we could take advantage of their absence."

Max choked as he inhaled a chunk of bread, feeling his ears burn even as he drained his water. "Advantage how?" he wheezed.

"We'll think of something. You still haven't been down to see my lair yet. I've got tons of games."

"Okay." He suspected Quinn didn't mean to play games, but he appreciated the option. He'd started to think Caius was full of it and that Quinn and Lukas weren't interested in him now that Caius had staked a claim, especially since Caius never brought it up again. He had to wonder if Caius really meant it when he said he wouldn't mind, or if Caius would stop wanting him.

"What are you worrying about?"

Max sighed and cursed Quinn's nose. "Caius said you might want to, you know, but…."

Quinn tilted his head. "But you're worried it'll change things between you two?" When Max nodded, Quinn smiled. "Max, he claimed you. Not even the Order is taking you from him."

"You mean the bite mark?" he asked, dragging his finger over the faint scar on his neck. Caius was obsessed with it, constantly touching or licking or kissing it. "I thought it was some territorial shifter thing."

"Well yeah, it's that too."

Max shook his head. "It can't be a claiming. I'm not a shifter."

"*A mhuirnín*, this isn't the Middle Ages. We can have a claiming with non-shifters." Quinn grinned and waggled his eyebrows. "Sometimes we even share."

"Really?" he asked, not sure he believed that.

"Don't believe the movies. Sure, some shifters are territorial fuckwads, but it's the twenty-first century. Cap wouldn't have let us bind you if he wasn't willing to share."

"Have you two…?"

"Had sex?" Quinn chuckled and shook his head. "No. He had a thing with a general a few years ago, but it didn't last long. He's not really my type anyway."

Unable to help himself, Max asked, "Lukas more your type?" He grinned when Quinn looked away, but not before Max saw the wistful smile. "If you're pining for him, why would you want to settle for me?"

"First off, I'm not settling." Quinn narrowed his eyes at him, and Max heard the distinct rumble of a growl. "Second, I'm open to a poly arrangement. I can handle a relationship with more than one person. The question is, do you want that too?"

Did he? Barely two weeks ago, Jake had betrayed him in every way possible and ended up dead because of it. He may not have thought Jake was forever, but he at least had trusted the bastard. The last thing he ever thought possible was that he'd Spark and then be bound to three shifters. Or have the Order after him, along with probably every corrupt person with any significant power in the damn city. "I've never even had a serious relationship before," he said, tearing pieces off his sandwich and feeding some to Aradia.

"We don't have to be serious. Cap is serious enough for all of us."

"Maybe," he said, watching Quinn from the corner of his eye, unable to believe he was really interested. He could barely believe Caius was, and he had the mark to prove it.

When they finished eating, he took the plates to the sink, his heart skipping in surprise when he turned to find Quinn behind him. He took the offered hand and let Quinn lead him downstairs, into what looked like an entirely different house.

Where the upstairs was dark wood floors and walls alternating between rich greens and off-white, Quinn's lair was light wood floors, with the back wall painted in a brilliant mural of the woods overlooking a lake at sunset. The walls on either side continued the motif with dense trees. The closer he looked, the more details he found—a deer grazing, a fox caught in a midair pounce, birds perched in the trees.

"Wow. Who painted all this?"

Quinn chuckled. "It was an expensive spell, but the scene came from me. This is where I grew up."

Max turned in surprise. "It's beautiful."

"Yeah, this part was."

When Max stepped farther into the room, he spotted a nook with a large L-shaped desk filled with six monitors and three towers under it. "Are you a hacker?"

"Something like that."

"Right." He didn't buy that at all. Not that it mattered. Hacking was usually one of the tamer crimes.

Quinn dropped onto a large leather sofa and propped a foot on the coffee table. "So, game? Movie?"

Max sank onto a knee next to Quinn and balanced with a hand on his shoulder, struggling to keep his breathing steady as nerves twisted in his gut. "It's... not cheating if he agreed to it. Right?"

Quinn's smile softened as he tugged Max closer, easily manhandling him until he was sitting across the shifter's lap. He held Max steady with one arm around his waist and pulled his phone out with the other hand.

Max made a sound embarrassingly close to a squeak when he saw *Cap* flash on the outgoing call. "What are you doing?"

"Shh." Quinn pulled the phone out of reach when Max grabbed for it, chuckling when Caius answered.

"What's wrong?"

"Nothing, except I'm trying to seduce Max and he's worried about cheating on you."

Max groaned and buried his face in his hands. And now Caius was going to think Max thought they were in a committed relationship when Caius had certainly not said anything remotely like that. For all Max knew, this was just a fling or a multi-night-stand.

"Max," Caius said.

He jumped at how close that sounded, lifting his head to find Quinn holding the phone near his ear. "Yeah?"

"Whether you sleep with Quinn or not, it won't change anything between us. It's your choice."

Max wanted to ask if Caius was sure, but he settled for an "Okay" instead.

"We'll be back in a couple of hours. Anything else?"

"Sushi for dinner," Quinn said. "Thanks, Cap." Then he hung up, cutting off Caius' exasperated sigh and tossing the phone aside as he turned his full attention to Max. "Satisfied?"

Max shivered, his eyes flicking to Quinn's lips. He'd wanted to kiss them almost from the beginning. "Fuck it," he muttered, ignoring Quinn's delighted laugh as he leaned in and kissed him.

He expected Quinn to take things slower than Caius did, but he was pleasantly surprised when Quinn gripped his hair in a tight fist and pressed his tongue past Max's lips. Quinn kissed like Caius, like he expected to be in control, and Max was fine with that. With a moan, he gripped Quinn's shoulder and hair and shifted to straddle his lap, grinding their hips together until Quinn finally broke away with a low growl.

His hazel eyes seemed to glow, but when he blinked, they were back to normal. "Bed," he ordered, not waiting for Max to get up. Instead, he gripped Max's ass and stood.

Max couldn't help the needy moan as his stomach swooped with desire. "Hot," he murmured, attacking Quinn's lips again.

Quinn laughed into the kiss, carrying him across the room and kicking a door open before tossing Max onto the bed. He wasted no time in stripping Max of his pants and underwear, tossing them across the room like he was personally offended by their existence.

Max was struck motionless by the intensity of Quinn's focus, unresisting as Quinn rolled him to his stomach. He shivered from the cool air on his back as his sweater was pushed up and over his head. Then his arms were tugged behind his back, trapped there by the sweater. It took a moment for his brain to catch up, the brief flare of panic at being restrained fizzling out beneath the kisses traveling down his spine.

"I bet even Caius hasn't done this for you yet," Quinn said, sounding smug as he gave a firm tug on Max's hips, dragging him to the edge of the bed before sinking to his knees.

Max squirmed, digging his toes against the floor as Quinn's hands settled on his ass, and then his brain turned to white noise as a hot, wet tongue licked him from his balls to his hole. "Oh my fuck," he gasped, his eyes rolling back when Quinn licked him again. Then that tongue teased past his entrance and he couldn't do anything more than make a desperate gurgling sound as his groans stuck in his chest.

Zings and sparks of ecstasy ignited through his body, lighting up all his nerves as if each and every one connected to his ass. He couldn't speak. Could hardly even remember to breathe beyond the intense pleasure coursing through him. At least until countless minutes later when his toes started to ache.

Finally, Quinn pulled back, leaving Max a gasping, shaking mess of too hot flesh teetering on the edge. His legs were shaking when Quinn maneuvered him back onto the bed, where he sprawled bonelessly on his stomach, his arms still trapped behind him. He might have minded, but he was far more interested in watching Quinn strip and the slow reveal of toned muscles covered in smooth, pale flesh.

Quinn grinned and winked before grabbing the lube from the nightstand. "You good?"

Max tried twice before he got his tongue to work. "Hurry up and fuck me."

Quinn chuckled, crawling onto the bed and settling between Max's legs. "Did I make you impatient?" He ignored Max's ass grinding against him in an attempt to urge him on, taking his sweet time with the lube, much to Max's annoyance.

"Quinn," he growled, two seconds away from setting his sweater on fire and taking care of things himself.

With a tsk, Quinn gripped Max's hips and finally pressed into him.

"Fuck, please," Max whined, tossing his head and arching in pleasure. "Please, please, please."

"Fuck, you feel so good," Quinn groaned, his fingers digging into Max's hips and ass as he sank in, inch by slow inch.

It wasn't enough. The restless itch plaguing him all day grew worse, and being trapped, unable to sink his fingers into hair or flesh, bordered on unbearable. "*Quinn*."

Quinn leaned over him, pinning him to the bed and pressing his face against Max's neck, burying himself completely with a quick, hard thrust. Hot breath washed across his throat before Quinn nuzzled against the mark Caius had left, dragging his tongue across it. "Can I mark you?" When he pulled back to look at Max, his eyes glowed, the faint light unique to shifters shining in their depths.

It was the same glow he'd seen in Caius' eyes most nights, especially when the alpha was focused on the claiming mark.

"Uh-huh," he said, hardly processing the words, but anything Quinn asked for right then was fine. "Only if you move."

Quinn snorted, but he got moving, driving into Max with deep, steady thrusts that blanked Max's mind with pleasure again.

He promptly forgot what Quinn had asked in favor of begging him to touch him, to move faster and harder, to let him come. The only response he got was murmured nonsense and soft growls against his neck, but Quinn slid a hand down, grasping Max's aching cock and giving him something to thrust into. Right before sinking his teeth into Max's neck, on the opposite side of Caius' mark.

He jerked at the sharp pain, his eyes flying open with a soundless scream. Max was no stranger to pain, but being bit by a shifter was something else entirely. The pain was temporary and quickly turned to a bright hot spark of pleasure that radiated through his entire body and into his core, like a thread of Quinn's essence was reaching for Max's flames.

His magic surged as the thread connected to him, stronger than it'd been when Caius bit him. There was an answering pulse as the magic Rían set in the foundation and amulet flared in response, channeling and diffusing the burst of excess energy before it could set the entire room ablaze.

Quinn tightened his grip on Max's cock and stroked faster, matching the speed of his thrusts, until Max tipped his head back with a loud cry as he shuddered with release. Quinn followed a few thrusts later, pulling his teeth from Max's shoulder with a sharp growl as he came.

Max's body turned liquid, small tremors of pleasure curling his toes, though it wasn't long before his arms and shoulders started to protest his position. "Arms," he slurred.

"Fuck, sorry." Quinn groaned as he pulled out before guiding Max's arms free of his sweater. Then he rolled off the bed and disappeared into a bathroom before returning with a warm cloth to wipe them both down. "You good?" he asked, sprawling out next to Max.

"Uh-huh." So good. Afterglow was awesome. He could see why people got addicted to sex.

Quinn chuckled and pulled the blanket over them, hooking an arm and leg over Max before nuzzling against his mark.

His claiming mark.

Fuck. Bound *and* claimed by shifters.

Max's last thought before he passed out was what the hell was his life?

HE WAS woken by a commotion upstairs and burrowed against Quinn's chest, dread swelling inside him before he fully regained consciousness. He was sure Caius would be pissed, despite saying he was okay with this.

Quinn stirred and tightened his arms around Max. "None of that," he murmured. "It's fine, you'll see." He rolled away with a yawn and started tossing clothes onto the bed. Once he dressed, he headed to the stairs like he had no care in the world. "I don't smell sushi," he called.

"Your nose is broken," Lukas called back.

Max chewed on the inside of his cheek as he lingered at the bottom of the stairs. A few moments later, Aradia sailed down and landed on his shoulder with a soft chirp, nuzzling into his cheek. "I'm fine," he murmured, stroking her soft fur.

He took a breath and headed up to the kitchen. Quinn was digging through food containers, and Lukas was hauling large pieces of what looked like a metal fence upstairs, but his attention zeroed in on Caius setting several bags on the table. Max froze when Caius turned and gray eyes focused on him. He didn't miss the quick glance to his neck or the way his nostrils flared as if scenting Max from all the way across the room.

Which he probably was. He could probably smell the grilled cheese Max had eaten for lunch.

Fuck, did he smell different since Quinn bit him? Did he smell bad? They hadn't showered; he must still smell like sex. Fucking hell, Caius could probably smell Quinn on him. Who in their right mind wanted to smell someone else on their…. What were they? Lovers, boyfriends? Bound and master?

He opened his mouth to say he needed to go shower, but all that came out was a strangled gurgle.

Both Caius and Quinn moved towards him, Caius gripping his shoulders as Quinn wrapped arms around his stomach from behind. Caius slid his hands up until they wrapped around the sides of Max's neck, tipping his head up with thumbs under his jaw.

"There's nothing wrong."

Max sagged against Quinn and nearly choked on a relieved gasp, latching on to Caius' wrists. "Really?"

Caius leaned down, claiming Max's lips and kissing him as thoroughly as he had the night before, leaving Max momentarily dazed. He lingered with another kiss before stroking his thumb against Quinn's mark. His nod of approval was the last bit of reassurance Max needed to relax into Quinn's hold with a shaky exhale.

"What's all this?" he asked, nodding to the bags.

"Supplies." Caius stepped away and pulled out boxes of pet food, treats, and toys.

Max's eyebrows inched up a bit farther with each one, until Caius had emptied all four bags.

Aradia launched off Max's shoulder and glided to the table, sniffing at the boxes until she found one she wanted and pawed at it.

Caius immediately opened it and shook what looked like bugs and small pieces of dehydrated fruit onto the top of another box.

"Oh gross," Max muttered, pushing back into Quinn. "I don't do bugs."

Quinn laughed and propped his chin on top of Max's head. "I think Cap can handle the bugs." He patted Max's stomach before he went back to sorting the containers with their dinner.

Max picked through the toys and supplies, finding a hammock, a hanging tent, hanging jungle gym, and various swinging toys, several forage toys and treat dispensers, and a giant chew toy. He turned an incredulous look on Caius. "You didn't need to get all this."

"I wanted to. Your familiar is part of the pack, just like you."

He blinked against the stinging in his eyes and reached out to rub one of Aradia's ears. "Thank you."

"Of course. If you want to have any say on where the cage goes, you should catch Lukas before he finishes setting it up."

Max hurried up the stairs and found Lukas putting together a large cage, tucked against the wall in Caius' room by the bookcase. "Shouldn't this go in my room?"

When Lukas glanced at him, Max got the distinct impression he was annoyed.

"This is your room."

He could have argued that, considering all his clothes and possessions were in the room he'd first woken up in, but he decided against it. He hesitated near the bed, wondering what he could have possibly done to make Lukas mad, or if it was only his imagination. "I can finish," he offered.

"I'm almost done."

Max nodded even though Lukas wasn't looking at him. "Okay. Thanks." He backed out of the room and headed back downstairs.

Caius was clearing off the table while Quinn set out their dinner.

Max desperately wished one of them could learn to cook, but at least sushi wasn't grilled cheese or greasy. Maybe after his finals, he'd look up some recipes. It couldn't be that hard to follow some directions, right? So long as he didn't have a hot guy dancing naked and distracting him from paying attention.

When he reached the table, Aradia raced up his arm to settle against his neck, thankfully no longer munching on bugs.

"Here," Caius said, handing over what looked like a stuffed sugar glider plushie with a long strap. Only when he turned it over did Max see it was a pouch. When he opened it, Aradia hopped right in, twisting around and around before finally curling into a ball with a contented chirp.

With a soft laugh, Max hooked the strap over his neck and adjusted it until it settled against his chest where Rían's own pouch had hung. "Thank you."

Quinn dropped into the seat next to him and popped a piece of sushi into his mouth, closing his eyes with a groan. "I've missed sushi."

Max rolled his eyes and reached for his own container. "You ate it last week."

"I'd eat it every day."

"You're ridiculous," he said, though as soon as he took his own bite, he had to fight against groaning like Quinn. It *was* good. But he still wouldn't want to eat it every day.

Lukas came downstairs and sat across from Quinn. "Cage is set," he said, digging into his own food. Not sushi. It looked like some kind of beef stir-fry.

Max watched him from the corner of his eye, but Lukas kept his focus on his food. Before the silence could turn awkward, he cleared his throat. "I have finals on Thursday, if I could borrow a car."

"I'll take you," Quinn said.

"I can drive myself. I'll be there for a few hours."

Quinn gave him a look and shoved another piece of sushi into his mouth, tucking it to the side to say, "You're not going anywhere alone while the Order is after you."

"Quinn's right," said Caius. "Until you've learned to use your magic properly, it's too dangerous. Especially when we don't know who all might be targeting you."

Max tensed, his fingers nearly snapping his chopsticks in half. He knew Caius meant well, but those were nearly the same words his father had used, always paranoid someone would attack them. Or target Max, even though his father had made it clear that Max would never inherit, even if he'd wanted to. His twelve-year-old sister, who he'd rarely been allowed to speak to, would inherit when she came of age.

Eventually, not being allowed to leave without a bodyguard turned into not allowed to leave without an escort to leave without his father's explicit permission to not allowed to leave at all.

He wouldn't be trapped like that again.

"I won't be held prisoner," he said, thankful when his voice didn't shake. Three pairs of eyes focused on him, but he kept his attention on Caius.

"You're not a prisoner," Caius said, meeting his gaze. "You can go wherever you need to go, so long as you have protection. If you'd prefer I hire a bodyguard until the Order is dealt with, I can."

"Once the Order is gone, I can travel alone?"

"Once we have established our territory and you're no longer a target, yes."

"How long do you expect that to be?"

"A few months, maybe." Caius held up a hand before Max could protest. "I promise you will not be a prisoner here. I'll hire a bodyguard so you don't have to rely on one of us if you need to go somewhere. For now, can Quinn go to the campus with you?"

Max stared at his plate, his instincts still raging at him to fight for his freedom before he fell into the familiar, bottomless hole of helpless despair. Where did he draw the line? Where could he? He'd already let them bind and claim him. He was pretty sure shifters and mages lived by different laws, and even if they didn't, Caius could order him to stay inside and the bond would ensure he obeyed.

"Fine," he said, hating how he felt like he'd lost. His appetite was gone, but he forced down a few more pieces of sushi before sliding the rest over to Quinn. He grabbed the bags of supplies and took them upstairs. Only when he got to Caius' room, he decided he really didn't want Aradia's cage in there.

He piled the bags in his own room and carefully set the pouch on his bed before heading back up and starting the arduous task of dragging the cage out and down a flight of stairs without drawing attention to himself.

Thankfully, the others were smart enough to leave him be if they heard anything. It took over ten minutes, and he nearly lost a finger in the process, but he managed to get the cage into his own room. He closed the door, wiggled the cage into place in the corner where sunlight wouldn't hit it too much, then set to work filling the bottom with litter and hanging the beds and toys.

Aradia came to inspect when he was finishing up and gave it her seal of approval, promptly climbing into the tent and going back to sleep.

"Well, at least someone's happy," he muttered. He set up the food trays and filled the bottle from the bathroom tap. He gathered up the trash to set by the door, then flopped onto his bed.

Had he overreacted? He didn't think so. He'd said from the beginning he wanted his freedom. Caius might mean well, but the Order hadn't come knocking on their door. They'd probably given up. Surely they knew he wasn't worth training this late in life.

Still, his father would come after him sooner or later, regardless of training or potential. It would be nice to have a shifter at his side when that happened.

He groaned, rolling from side to side before pulling his pillow to his chest and shoving his face into it. "Fuuuuuuck."

A knock at the door made him freeze, and he slowly lowered the pillow to peek over it. "Yeah?"

The door opened enough for Caius to poke his head in. "You okay?"

Max sighed and sat up. "'M fine."

Caius raised an eyebrow, glancing at the cage, though he didn't comment on it. "If you're sure."

He tightened his arms around the pillow and nodded. He'd be fine, so long as they kept their word. The moment they tried to tell him he couldn't go somewhere or do something, then they'd have a problem. Of the house burning to ash variety.

"Are you sleeping here?"

"Probably," Max said after a moment. "I need to study more." And he needed a shower and some quiet time to himself.

"All right. Good night."

"Night." He waited for the door to close before flopping onto the bed again. He felt like a dick, but he refused to wallow.

He showered, put on some music, and pored over his notes for a few hours. His studying had gone well enough the past week that he was confident he could pass the finals. Amazing what a change in environment could do. Even if he was bound to shifters, at least they weren't telling him how disappointing his entire existence was.

Only time would tell if they would keep their word. By the time they showed their true colors, he was determined to have learned enough magic to break the bindings and make it on his own if he had to.

CHAPTER 14

MAX FINISHED his last test and sat back with a groan. Fuck finals. And fuck his brilliant idea of keeping them all scheduled on the same day so he only had to make one trip to campus. He eyed the clock and saw he had about half an hour of his allotted time left, but he couldn't bring himself to care enough to double-check his answers. He was done.

He gathered everything up, hooking Aradia's pouch around his neck again and peeking inside. She was still asleep, so he settled it against his chest and took the tests up to the monitor to hand over, then made his escape.

Quinn had his legs stretched out on one of the benches down the hall, absorbed in his phone. When Max peeked over his shoulder, he saw Quinn type out *on our way back* in a text to Caius before hitting Send.

"Stupid shifter hearing," Max muttered, ignoring Quinn's laugh as he headed for the exit.

"Hungry? Why don't we order food from that steak place and grab some ice cream to celebrate you finishing the semester?"

Max slipped his sunglasses over his eyes as they stepped outside. "You mean the steak place Lukas has an orgasm over whenever it's mentioned?" He glanced over when Quinn growled, snickering at his glare. "Gods, when are you gonna make a move?"

Quinn groaned, his head falling back as he muttered the same curse Rían had favored under his breath.

Whatever else he said was lost in the sudden burst of white noise in Max's ears as he saw a forest green Firebird driving across the parking lot towards them. He knew that car. It belonged to one of his father's men.

He reached for Quinn, a dozen different warnings fighting over his tongue as fear squeezed his chest. He didn't get a chance to do more than latch on to Quinn's arm before the car's window rolled down as if in slow motion, the muzzle of a semiautomatic gun sticking out.

Quinn's curse was loud and broke the strange stretching of time. The sharp, echoing retort of gunfire cracked through the air at the same time the trees spun around him and his back hit the ground.

The gunfire continued for an endless second. Max's amulet flared bright, creating a force field around them that stopped the bullets. Then car doors squeaked open and footsteps pounded on the pavement. Coming for them. Coming for him.

No, no, no.

Max tried to get up, but Quinn was a heavy weight on top of him. "Quinn," he said, pushing at the shifter's chest. His fingers met wet fabric, and his thoughts stuttered to a halt. No. He refused to look and redoubled his effort, finally managing to push Quinn off, where he slumped with a groan, weakly pressing a hand against his side.

His shirt was soaked through with blood.

"Quinn!"

The shield faded with the stop of gunfire and hands grabbed his arms, dragging him back. He screamed, and the pouch around his neck wiggled. Aradia poked her head out with a sharp bark before launching herself into the air as her wind magic circled, coaxing her higher. Then she dove at the man dragging Max towards the car.

The man swore, slapping at her like a fly. When he clipped her side and sent her spiraling, the anger finally broke through Max's shock.

His flames surged inside him so fast he was sure he'd burn to ash, the amulet at his throat flaring bright again as it kept his magic in check. For a moment, panic froze him, but Quinn's life depended on him controlling his magic. He couldn't let his father's men get hold of him.

Unable to think of any other way to release the building flames, he opened his mouth and breathed fire in the man's face. He jerked his arms free when the man screamed and twisted away, kicking the man's knee to send him to the ground, where he kept screaming and writhing as the flames spread.

Max fought his gag reflex at the smell of burning meat. He looked at the car near the curb, his flames surging again when he saw the driver watching with a sneer. "Aradia!" he yelled.

She chirped and wind rushed around him, gaining enough strength his shirt snapped from side to side. He brought his hands together and aimed his palms at the car like a fucking anime character, but there was no time to find a better pose. Fire erupted from his hands, and with the help of Aradia's wind, a horizontal fire tornado spiraled through the air. When it hit the car, it immediately took root and reached towards the sky.

The man who'd grabbed him was still on the ground, still on fire, but no longer moving. Max turned to Quinn, surprised to find him already struggling to his feet. "Are you okay?"

"Yeah," Quinn said, though he was pale and leaned most of his weight against Max when he offered his shoulder. But he was up and moving. "Can you drive?" he asked, voice tight with pain.

"Yeah." Max filched the keys from Quinn's pocket as the Firebird exploded in a spectacular fireball and the smell of burning gasoline. "Fucking assholes," he muttered, before getting Quinn to the car and into the passenger seat. He paused long enough to let Aradia back into her pouch before getting in, then peeled out of the parking lot without buckling.

"Where's the nearest hospital?" he asked, his knuckles white on the steering wheel.

"Go home."

"Quinn—"

"Max," Quinn said, voice sharp. "I'm fine. I don't need a hospital, promise. Just get us home."

Max snarled against the press of the bond, but he didn't have the focus to spare to argue.

Quinn was on his phone, smearing blood across the screen as he typed message after message, his phone chiming almost constantly with the responses.

A firetruck flew past as Max turned onto the main street, followed by two police cars a moment later and an ambulance a minute after that. He kept checking the mirrors for any police coming for him, or one of his father's men tailing them, but it seemed they were in the clear.

"Shouldn't we have stayed there?" he asked, belatedly realizing they'd fled the scene of a crime.

Quinn snorted. "Pretty sure you killed those guys. Even if it was self-defense, the Order would have swooped in by the time they got you to the station. I'd rather be in our own territory by the time they realize what the fuck is happening."

Max frowned and glanced at Quinn, the color already returning to his face, and it didn't look like fresh blood was soaking his shirt anymore. "How are you still conscious?"

"I'm a shifter," he said, still texting.

"No, *really*?" he snapped sarcastically, grinding his teeth as he checked the mirrors again. Was that black SUV following them, or was he being paranoid?

"We heal fast," Quinn replied, but Max hardly heard him.

The light ahead turned yellow and he stepped on the gas, passing through the intersection as it turned red. He glanced back and breathed a soft sigh when the SUV stopped instead of trying to keep up.

He didn't stop looking for an ambush the entire twenty-six minutes it took to reach their neighborhood, and even then he didn't get a decent breath until the garage door screeched closed behind them.

He slumped against the steering wheel as the adrenaline vanished, leaving him cold and shaking. He heard Quinn curse and get out of the car, and then an eternal minute later the driver's door opened.

Caius pulled him out of the car and picked him up in a bridal carry before heading inside. "Are you hurt?"

Max shook his head and buried his face against Caius' chest, fisting a hand in his shirt. He was distantly aware his fingers were still tacky with blood and swallowed the lump of guilt in his throat. It was his fault Quinn nearly died. He should have rescheduled his finals. Of course his father would have ransacked his room and snooped through everything on his computer. He'd used the university portal to schedule his finals, and the login was saved.

Aradia stirred in her pouch, wiggling out of it and tucking herself against Max's neck. He blinked and lifted his head as someone tugged at his hand.

Lukas sat on the coffee table in front of him, attacking the blood on Max's fingers with a hot, soapy cloth, glaring at them like he wanted to rip them off. "Who did this?" he snarled.

"Lukas," Caius said, his voice calm, but Max felt the anger beneath it.

Lukas' lips twitched into a sneer before he forced out a slow breath, easing up on his scrubbing.

"My father's men," Max said. "They shot at us and grabbed me." His voice hitched, and he slumped against Caius when arms tightened around him. "I burned them. 'M pretty sure they're dead."

"Good," Lukas growled, finishing with Max's hands and sitting back as Quinn joined them.

He'd ditched his bloody shirt and at least wiped himself off.

Max stared at his chest and stomach, looking for the bullet wound, but other than a few smears of drying blood and a scabbed-over splotch of bruised and angry red flesh, he looked unharmed.

Quinn handed over a steaming cup of tea, before carefully sinking down next to Max with his own cup. His expression pinched with discomfort, which was somehow reassuring.

At least Max hadn't imagined the last hour in some psychotic break. He might have been stressing over finals, but not that badly.

Quinn gave him a faint smile. "By tomorrow I'll be good as new." He cleared his throat and glanced at Caius before ducking his head. "Sorry," he said quietly. "I shouldn't have been taken down by a single bullet. It caught me by surprise."

Max frowned at him, about to tell him it wasn't his fault and he was lucky to be alive, but Caius sighed and reached out, pressing his hand against the side of Quinn's neck.

"You're both safe. That's all that matters. You're lucky they were regular bullets."

Quinn shuddered and closed his eyes, leaning into Caius' touch as the tension seemed to melt out of him.

"So, what's the plan?" Lukas asked, glowering at Quinn's stomach before reaching over to wipe away the missed blood. Once satisfied, he got up to toss the cloth in the kitchen sink.

"There's not much we can do right now," Caius said, nudging Max's cup until he got the hint and took a sip.

Belatedly, he realized he was sitting in Caius' lap and tried to slide off, but Caius kept him locked in place with a soft, warning growl that somehow went straight to his dick.

"We don't have the numbers to declare war. Unless the police tie the dead men to Savino, we have no recourse."

When Caius flexed his fingers, Max caught the way they shifted from human nails to dark claws and back again. A quick glance at Lukas showed the same, both of them clenching and unclenching their fists as if they wanted to strangle someone. Even Quinn, who was pale where he slumped into the sofa, looked furious. That was new. Max wasn't sure he'd ever had someone genuinely worried about his safety before. Ironically, surrounded by three pissed-off shifters was the safest he'd ever felt.

"The security cameras should at least show they attacked first," Quinn said.

Max groaned and buried his face against Caius' chest. "Fuck, they're gonna know it was me. They're gonna kick me out, and I'll never finish my degree."

"They're not going to kick you out," Caius growled.

Max was sure Caius fully believed he could threaten the university into letting Max stay if they tried anything, but he wasn't so sure.

"You are part of our pack. You're protected against discrimination even if you're not a shifter."

Max scrubbed at his face and took another sip of tea. "I think you need to give me a crash course in Pack 101."

"Sure," Quinn said, "but maybe tomorrow."

"Yes," said Caius, standing with Max still in his arms. "You need a shower and rest."

Max huffed. "I'm fine. Quinn is the one who got shot."

"You smell like ash and Quinn's blood."

He winced. "Fine," he muttered, sipping more of his tea rather than trying to tell Caius he could climb the damn stairs by himself. If he were being honest, it was kind of nice being fussed over. And when Caius pulled him into bed after his shower, he was certainly not saying no.

CHAPTER 15

QUINN'S WOUND was completely gone by morning thanks to his shifter healing, though he'd never healed so quickly before. He'd been shot in the leg once. It'd taken two days for the wound to heal, and he'd been tender there for a week. He was sure it had something to do with binding Max, but whether it was simply from having a mage bound to him, or because Max was so powerful, or because the three of them had bound him, he had no idea.

Not that he was complaining about a boost to his abilities. Honestly, some of the best things about being a shifter were the enhanced senses and healing. He'd seen men die in battle from a GSW to the chest or stomach. Sometimes he wondered how humanity had survived to become the dominant species when it took them months to heal a broken bone, or a single virus could wipe out a fifth of the world's population in the same amount of time.

Not that the population couldn't do with a bit of trimming. Magic could only do so much to curb the damage people were doing to the planet.

Fuck, he was grim today. He decided to blame it on Lukas and his weird mood the last couple of days. If he didn't know better, he would have thought Lukas was jealous, but Lukas had never shown any interest in him. Certainly not like he had Rían. If anything, he was probably jealous over Max.

Quinn was starting to think Lukas had a thing for mages.

With a groan, he rolled out of bed and dressed, heading upstairs for a large mug of coffee before settling at his desk to check through his alerts. He had several deep and dark web crawlers set up to notify him if anything triggered off his few hundred key words and phrases, from anything of interest in Denver in general, to changes in political power or social status, and narrowing down to changes in shifter and mage laws, chatter about his pack, the mob, or the Order, and further down to bounties or hits put out on them.

Max's name was still clear for the most part. However Wright had heard of him, it had to have been from direct contact from someone. Like the Order.

He switched over to his backdoor monitor in Savino's network, but even after the attack, there was no mention of Max or mages there either. The only thing of any interest was a brief conversation in Italian from two days ago that his system translated to needing to pick up a package. Which likely referred to Max.

Quinn cursed himself for not realizing it sooner. Caius had made it clear they weren't in any position to antagonize the family currently running the city's underworld, but he saved the conversation for his records anyway. Not that they'd be able to do anything with it. Even if they'd had a decent-sized pack, or any standing in the city, it would take something more than an attack on his own son to finally tip the scales enough for the government to get involved.

He'd already found two cops and a judge on Savino's payroll, but that wasn't enough to do more than paint a target on their backs if they tried to do anything with that information either. With a huff, he finished his coffee and went upstairs for a refill. He paused as he found Lukas, fresh from his run, his hair plastered to his face with sweat, head back and throat working as he drained a glass of water.

He'd made no effort to hide his attraction before now, so he had no problem enjoying the sight for a moment before continuing to the coffeepot. "Uneventful run?"

Lukas grunted something like an affirmative and refilled his glass, then lingered there as if debating saying something.

Quinn watched from the corner of his eye as he doctored his coffee with too much pumpkin spice creamer.

"We should have a game night," Lukas finally said.

He turned and nodded, far too excited for something that was usually a biweekly thing for them. "Yeah, sounds good. Just us, or Max too?" he asked casually, propping his hip against the counter and sipping his coffee.

"Max can join if he wants." Lukas glanced at him before quickly looking away and heading to his room.

Weird, but at least Lukas wasn't completely ignoring him. Quinn watched him go, decided not to poke the wolf, and turned to get started on breakfast. Except the early-morning light breaking over their property caught his eye, and he realized how long it'd been since he'd shifted.

The others could fix their own breakfast.

He slid the door open and tipped his head back, breathing in the crisp winter air. He shed his clothes and dropped them inside before closing the door. Then he let his shift ripple over him and dropped to all fours, giving himself a vigorous shake.

The urge to howl was strong, but he swallowed it down. They might have lucked out with finding property with a backyard tucked against a national park, but they were still close enough to the heart of the city that a wolf might draw unwanted attention.

He raced along the perimeter of the tall privacy fence. It was high enough to keep people from prying, with several passageways at the bottom for small animals. He caught the scent of squirrels, rabbits, possums, foxes, and a skunk that had passed by recently as he patrolled. Once he was satisfied that no threats had entered their home territory, he found the hole hidden behind two large bushes at the back and wiggled through.

He was almost too large to fit. His family had always said he was too big for a wolf, that he must have inherited some Irish wolfhound hidden in their bloodline. He'd never minded, considering he was short for a shifter in his human form. His wolf more than made up for that, dwarfing most wolves.

Then he was off, crashing through snowdrifts that reached his chest and following the scent trails of foxes and raccoons left the night before. The *scrunch-scrunch, scrunch-scrunch* of fresh snow beneath his paws was one of his favorite things about winter. The sharp scent of pine grew stronger as he ventured farther into the woods.

He lost track of time as his wolf took full rein, annoyed at being locked away for so long.

He tracked the flight of birds through the sky and turned away completely when he caught the musty scent of a bear. His ears pricked when he heard a wolf, then another answer its call, and he tipped his head back to add his own voice to the song.

He stumbled across a pair of juvenile foxes and spent what seemed like hours chasing and playing with them before he realized the afternoon light was fading.

Fuck. Caius was going to chew him out. Except there was no mission, and he had nothing planned for the day aside from game night.

He headed for home as it started snowing again. They'd definitely have a white Christmas.

They needed to get a tree. He hadn't properly celebrated the holiday in years. Not since before he joined the Marines. He had a feeling Max hadn't had a proper Christmas his entire life, and he was sure Lukas hadn't either.

By the time he caught the familiar scents of the city and home, twilight had settled. Apparently he'd gone farther than he thought. He glanced back to make sure his tracks were being hidden by the fresh snow, then wiggled through the hidden hole into their backyard, shaking clumps of snow from his fur as he trotted up to the porch.

A breath and twist of magic and he stood on two furless feet once again, shivering from the cold bite of air as he pushed the sliding glass door open and slipped into the heat of the house. The others were at the table, but he ignored them for the moment. His clothes had been folded and left beside the door, and he pulled them on, feeling far more settled in his skin than he had in weeks.

The scent of burgers and fries made his stomach growl, and he turned for the table. He draped himself over the back of Max's chair and kissed one of his red ears before snagging several fries to stuff in his mouth.

"Nice run?" Caius asked.

"Awesome. We really need to schedule pack runs from now on."

Caius grunted under his breath, and Quinn rolled his eyes. He couldn't blame Caius for being hesitant to shift with his injury, but all the doctors were sure it could only help with the healing process.

He dropped into his chair next to Max and snagged the last two burgers and fries. "So, game night tonight," he said, elbowing Max's arm. "You in?"

"Um, sure?" Max glanced from him to Lukas and back again, then to Caius. "All of us?"

"I don't play," Caius said.

"Don't lie." Quinn took a too large bite of burger, barely chewing before swallowing. "You got banished from the barracks for being too competitive."

Max coughed in a terrible attempt to hide his laugh.

Quinn smirked in the face of Caius' glare before focusing on his food. He might have asked Caius to join them anyway, if Lukas hadn't been acting so weird. When he glanced across the table, he found Lukas intently focused on the last few fries on his plate. Beneath the scent of beef and grease, he swore Lukas smelled anxious. Which didn't happen.

Lukas was a fucking sniper. He was the calmest shifter Quinn had ever met, to the point he was convinced Lukas' wolf was far closer to the surface than most. Few humans could ever manage to sit still for hours on end, waiting for one specific target to be in one specific spot. Shifters tended to have a bit more patience than humans, even alphas, thanks to the wolf in them, but more than once Lukas had scouted a mission for twelve or more hours.

Quinn didn't have that in him. He needed to move and burn off excess energy. The only exception was if he was on a computer or playing a game, but that was his human hyper-fixation at its finest.

He polished off his burgers and snagged a beer from the fridge, then went back for the leftover sushi he'd ordered too much of yesterday. More than once, Caius had asked if he had a sushi tooth instead of a sweet tooth over the years. He was always glad to report that yes, yes he did.

Max's eyebrows went up when Quinn sat back down and popped the lids off three different rolls, but he'd been with them long enough by now to know how much a shifter could eat.

After spending all day running around the woods as a wolf, he was starving.

He went back for a small dish, poured a generous amount of soy sauce into it, then mixed an entire wasabi ball into it. "I was thinking we should get a tree," he said, eyeing Caius as he popped a large bite of delicious roll into his mouth.

Forget finding a cook. He really could eat sushi every day for the rest of his life.

Caius glanced at him before, unsurprisingly, looking at Max. "Do you want to pick one out?"

Max blinked when he realized Caius was talking to him, tearing his eyes away from Quinn's sushi. "Really?"

Quinn hid a smile by shoveling more food into his mouth. Max's excitement was palpable, and he nearly vibrated with the effort to keep still. "We should all go. We need decorations and shit too. Can make it a new pack tradition." If they were going to make this their home, they needed to start it off right. They couldn't spend all their time worrying about the Order or the next mob hit.

He'd make some changes to his scrubbers so they weren't taken by surprise again. Maybe even reach out to one of his friends who'd gotten into info brokering to help.

Lukas was oddly silent as he sipped the last of his soda. More silent than usual. He doubted most people would even notice since Lukas kept to himself most of the time. Sometimes Quinn was surprised he'd even joined the pack, but even a lone wolf knew better than to go packless.

Humans may have deceived themselves ages ago that they could exist as islands without unraveling, but shifters relied on pack more than humans ever relied on family.

Quinn stared and ate his sushi as Caius and Max worked out tree details, but Lukas never looked up. He knew the moment Lukas realized he was being watched when he went absolutely still, like when he settled in for a long wait with nothing but his gun and the other end of his viewfinder.

That was fine. He'd get some answers soon. Lukas wouldn't have suggested game night for no reason.

He polished off the last bite of sushi and sat back with a groan, rubbing his food baby.

"Can't believe you're not sick," Max muttered.

"You should try it sometime. You need some meat on those bones."

Max scoffed. "I don't see how you all eat enough for twenty people and aren't fat."

Quinn laughed. "Shifter metabolism."

"Exercise doesn't hurt either," Lukas said, standing and dumping his trash.

"I exercise," Quinn protested, crossing his arms when Lukas raised an eyebrow at him. "Fuck you." He picked up the empty containers and bottle and tossed them in the trash before glancing at Max. "Games?" It was almost sickeningly cute when Max and Caius lingered a few more moments, their fingers locked together on top of the table.

Nothing like being attacked and nearly kidnapped to make one sentimental.

He headed downstairs and sprawled into the corner of his sofa, propping a foot on the edge of the table. "You two can pick," he said, once Lukas and Max joined him.

"Anything but zombies," Max said.

"I think that's doable." He motioned to the large cabinet that Lukas opened next to the TV, grinning when Max looked over and froze. Inside was almost every console ever made, and all the games Quinn could get his hands on. There was even an ancient Atari that once belonged to his older brother.

"Holy shit," Max breathed, stopping a few inches away as if scared to touch anything. That only lasted a moment before he grabbed the newest *Mario Kart* and spun with a grin. "This?"

Quinn's attention snagged on Lukas where he'd gone still again, his fingers lingering on the knob of the cabinet. "Oh, right. So, usually we make a bet," he said, winking at Max's suspicious look. "Since Lukas called for game night, he gets to set the terms."

Lukas finally glanced at him, albeit briefly, before staring through the rows of games. "Loser blows the winners."

Max fumbled the game as he whipped around to stare at Lukas, his eyes wide and a flush creeping up his neck.

Quinn couldn't blame him; he was even more surprised. Usually their bets were making the loser eat some weird-ass food or doing the winner's laundry for a week. Not once had they ever traded sexual favors, and he didn't need to be a genius to realize the only difference this time was Max.

He ignored the sting of jealousy and grabbed the remote. "Fine with me. Max?"

Max made a high-pitched wheezing sound before coughing. "Sure?"

Quinn raised an eyebrow and motioned Max over, taking the game from him before grasping his chin. "You sure?" he asked. "You're good regardless of who wins or loses?"

His face burned redder, but he met Quinn's eyes. "Yeah. Sounds good."

Quinn forced a grin and turned on the TV. "You good with the game?" he asked, glancing at Lukas, who hated racing games. Lukas, surprisingly, preferred co-op games, though Quinn supposed when you could shoot a target from two miles out in real life, shooter games lost their appeal. He preferred the zombie games himself. Eight years in the Marines with some asshole teams made the jump scares seem like child's play.

"Yeah," Lukas said, grabbing the controllers to pass to Max before hooking up the console.

Once they were set up, Quinn eyed Lukas again, tucked into the other end of the couch with Max between them. He still refused to look at either of them, but that was fine.

They took one practice round to let Max get familiar with the controls, but it was obvious from the start that he'd played before.

By the second round, Quinn realized Lukas was intentionally losing. Not that he really stood a chance with Max playing dirty despite claiming innocence, but Quinn knew Lukas' play style. He would never hold on to a blue shell if he was actually serious about the game. He'd never met *anyone* who could resist using the blue shell, even if they blew themselves up with it.

That was all the proof he needed. He might not have much of a chance of beating the cheating demon himself, but if Lukas wanted to lose to Max that badly, Quinn could at least ensure it happened without too much of a fight.

Max won three rounds before side-eyeing Quinn. "Are you letting me win?"

"No, you're cheating." He grunted as Max's elbow jabbed his rib. Just for that, he won the next round by flopping onto Max halfway through the track and squishing him into the sofa.

Max lost his controller, trying in vain to push Quinn off. "Lukas!" he called, laughing as Quinn wiggled and shoved a pillow over his face. "Help!"

Lukas reached over and shoved a hand in Quinn's face to push him off, his scent spiking sharply with annoyance as he glared at the screen. "We gonna play or what?"

Quinn winced and sat back, clearing his throat as he started up the next race. "Yup, sure. Final race. Winner takes all," he said, ignoring Max and the confused look he shot at both of them. He'd figure it out himself shortly how territorial Lukas could apparently be.

They were all deathly silent for the final race. Quinn even managed to snag one of the shortcuts Max had been using the entire time, taking first for a few moments before a blue shell knocked him out. He thought it was Lukas' for a moment, but then Max sped by him, cackling like a madman and crossing the finish line a few seconds later.

"Little cheat. How'd you get that?"

Max stuck his tongue out in answer, and Quinn nearly retaliated by biting it, but he didn't want to risk losing his head.

"Enjoy your blowjob. I need some ice cream," he said, setting his controller on the table as he got up.

Max squawked and grabbed his hand. "You're not leaving," he said, his voice a couple octaves higher.

Quinn risked a glance at Lukas, whose knuckles had gone white on his own controller. "You're the winner."

"I said *winners*," Lukas snapped, his amber eyes flashing with his wolf as he finally looked at Quinn. "If you weren't okay with the bet, you should have said so."

"I am fine with it, but you two should enjoy yourselves." Why were they both making such a big deal about this when he was trying to give Lukas what he wanted?

Max gave a sharp tug on his hand that brought him back down to the couch. "What is going on?" he demanded, looking from Quinn to Lukas. Quinn wasn't sure what he could have possibly seen with his inferior human senses, but the long, drawn out, "Ohh," was irritating enough that he glared.

"Ohh what?"

Max smirked at him before turning to face Lukas, placing both hands on his cheeks and making Lukas face him. "Kiss me."

Quinn bristled, digging his nails into the arm of the sofa.

Lukas glanced at him over Max's shoulder before Max slid a hand to Lukas' chin.

"Eyes on me," he ordered.

Well, that was surprising. Max had seemed anything but dominant the entire time he'd been here, except when he got mad. Granted, it had only been a few weeks. Max was still feeling out his place with them.

He looked away as Lukas leaned in for a kiss, forcing his claws to recede when he realized they were on the verge of ripping his sofa to pieces. He pressed his palm against his mouth and tried to ignore the fact that Max was kissing the man he'd been pining over for years. Who was only interested in mages.

"Now kiss Quinn."

Quinn froze, his entire being locking up and his thoughts screeching to a halt. Even his lungs refused to work for several painful heartbeats. Then Lukas was standing over him and he dragged his eyes up the lean, toned body he'd had more than a few fantasies about.

Lukas' eyes were intense and glowing, completely focused on Quinn as he pressed a knee between Quinn's thighs and leaned down. He braced a hand behind Quinn's head, using the other to tug his hand away from his face.

He was peripherally aware of Max squirming with excitement, but the rest of his attention was on Lukas' lips and the way his tongue darted out to wet them as he leaned closer. When his lungs decided to work again, he got a deep breath of the lingering scent of metal, oil, and gunpowder beneath the richer scent of Lukas himself. Like fresh rain on warm concrete and his coconut shampoo.

A deep groan ripped out of Quinn's chest as he grabbed Lukas' shirt with both hands and yanked, crushing their mouths together. Every time he'd fantasized about kissing Lukas, it was always a fight for control, but there was no resistance as Quinn pressed his tongue past Lukas' lips. All he tasted was sweet submission, and that explained and changed everything.

He slid a hand into Lukas' hair and curled it into a tight grip, echoing Lukas' moan and pulling him closer, seeking out the heated flesh beneath his shirt.

Lukas shivered and straddled Quinn's lap until their chests were pressed flush together, his arms wrapping around Quinn's shoulders. When Lukas started grinding against his body, Quinn tore his mouth away with a groan.

"Too fast." Quinn was partially convinced this was some fever dream. Maybe he'd been shot with aconite and he was dying and this was his mind's gift to protect him from reality. He intended to enjoy it either way; he just needed a minute.

He nipped Lukas' lip before tipping his head back. "Take care of Max first."

Lukas' darkened eyes flicked over him, his slight frown shifting into a smirk. "You want to watch."

Quinn tried to glare, but fuck, he couldn't deny it in the least. And it sounded better than he needed a second before he came in his pants. "Yeah, so get to work." He didn't miss the way the amber of Lukas' eyes shrank further, and he definitely didn't miss the sharp spike of arousal in his scent. He never would have pegged Lukas as such a submissive, but he certainly enjoyed the revelation.

Lukas tipped off his lap and onto the couch, then rolled partially over Max and slid to the floor onto his knees.

Max's eyes went wide at the sudden change in Lukas' focus. "You really don't have to if you don't want to."

Lukas tilted his head, resting his hands on Max's thighs. "I want to."

With a hum, Quinn slid across the sofa and grasped Max's hand before he could freak out too much, pressing a kiss to his palm. "Whether you want to or not, it's okay." Max still didn't look convinced, so he brushed kisses across Max's fingertips as he added, "Lukas and I can figure out something between us, even if you want to figure out something between the two of you."

"Like Caius," Max said with a shaky breath, squeezing Quinn's fingers before hesitantly running his other hand through Lukas' hair. "I don't get how you can do this so easily."

Quinn shrugged and continued trailing kisses over Max's fingers and knuckles. "My mom has two mates," he said, grinning when they both looked surprised. "One is a human. I guess I grew up knowing love wasn't finite, and society only pretends to know how things are supposed to work. And you're stalling," he added, wrapping his lips around Max's finger and sucking. The strangled moan drowned out the idle music of the game and he smirked against Max's palm.

Lukas tilted his head, rubbing small circles into Max's thighs with his thumbs. "So, yes or no?"

Max glanced between them one more time before nodding.

When Lukas smiled, it wasn't his usual mocking or sarcastic one, but a slight, pleased upturn of his lips that made him seem younger. More his age.

It was easy to forget that Lukas was a few years younger than him, closer to Max's age.

The small spark of jealousy at seeing that expression focused on Max didn't even get a chance to ignite before Lukas turned the same expression on him, before it was ruined by a hint of smugness. As if Lukas knew exactly what he was thinking.

Quinn narrowed his eyes and decided to test some buttons. "Get to work, pup."

Lukas' eyes widened in surprise before he snorted. Apparently that was a no.

"Ooh, can I try?" Max grinned, still playing with Lukas' hair. "Mm, pet seems derogatory. How about *kitten*."

Quinn laughed, then laughed harder still at the look of horror on Lukas' face.

Lukas glared at both of them when Max started snickering. "Are you assholes done?"

Quinn wiped tears from his eyes, tucking away that little nugget of gold for later. He cleared his throat. "Waiting on you," he said, managing to keep most of his laughter contained. He pitched his voice lower as he added, "Your mouth should be full by now, slut."

That got the reaction he'd been looking for. Lukas' pupils dilated, and his scent thickened, his lips parting on an inaudible gasp.

"Oh, I think he likes that one."

He hummed in agreement and trailed his fingertips along Max's hand. "Maybe we need to give him some encouragement to get to work." He nuzzled Max's ear before tracing his tongue along the edge.

Max shivered, relaxing into the cushions with a sigh, his fingers twitching in Quinn's hold. "Yeah," he breathed, tilting his head to meet Quinn's lips with his own.

Lukas let out a soft half growl, half whine before the sharp sound of a zipper followed. A moment later, Max gasped against Quinn's lips, arching with a sweet moan.

Quinn took the advantage to deepen the kiss, pressing Max's hand against his thigh before releasing it. He slid his freed hand beneath Max's shirt, lightly dragging his nails against heated flesh before breaking the kiss long enough to glance at Lukas.

"Fuck," he breathed, unprepared for the shock of desire at the sight of Lukas' lips wrapped around Max's cock.

Long eyelashes fluttered as Lukas tipped his head to look up at them, the amber of his eyes brightened to glowing rings of molten gold.

"You're a good little slut, aren't you." He didn't bother holding back the growl in his voice.

Lukas groaned, which caused Max to gasp and rock his hips into Lukas.

"Please."

"Not yet," Quinn murmured, sliding his hand down Max's stomach to wrap two fingers around the base of his cock.

Max whined in protest, tossing his head and digging his fingers into Quinn's thigh.

He worked his other hand into Max's hair and tugged his head back, capturing his lips again. Like this, he could match the thrusts of his tongue to the pace of Lukas' lips brushing against his hand. Between the two of them, it didn't take long to reduce Max to a squirming, needy mess.

When he reluctantly pulled away, he caught Max's lower lip with his teeth before focusing on Lukas. "Swallowing?" he asked, taking

Lukas' groan and the flex of his fingers against Max's inner thighs as a yes. That was the only warning he gave either of them as he released his tight grip on Max's cock, dragging his nails up Max's stomach to his chest and tweaking a nipple.

Max shuddered, his mouth open on a mostly silent scream as he came.

Lukas swallowed, keeping Max in his mouth until he slumped into the couch, fully spent. Then he pulled away, sitting back on his heels and licking his lips, eyes still burning gold.

Unable to resist, Quinn leaned forward and dragged Lukas in for a kiss, sweeping his tongue past unresisting lips with a soft growl. When he pulled back, Lukas' eyes were glassy, and he chased after Quinn's lips with a moan of protest.

Who was he to deny such a sweet request?

He curled his fingers into Lukas' hair and kissed him until the lingering taste of Max was long gone. Until the fingers on the waistband of his sweats distracted him enough to come up for air. When he glanced down, he found Max recovered enough to get a hand down his pants.

"Your turn."

"Yes," Lukas hissed, abandoning his attack on Quinn's neck to help Max instead.

Quinn had little choice but to sit back and let them strip his pants off, swallowing a protest when Lukas dragged his sweats and boxers off as one and tossed them aside.

Lukas licked his lips as he focused on Quinn's dick, sliding his hands up Quinn's legs and nudging them apart. Then he leaned in and nuzzled his way up an inner thigh until hot breath ghosted against Quinn's cock.

Just that was enough to make his toes curl. Fuck, he wasn't going to last long at all.

He buried one hand in Lukas' hair and stretched the other arm behind his own head, raising an eyebrow in his best *I'm waiting* expression.

Lukas smirked, dragging his tongue up the underside of Quinn's cock. Then the wet heat of his mouth enveloped Quinn and his world fractured.

As many times as he'd imagined this, it was nothing compared to the real thing. Especially with Max pressed against his side, trailing lazy kisses along his neck and jaw. The mix of Max's campfire-and-citrus and Lukas' petrichor was heady and intoxicating. He wouldn't mind getting drunk off it.

A half moan, half sob escaped him as Lukas did something with his tongue that made sparks burst along his nerve endings, and that was it. He was gone, shuddering with an orgasm so intense he lost his breath long enough for gray to creep into the edges of his vision.

His body went limp as he sucked in a few desperate breaths, pressing his arm over his eyes with a groan. Fuck, he hadn't come that fast in years. "Sorry," he murmured, resisting the hand tugging at him and keeping his arm firmly in place.

Max huffed against his shoulder before jabbing a finger into Quinn's ribs, making him jump and shoot a glare from beneath his arm. With a smirk, Max pointed his chin towards Lukas.

Quinn braced himself before slowly focusing on the other wolf.

Lukas was flushed, his hair a mess from both Max's and Quinn's fingers, his lips swollen and eyes nearly black even with the wolf glow behind them. With barely a tug to his hair, Lukas crawled into Quinn's lap, a whine at the back of his throat that squashed Quinn's embarrassment.

"You poor thing," Max murmured, sliding a hand under Lukas' shirt. "Do you need a turn now?"

Lukas shivered as he arched into Max's fingers. "Please."

Max glanced at Quinn and snorted at whatever he saw.

Quinn couldn't blame him; he probably looked like a mess. He could hardly even think clearly beyond the fact he had a hot, needy Lukas squirming in his lap. When Max crowded said lap, settling behind Lukas and peeling his shirt off, Quinn found himself transfixed by Max's fingers exploring the bared chest and stomach. When they reached the jeans and palmed the large bulge there, Lukas groaned, tipping his head back with a roll of his hips, and Quinn finally regained enough sense to put his hands on Lukas.

He made short work of the button and zipper and yanked both pants and boxers down, a soft growl building in his chest as he pulled Lukas free and wrapped a hand around the hot, thick length of him.

"Yesss." Lukas pushed into the grip, leaning into Max and turning his head enough their lips met in an open-mouth kiss.

Before Max entered their lives, Quinn had never imagined a poly relationship for himself, but he could admit he liked the sight of them together. Even if that was only because he now knew he had a chance at something with Lukas himself.

He tightened his fingers around Lukas' cock as he began stroking, grinning at Max when his fingers joined in.

Lukas moaned, long and throaty, before pitching forward and crushing his lips against Quinn's. His hips jerked before he found a rhythm, thrusting into their grips and biting Quinn's lower lip with sharp cutoff growls.

"Fuck," Quinn breathed, burying his free hand in Lukas' hair and dragging him into another kiss, dominating it, keeping Lukas exactly where he wanted until the other wolf whimpered in surrender. "Good boy," he murmured against Lukas' lips, curling his fingers tighter in his dark hair as he glanced at Max.

With a grin, Max dragged his teeth across Lukas' shoulder. "Good little slut," he purred.

Quinn nearly laughed at seeing this side of the mage. He'd have to ask exactly how he knew how to read Lukas at the start, but that could wait. For now, they turned their attention to pleasuring Lukas, marking him and repeatedly pushing him to the edge of bliss, before finally letting him fall over the edge with a hoarse scream.

He licked into Lukas' mouth when he came, muffling his cries as he covered Quinn's stomach and chest with an obscene amount of spend.

Lukas shook between them, panting against Quinn's lips with a dazed, blissed-out expression. When Max pulled away and disappeared into the bathroom, Lukas tipped to the side, collapsing next to Quinn as if Max had been the only thing holding him up.

Quinn was so distracted by Lukas curling into his side with a sigh and a scent of contentment that he hardly noticed Max's return until a damp cloth swiped up the mess cooling on his stomach. "Thanks," he murmured, hooking an arm around Max's waist as he sank into Quinn's lap and stretched his legs out over Lukas. "Okay?" he asked, nuzzling into Max's shoulder.

"Mm, yeah." Max smiled and kissed Quinn's nose before sliding across both of them and snuggling into Lukas' other side.

Lukas grunted when Max got a knee in his stomach, but otherwise was doing a great job at playing a blacked-out druggie.

Quinn shifted enough to pull Lukas closer, wrapping one arm around him and resting his other hand on Max's arm when it draped over Lukas' stomach.

It may not have been a typical pack or relationship setup, but Max and Lukas both smelled happy and content and satiated, which was all that really mattered.

CHAPTER 16

LUKAS' PHONE ringing jerked him out of sleep sometime later. He winced as he sat up, his neck protesting the awkward angle he'd been resting in. He fumbled his phone from his pocket, squinting at the too bright backlight and cursing when he saw his CO's name on the screen. He might have gotten back from a mission less than forty-eight hours ago, but sometimes that couldn't be helped.

He carefully extracted himself from Max and Quinn, hitting the Answer button as he headed up the stairs. "Hunt," he answered, grimacing at the gravelly edge to his voice. The pause on the other end burnt away the remaining fog of sleep, and he hurried up the last few steps until he was in the kitchen. "Sir?"

"You really should have put in for another leave," Adams replied with a sigh. "Just got a mission from the brass, and they're requesting you specifically."

Fuck. That couldn't be good. Nothing good ever came of being recognized, either for failure or success. "Okay," he replied slowly, pressing his fingers into his eyes until he saw spots dancing in his vision.

"I've been keeping apprised of your situation. I don't know why the Order is so obsessed with your mage, but this mission can't be a coincidence. I'd flag it and send it up the chain, but this is coming from so far over my head I'm getting chills. But since it reeks, I'm sending you some additional support."

"All due respect, sir, if this is a trap, they may end up a casualty."

"You saying you don't want the Rabid Ghost watching your six?" Adams asked, smug amusement in his voice.

Lukas froze. Of all the mages he knew of, the Ghost was the only one who had never been bound to or trained by the Order. They worked exclusively for the armed forces and were barely more than a myth among the lower ranks. But he knew of their work, and they weren't called Rabid for no reason. Some of the stories sounded like the military barely had any control over them and used them only as a last resort.

"Corporal?" Adams prompted. "Do you want the assist or not?"

"Yes," he wheezed, ignoring Adams' snicker. If nothing else, he at least wanted to meet the mage who'd destroyed the Russian government within twelve hours last decade. If he was lucky, they'd both survive this mission unscathed.

"Good. And Lukas…. Live. That's an order."

That was odd enough to fuel Lukas' unease even further.

He woke Caius long enough to let him know he'd been called for a mission, changed into his fatigues, and grabbed his bag. He debated waking Quinn and Max but settled for texting Quinn instead.

This time of night, it was a quick drive to Buckley, where a ride was waiting for him. Not a C-17 like he was used to. Instead, he was directed to an actual fucking Nighthawk. He'd flown in jets before, but never supersonic. This was one of the new models with two seats. He could smell the magic wrapped around the entire jet and knew the newer planes were supposed to be warded for structural integrity, lower air resistance, and better fuel consumption.

The pilot was waiting beside the stairs and held a helmet out to Lukas as he approached. "Supposed to drop you off in Rasht," he said by way of greeting.

"Iran?" Adams was right about the reek. If he was needed overseas, why didn't he have a team with him?

He took the helmet and found a dossier tucked inside it. He headed up the metal stairs and tossed his bag in, pulled the papers out, and got his helmet on. He found the switch for the comms and heard the static pop as they switched on. Before he could climb into the jet, a soft voice spoke.

"*Do not get on the plane.*"

Lukas tensed and turned, opening his mouth to ask who the hell was talking to him, but he didn't get a chance.

"*Do not speak. If you get in, you will die. Make your choice. Get in or put your belongings in the seat and walk away.*"

He glanced at the pilot, but the man showed no sign of hearing the same thing in his headset. Which wasn't as surprising as the fact that it didn't feel like the voice was coming from the headset at all, but inside his head.

"*Tick tock, wolf. I'm dying of suspense.*"

Lukas hesitated. Even if he might die, walking away would certainly end with a dishonorable discharge or court-martial. Unless Adams knew. That would explain the cryptic parting.

He tossed his phone into the seat, pulling out what cash he had on him before tossing in his wallet, then the helmet. When he went back down the steps, the pilot flicked his cigarette away.

"Good choice. Get the stairs, would ya." The pilot climbed in and settled into his seat, the cockpit sliding closed over his head.

Lukas grabbed the stairs and wheeled them away, then stopped to watch the Nighthawk take off from a near standstill. There was a shimmer of magic, and then it vanished from sight completely. The only indication it had been there at all was the sonic boom a long moment later as it broke the sound barrier.

A black SUV careened around one of the hangars and headed for him before screeching to a stop a few feet away. The back door popped open, and Lukas took a breath before climbing inside. They were moving again before he even got the door closed.

A man sat in the back beside him, wearing sunglasses despite it being the middle of the night. He didn't say anything, but Lukas could feel the man's eyes on him.

Surely this wasn't the Ghost? Except he couldn't fathom they would have let him fly halfway around the world only to bring him back. Nothing suspicious about this at all. If the Order was behind any of this, this would be the perfect time for them to make their move.

He cleared his throat. "Thanks?"

When the man didn't respond, he glanced at the driver. A woman with long dark hair, also wearing sunglasses. They were both wearing leather, which was giving him strong Matrix vibes. He couldn't see much of the person in the passenger seat, aside from bright, spiky blue hair.

"Care to explain what's going on?"

"What's going on, wolf," the blue-haired passenger drawled, "is your pack has pissed off the Order and the underworld of this city. Quite a feat. You've only been here a few months." She sounded impressed.

Lukas was shocked to hear a young feminine voice that matched what he'd heard in his head. "You said I'd die if I got on that plane."

"Yes, it's rigged to explode in a few hours when it's over the Pacific.

"And how do you know that? What about the pilot?"

She flicked her hand, a lollipop held between her fingers. "The pilot will be fine. And I know because I'm the one who was hired to sabotage it."

Lukas instinctively reached for a gun that was currently several thousand feet in the air, silently cursing himself for being so careless. He had a small combat knife tucked into a boot sheath, but doubted he would get far with it. Tight, cramped spaces against three opponents in a moving vehicle when he smelled guns on at least two of them would be a challenge, but if this was really Ghost's team, they were here to help him. Unless they were playing both sides. This was why there weren't many mages he trusted; the Order always got to them eventually.

The SUV reached the highway and picked up enough speed that even he was leery of jumping. Shifter healing would keep him alive, but he risked being incapacitated long enough they could grab him again. And road rash was a bitch.

The woman shifted in her seat, turning and leaning over the center console to face him, lollipop back in her mouth as she propped her chin on her fist. She tucked her sucker into her cheek. "Relax. If I wanted you dead, why would I have gotten you off the plane?"

"Why don't you want me dead?"

"Honestly, whether you live or die is irrelevant to me. But Adams called in a favor and made a few promises." She studied him as she shifted her hand to twirl the stick of her lollipop a few times before pulling it free, pointing it at Lukas. "Ghost, at your service."

He couldn't help his snort of disbelief. She couldn't have been much older than seventeen, and the Ghost had been around for decades.

She narrowed her eyes at him, lifting her chin. "I could always toss you in the ditch. Leave your pack to be annihilated."

Lukas opened his mouth to ask how old she was before his sense of self-preservation kicked in. "You're not old enough."

She smirked at him as if knowing exactly what he'd meant to say. "I'm older than I look."

"There's no way you took down the Russian government when you were seven or eight years old."

"True. I looked the same then as I do now. Except for the hair."

"How?" There was no way. Mage lifespans might be longer than normal humans, but they still aged noticeably in ten years.

With a thick Russian accent, she replied. "Even most strong defense crumble before beautiful woman." Then she batted her lashes and curled her tongue around her sucker in a way that made him feel skeevy.

"Please stop," he said with a grimace.

She turned back around with a cackle, muttering something in Russian he was sure was derogatory.

Lukas reached for his phone before tipping his head back with a groan when he remembered that was gone too. "I need to call my alpha."

"No."

"Excuse me?"

Ghost let out an exaggerated sigh. "The Order is calling in favors to ensure you're dead. What do you think they're going to do when your alpha doesn't react to the news and they realize you're still alive? The *only* reason they haven't abducted all of you is your military connections. And the fact Max is legally outside of their grasp."

Lukas flexed his fingers when his claws dug into his flesh and drew blood. He took several deep breaths before he could retract his fangs and claws. He suspected Rían's wards and protections also had something to do with the Order not trying to take Max directly. He could only hope the Order couldn't trace the wards back to the mage.

"I'm not going to sit with my thumbs up my ass while the Order comes after my pack."

"Of course not," she scoffed. "You're going to help me finally get my revenge. Starting with Helga Fuchs."

"And who the hell is that?"

"The bitch who made me," Ghost replied brightly.

CHAPTER 17

SOMETHING WAS wrong.

Caius woke before dawn as usual, with a pit of dread in his stomach that he knew well. During his years of service, he'd learned to trust his instincts, and his instincts were currently screaming at him that his pack was in danger.

He headed downstairs and across the den, lingering at the second set of stairs leading to Quinn's lair as he breathed in. He smelled Quinn and Max, and the lingering scent of Lukas. And sex.

The dread lessened a bit at knowing at least those two were safe and where they belonged. Lukas was routinely called away for missions, but this felt different, a shiver of unease along his nerves that only worsened when his phone rang.

The name of Lukas' CO flashed on the screen.

"Ward," he answered.

"Colonel," Adams said, tension in his voice.

"What happened?" He didn't appreciate the sigh or the long pause before Adams responded.

"At 0530, we lost contact with Corporal Hunt's plane over the Pacific."

Caius didn't hear much after that. Adams' words became muffled white noise for an eternal moment.

Lukas wasn't dead. He knew that much at the very least, thanks to their pack bond, but he could very well be dying, and Caius wouldn't know until that tenuous bond snapped and disappeared.

Someone shouted his name and he blinked, finding Quinn's hazel eyes an inch from his own. Quinn's wrist pressed against his neck, the subtle scent of cinnamon and pack warm between them.

He grasped Quinn's wrist and breathed deep, grounding himself in the here, in pack. The phone was still in his hand, but the call had disconnected at some point. He couldn't blame Adams for that; he'd been on the other end of those phone calls before, when he'd lost men in the line of duty. He'd hoped to never be on the receiving end.

"What's going on?" Max asked, standing by the table, arms wrapped around himself.

Caius instinctively reached for him, relieved when Max sat beside him. "Lukas was called for a mission last night." He hesitated to say more, wishing modern pack bonds were strong enough to give more information than alive or dead and a general sense of direction. Maybe they had offered more centuries ago, but whatever magic was inherent in them had faded with time. Or maybe was lost with the advent of technology.

"His plane went down." The sound Max made threatened to rip his chest in two, but he kept most of his attention on Quinn, wincing at the bite of nails on the back of his neck.

"He's not dead," Quinn said, desperation in his voice.

"No." Caius moved his grip to Quinn's neck in return. "He's alive."

Quinn let out a shuddering breath and grabbed Caius' phone without pulling away. He dialed Lukas' number, but the phone went straight to voicemail.

"How do you know he's alive?" Max asked, pressing into Caius' side.

"The pack bond is still there."

"I thought that was something Hollywood made up."

Ironically, that was one of the few things they got right.

The fifth time Quinn dialed into Lukas' voicemail, Caius gently took the phone back and disconnected the call. "We'll find him," he said. He didn't believe this was a random accident. Technology might fail them at times, but magic was more than enough to supplement and protect against a military plane going down outside of battle.

The Order was behind this somehow, which meant they'd dug their poisonous claws into the US government or military far deeper than he'd ever anticipated.

Quinn finally let go and stood. "I'm going to try tracking his phone."

Caius nodded, waiting until Quinn disappeared downstairs before turning to Max.

"How can I help?"

"I don't know yet." Caius pulled him closer, breathing in his scent, the mix of Lukas and Quinn beneath it. It should have irritated him, but if anything, it grounded him further. "I need to make some calls." He had a few contacts he could still trust to tell him what they knew, even if he was technically a civilian now.

"I'll make breakfast."

"Thank you." He pressed a quick kiss to Max's lips before heading to his office. He sank into his chair with a sigh and pinched the bridge of his nose, focusing on breathing through the panic and fear and anger trying to claw its way up his throat. He'd known this could happen the moment he decided to claim a newly Sparked mage, but he hadn't expected what Max would come to mean to him or his pack. The three of them had worked well together from the beginning, shifters isolated or exiled from their original packs, grabbing on to the first life raft they could find.

Max was no different. Once he'd started to believe he was safe here, he'd drawn the rest of them even closer together. Knowing Max had finally brought Lukas and Quinn together was a miracle; Caius had started to despair they'd ever get their heads out of their asses.

He couldn't let that all be in vain. Losing even one of them would tear his pack apart.

Lukas was alive. He was well trained, in his prime, healthy. If he survived the initial crash, there was a chance he'd survive until the coast guard or a rescue op found him.

He had to believe that.

With a deep breath, Caius pulled up a contact he never thought he'd use again. The name Charlie Savage flashed on his screen, the number ringing three times before a woman answered.

"Savage."

"It's Ward."

A brief pause, then, "Calling for business or pleasure?"

"It's personal. I need a favor."

A low whistle followed that. "Five years and you call asking for a favor."

He'd expected annoyance, but she sounded amused.

"Never did learn to pull your punches."

"You never asked me to."

Charlie snorted. "And you're still a dick. What do you need, Cai?"

"I need to know about the plane that went down over the Pacific this morning."

"What?" she snapped. There was a sound like her phone clattered to a table, and then the sound of furious typing.

"It should have left Buckley around one or two this morning."

After a few tense moments, she hissed. "A fucking Nighthawk went down." More typing. "Pilot Wren Taylor and Corporal Lukas Hunt. These boys yours?"

"Lukas is pack."

She hummed but didn't ask for details. "Doesn't look like an attack…. There's no mission file attached to this flight. Cai, what the fuck is this?"

"Fuck," he breathed, pinching his nose again. "Can you see who authorized it?"

After another few moments, she swore. "General Graves."

"Rhys Graves?" Caius had met the man only once, and that'd been more than enough. He couldn't say exactly what about the man raised his hackles, but surely that didn't mean Graves was willing to murder his own men. That was something the Order was rumored to do.

"It's being listed as faulty wiring," she said, incredulous.

"No chance of it being true?"

Charlie scoffed. "These new models are more secure than Air Force One. Even if it was the wiring, the spellwork should have kept it from crashing."

"Sabotage?" Even as he asked, he knew it was true; he just hadn't wanted to believe the Order could orchestrate something so far outside their jurisdiction. If one of their highest ranks was compromised, how far did the Order's reach truly go?

"What the hell did you get caught up in, Caius?"

He considered telling her the truth, but the less she knew, the safer she'd be. "I'm handling it."

"Right," she said, her tone dripping derision. "That lone wolf thing is gonna get you killed someday."

"Not today." He hoped, anyway.

"Right. If you live, maybe we can catch up over drinks."

Despite how long it'd been since they'd spoken, Caius was tempted. If not for Max, he might have accepted outright. As it was, he hesitated too long.

"As friends," she added dryly. "Or maybe as a double date?"

"You're seeing someone?"

"I'm engaged, you ass."

"Congratulations."

Charlie's eye roll was audible. "God, how did I put up with you? If you get yourself killed doing something stupid, I'll find a necro to raise your sorry ass."

Caius sank into his chair, a smile tugging at his lips. "Necros don't exist."

"Fine, die and stay dead, then."

He laughed despite himself. "I think I remember why I stopped calling."

"Don't lie to yourself, you love me."

"Yeah," he agreed. They'd been good together. They might have even worked out if they'd met a few years earlier than they had, but it'd been the wrong time for both of them. He was thankful they'd both agreed on that.

When she spoke again, her voice was softer. "I'm serious about the drinks, Cai. It would be nice to see you again."

"I'd like that," he said, clearing his throat as he straightened. "I'll call you when I've taken care of this mess."

Once they'd hung up, he debated reaching out to any of his other contacts, but he doubted they would have any new information. If anyone actually knew anything, it was going to be Adams. He knew Lukas trusted him, but Caius had never met the man.

He stepped into the kitchen and hooked an arm around Max's shoulders, burying his nose in the mage's neck and his claiming mark and breathing in his scent.

"Everything okay?"

"No," he murmured before he could stop himself. He refused to lie to his pack, but he didn't want to worry Max about something he could do nothing about. At least not yet. Something was happening, but nothing made sense.

A fire mage Sparking in his twenties wasn't worth all this trouble. At least not for the Order. They preferred children they could mold into their perfect magical soldiers. He could understand Savino wanting his son back for the sheer power. And the war no doubt brewing in the underworld as every faction, big or small, planned to make a grab for Max. But none of them should have the ear of a general.

Caius sighed and pressed a lingering kiss to Max's temple. "We'll figure it out."

Max leaned his weight into him. "You're really sure he's still alive?"

"Yes." He had no doubt about that and didn't hesitate to answer. "He's alive. We just need to find him."

Max nodded and straightened, and Caius was equally relieved and surprised that, despite the hint of worry, his scent remained calm.

He left Max to his cooking and didn't dare comment on the rubbery look of the scrambled eggs. Maybe Quinn was onto something about hiring a cook, but at this point, he couldn't trust a stranger that close to the heart of his pack.

He descended the stairs to find Quinn furiously typing at his computers, screens of maps with geographical overlays, and footage of road and highway cameras flicking across the screens. "Any luck?"

Quinn snarled. "No."

Caius stood behind him and watched in silence for a few moments, until Quinn shot him a look, his scent thick with frustration. "Can you open a secure line to Adams?"

Quinn sighed and opened a new screen. A few moments later, the call went out. When it connected, Adams didn't say anything, likely because it was an unknown number.

"This is Ward."

"Still no news, Colonel."

"Did you know this order came down from General Graves?"

The only sound on the other end was the heavy tread of boots for a drawn-out minute, until they were muffled by carpet and a door swung shut. There was a familiar burst of quiet static as a privacy spell activated. "Yes, I saw the signature," Adams finally said.

"Is the Order behind this?"

The silence was telling. "I can't confirm anything."

Caius forced out a calming breath while grinding his teeth. "Did you knowingly send Lukas on a bogus mission to die?"

"Of course not," Adams snapped. "I warned him as best I could and sent someone to help, but I haven't heard back yet."

Quinn scoffed but held his tongue.

"Who?"

Adams sighed. "Ghost."

Fucking hell. Lukas was as likely to end up dead thanks to that maniacal pixie as if he'd been on the plane. "What did you promise her?"

"An unsanctioned mission to take out her creator."

"And who is that?" There were rumors that the Ghost was decades older than she appeared, but her file wasn't just top secret; it didn't seem to actually exist. He knew. He'd looked.

"Helga Fuchs."

Caius looked at Quinn to find him already typing away. The screen that popped up a few moments later showed an elderly woman well into her eighties or nineties. Her information listed her as one-hundred-one.

"You put a hit out on someone's grandma?" Quinn muttered, incredulous.

"She was rumored to be a Nazi scientist. When the Order refused to sanction her experiments after the war, she vanished. Popped up again about forty years ago, shortly after Ghost was found."

"If Lukas is involved in murdering—" Caius started with a growl, but Adams cut him off.

"He won't be."

Caius growled again, low in his throat. He knew Adams would do what he could to protect Lukas, but he also knew if there was even a whiff of Lukas being involved, it would be included in a report somewhere, even if it wasn't official. As much as he believed in serving his country, he knew how deep and dark that service could pull someone, and he wasn't going to let that happen to anyone in his pack.

But that was something to be dealt with after they found Lukas.

"Does General Rhys Graves have ties to the Order?" he asked, ignoring the sharp look Quinn gave him as he listened to the silence on the other end of the phone.

Finally, Adams said, "I can't confirm anything."

Which was all the confirmation Caius needed. "Please keep me apprised."

"Of course."

Once Quinn disconnected the call, Caius let out a slow breath, but before he could think of possible next steps, Quinn swiveled his chair towards the stairs and sniffed.

"Something is burning."

Caius' heart lurched as he smelled burning bacon. He dashed up the stairs, sure it was another kitchen SNAFU, but when he reached the kitchen, the pan with bacon was charred black, and there was no sign of Max.

CHAPTER 18

ONCE THE eggs were finished, Max put them in the oven to keep warm until Caius and Quinn were ready to eat, turning the bacon down to let it cook a bit longer. Then he turned on the news on the off chance there was anything being said about Lukas' plane disappearing.

What he found was so much worse.

On the screen was a video of a pillar of flames, one he recognized as his, from when the Order first approached them. His magic had reacted on his instinct, afraid the mage would hurt Caius and Quinn before dragging Max off to be forced to fight for the highest bidder.

When the flames vanished, the clip switched to another, this one of the attack outside the college. Conveniently, the part where his father's man shot Quinn was edited out, and it only showed him burning the men to ash with a raging inferno. The anchor was talking about a rogue mage and a new, feral shifter pack trying to settle in the city, blatantly flaunting their power and ignoring even the most basic laws.

"What the fuck," he whispered, the remote creaking in his grip. He really wished some of his father's men were around so he could burn them down again.

His phone chimed, and he dug it out of his pocket, frowning at the unknown number before opening the text.

If you want this to stop, come outside.

"Fuck." He tossed the remote on the couch before stalking to the door and throwing it open. He didn't bother finding his coat as he hopped down the stairs and found a black SUV at the curb. He strode all the way across the yard and stopped while still inside the warding Rían had put in place, crossing his arms and glaring at the short woman standing beside the back door. "The fuck do you want?"

"My contract would like to speak with you."

Max narrowed his eyes. She was a mage, he could sense the magic around her if he focused, but there was no way he was getting in that car. "Where are they, then?"

She opened the door, revealing an older man with more white than black in his hair and storm-gray eyes. The man may have been smiling, but Max recognized a predatory smile when he saw one.

"Please, get in so we can chat."

Max laughed in his face. "I'm not that stupid." He was, however, stupid enough to have come out here without even his familiar, much less letting Caius know the Order was apparently at their doorstep.

The man's smile tightened as he reached across the seat and, like an actual villain, pulled a young woman with a gag forward enough that Max could see her.

"No," he breathed, taking an involuntary step towards his sister.

"Now, get in the car," the man ordered. "Or I'll give her to my men."

Angelica's yell was muffled by the gag as she twisted away from the man, but she didn't get far.

Max didn't realize his hands were on fire until the other mage summoned water around her own.

"We don't want a fight."

He sneered at the lie, but there wasn't much he could do with his magic. Not with Angelica in the way. Even if he only blew their tires, unless he could get her out of the car, she'd get hurt. Or worse.

He flexed his fingers as he forced his lungs to work and released the flames into harmless smoke. "Let her go."

The man sighed and pulled a pistol from his suit jacket.

"Stop!" Max yelled, stepping forward before the man could point the gun at his sister. "Fine. I'll get in." Even though his entire body ran cold at the thought of getting in that car, he forced his feet to move him forward. There was a tug along his familiar bond as Aradia clued in that something was wrong, but he urged her to stay away. If he was lucky, she'd be able to guide Caius to wherever they took him, even if it was only to his corpse.

He climbed in and reached for Angelica's clenched fists, ignoring the man facing them as he burned through the zip ties and then pulled away the gag.

Angelica surged forward and threw her arms around Max's neck.

Max froze. They'd rarely even spoken to each other without their father present, and she'd certainly never been allowed near him, as if his gayness were contagious. He'd been sure she didn't even see him as a brother. He hesitantly wrapped his arms around her back, the shock twisting inside him when he felt a sharp, tiny stab of pain in his neck.

He flinched away, grabbing at his neck and knocking her hand away. The syringe clattered to the floorboards. No. No, no, this wasn't happening.

"Papa was right," Angelica scoffed, and Max looked up to see their father's sneer on her face. "You're a disappointment."

A strange sound escaped his throat as a familiar cold numbness crept through his limbs. He should have known better. His father never let Angelica go anywhere without at least three bodyguards. There was little chance anyone could take her by force and make it here without retaliation.

Panic and adrenaline tried to kick his heart into overdrive, but the sedative was already taking hold. He didn't have more than a few seconds. He'd been drugged and kidnapped enough times to know that. More than once on his father's orders, even.

The first time he'd been in kindergarten. He left school and climbed into the usual car waiting for him. The guards were different, but his father routinely moved people around, so it hadn't worried him until one of them jabbed a needle into him.

Despite how careful he'd been after that, he'd still been taken twice more by his father's men. The last time, they'd chased him for seven blocks before catching him. That was one of the reasons he preferred his motorcycle. It was faster and more maneuverable, and no help to him now.

He managed to get one foot out of the car before the mage pushed him back inside and slammed the door shut.

The last thing he saw before he blacked out was the man with storm-gray eyes smirking at him.

CHAPTER 19

"YOU WANT me to shoot a kid?" Lukas looked up from the photos he'd been given. One of an elderly woman who looked one wrong step from shattering a hip, one of a classically beautiful woman in her late twenties, and a third of a young man who didn't look any older than Ghost.

"Problem?" Ghost asked around her sucker.

He wondered how she didn't have a mouth full of dentures by now, but he kept that thought to himself. "You're one of the most notorious mages around. What exactly do you need me for?"

She spun the sucker against her tongue before pulling it out with a dramatic sigh. "Nikolai is not a kid. He is older than me, and more powerful. My powers won't work on him, but a speeding bullet shot from a block or two away should be enough." She motioned to one of the tables of the safe house they'd brought Lukas to with her chin. "I'm sure you'll find one of those to your liking."

Lukas eyed the large assortment of guns, his eyes immediately catching on a fully outfitted AXSR rifle. His fingers twitched to get a hold of it, but he refrained for the moment. "Just so I'm clear, I shoot this Nikolai for you, and we're done and I can go back to my pack?"

Ghost popped her sucker back in her mouth with an air of amusement. "I won't stop you. It's your funeral."

He turned towards the table to hide his sneer, digging his tactical gloves out of his pocket before yanking them into place. He was starting to think most of the rumors about the Ghost being rabid were due to how much of a bitch she was.

As soon as he was close enough, he picked up the AXSR and immediately sank into the rhythm of taking it apart, checking it over, and reassembling it. He went through the full process three times before he was satisfied and packed it into the large duffel with some bullets.

His watch said it was still early enough for brunch, but his eyes were gritty from lack of sleep. He didn't trust Ghost or her team well enough to nap around them, even if they had saved his ass. Especially since neither of the other two had deigned to give him their name.

They hadn't even spoken a word since Lukas got in the SUV, which helped explain how there was so little information about them outside of rumors.

Honestly, it was disturbing as fuck and put him on edge. It wasn't just that the lack of trust made it clear that he was the expendable one here. The man and woman both kept their sunglasses on inside and didn't move once they were sitting. Their scent was all wrong too. No hint of emotion or stress, despite the fact they were about to go into a fight. If he couldn't see for himself that they were breathing, he might have believed they were corpses.

The sooner they got this over with, the better.

"When are we doing this?"

"Soon." Ghost paced near the wall, one hand attached to her sucker, the other to her phone, typing quickly with her thumb. Whatever she saw on the screen a few moments later put a manic grin on her face, and she spun towards him. "Now. Two minutes!" she called, and there was an immediate response as the other two pushed to their feet and grabbed their weapons, completely in sync.

Creepy as fuck.

Once they were in the car, the man handed over an earpiece.

From the front, Ghost piped up. "We have half an hour before they're due to arrive. You'll need to find a spot and set up before then."

Less than thirty minutes to find a vantage point and set up a shot? Were they insane? He had zero intel, had what he was sure were outdated photos, and a gun he'd never shot before. But saying any of that was sure to get him killed, so he kept silent.

His best bet was to do the job and slip away while they were dealing with the aftermath. He didn't have his ID or phone, but he always kept at least fifty bucks tucked into a hidden pocket when he could. And since joining Caius' pack, he was never hurting for money or a meal and rarely touched his stash.

He itched to contact Caius, to let his pack know he was alive, but was sure Adams had made a call by now. But would he have told the truth or let Caius think he was dead? Would Quinn hack into the systems and find where he'd gone?

He flexed his hand against his leg, claws sprouting from his fingertips before he got himself under control.

He couldn't shift here. No matter how much his instincts were screaming at him that this was all wrong. Only the fact that Adams had told him he'd called in the Ghost and to stay alive kept Lukas from doing anything stupid. Or more stupid than shooting a foreign civilian on US soil. In broad daylight. Something stupid like attacking the most notorious mage in the country, if not the world.

The SUV slowed to a stop and pulled into a parking area.

"They always use that entrance," Ghost said, pointing across the street to a large tinted-glass building a dozen stories tall. The logo declared it as Magierseele.

His bad feeling intensified further. No way in hell was a sniper rifle taking down anyone associated with this place. "You expect me to believe Magesoul employees aren't going to have some kind of protection?"

Ghost flicked her hand. "It's taken care of. All you need to do is take out Nikolai."

Lukas really had to wonder if Adams had pulled Ghost in expecting Lukas to shoot her instead of help her. Before he could give in to that temptation, he kicked his door open, grabbed the duffel, and slammed the door. The tires squealed as they sped away before it even shut completely.

"Fuck," he breathed, the chill air fogging his breath in front of him. He stared at the Magesoul building for a long moment before turning a slow circle. The target area was on the corner of an intersection, with a small half-circle drive-thru to keep from blocking traffic. The only building with an easily accessible vantage point was the roof of the café across the street, and no way in hell was he shooting from such an open space.

The building next to him looked like a hotel, with what looked like corporate offices beside it. The other corner was open space with a street taco cart.

He'd have to take his chance with the hotel.

He slipped inside, tipping his head down and away from the cameras as he went straight for an elevator and pressed a button for one of the top floors with his gloved knuckle. The floor was deserted when he stepped off and turned for the stairs, taking them the last three flights up. By the time he found the door to the roof and stepped back out into the chill, he estimated he had about fifteen minutes left.

He moved like he'd been trained, finding the target area and crouching near the edge of the roof to set up the shot. There was a breeze this high up, but he spotted a pride flag hanging over the café entrance and watched it for a moment to judge the wind speed.

He should be able to make the shot. He'd shot from farther in worse conditions. He only wished he could contact his CO to make sure he'd be protected. It was only in the past forty years that shifters were even allowed in the armed forces, and public opinion on them still swayed from one extreme to the other, depending on which spin the news decided to put on a story. The last thing he wanted was to cause issues for Caius.

Caius was a great alpha. He had enough to deal with right now with Max and the Order. He certainly didn't deserve an assassination scandal on top of everything else.

Lukas blew out a breath, ignoring the chill biting his face as he shook out his limbs. His breathing and heart rate slowed as he fell into the familiar routine of checking his sights and lining up the target area. He scanned the street, thankful the weather looked like it would turn severe again since it kept most people inside.

He didn't have long to freeze before a red Ferrari pulled into view. He let out a low whistle, taking a moment to admire the car before focusing on the doors.

Nikolai climbed out of the driver seat and straightened his suit as he surveyed the street. Only when he'd looked from one side to the other and back again did he move around to the passenger door.

Lukas glanced at the flag, verifying the wind was still blowing the same, before settling his finger on the trigger. When he had Nikolai in sight, he breathed out, slow and steady.

Sharp, visceral pain lashed through him, his nerve endings lighting up like they'd been doused in acid. Only his training and the need to not give away his position kept him from shouting in pain, but he couldn't control the spasms or the way his finger squeezed the trigger.

The rifle went off, and a second later there were shouts and screaming from across the street.

Lukas heard them as if from underwater, the pain lancing through him again and stealing his breath.

Max.

Instinctively, he knew this was a result of the binding. It felt like someone was trying to burn through the magic. To sever it. Fuck, he had to find Max. If someone had gotten to him, that meant—

No, he refused to believe either Caius or Quinn could have been taken out, even by surprise. Surely he would have felt that too.

Tires squealed against pavement, and he finally caught his breath enough to look over the edge of the roof.

Nikolai wasn't dead, but his left shoulder was drenched in blood, his arm hanging useless at his side.

Technically, Lukas hadn't missed, so he considered it a job well done and packed up. He wasn't about to stick around for a battle between mages. He found the bullet casing and tossed it in the duffel before standing.

He couldn't risk going back through the hotel. He eyed the office building next to him. It was slightly taller and had a metal drainpipe. Good enough.

He slung the duffel bag over his shoulder and ran for the ledge, launching himself towards the pipe and grunting as he slammed into brick. His fingers slipped against metal and his feet skidded before he found purchase, bracing his toes against the wall to slow his descent.

He was still four stories off the ground when the screech of twisting metal echoed through the area. When he reached the second floor, he jumped the remaining distance and risked looking across the street to see Ghost's SUV crumpled, as if hit by a speeding semi from all four sides.

Ghost herself was floating several feet in the air, feet kicking, hands scrabbling at her throat as if she were being choked.

A quick glance at Nikolai showed his arm still hanging at his side, but his other was raised in the air, his fingers curled like he was gripping something.

As Lukas watched, a security guard from the Magesoul building shuffled through the door, his motions jerky like in the bad zombie movies. He unholstered his gun and pointed it at Nikolai's head. When he fired, his arm went wide as if it'd been shoved aside. Ghost dropped half a foot in the air before flying through the glass doors and sliding inside.

Lukas decided now would be a good time to run. Already sirens ricocheted off the buildings, and he couldn't afford to be detained here. He had to find Max and the rest of his pack. If he concentrated hard enough, he could almost sense what direction they were in.

He made it about two blocks before the pain came again, knocking him to his knees as he gasped. The frigid air burned his lungs, but it was almost a relief against the fire eating his insides. The agony vanished as quickly as it came, and he listed to the side, hardly noticing the snow soaking into his pants before he struggled to his feet.

An old Pontiac sat in a small parking lot next to an alley ahead of him. Lukas glanced around and didn't see or smell anyone. There were a few cameras at the convenience store, but it was worth the risk. He elbowed the glass out and reached inside to pop the lock, only to find it unlocked. With a curse, he threw his bag into the passenger seat and checked the visor for keys, but his luck didn't hold. He popped the panels beneath the steering wheel, found the wires he needed, and got the car started.

"Hang on, Max," he murmured, pulling onto the street. "Just hang on till I find you guys."

CHAPTER 20

CAIUS WAS going to burn the entire Order to the ground. They were the only ones who could have orchestrated taking Max so quickly and easily, though Savino was a close second. It was a toss-up on which had researched Caius and reached out to his old pack.

He'd caught his uncle's scent where Max's ended, and he wasn't as surprised as he should have been. Kostas hadn't been happy at all when he'd taken over the pack, only to learn that all the assets had been legally transferred to Caius upon his father's death.

Caius had struggled with the guilt over leaving those loyal to his father behind when he'd stayed with the Marines, then later formed his own pack, but they'd had a chance to leave. He'd sent word to Leon, one of the few he trusted implicitly, that any who wanted to join his pack would be welcome, but the response was radio silence.

If Kostas was here now, declaring war on his tiny pack, likely in the hopes that all the assets would return to him as next of kin, then he certainly didn't know that if anything happened to Caius, or subsequently his pack members, all the money was set to be distributed into various charities to help packless teens and disabled veteran shifters.

Kostas would never see a cent. Especially since Caius intended to rip his uncle's throat out with his own teeth before the day was over.

The surges of pain only confirmed his suspicions. A mage was helping Kostas try to break the bindings, and only a mage with explicit instructions from the Order, or by request from the bound mage, would ever attempt such a thing. With how bad the last one was, he was surprised Max was still holding onto them. The fact the bonds were still intact despite the pain was a relief and proof that Max wanted to remain with them.

If they did break, he had no doubt Kostas would bind Max by force, and the idea of a mage under his uncle's control was almost as horrifying as knowing it would be Max.

Aradia chirped impatiently from her perch on the dashboard.

"I know," Quinn snapped. "Just give me a sec." He was still slumped against the steering wheel, knuckles white where he gripped it.

Somehow, he'd managed to pull over and stop when the pain hit instead of crashing. "They're trying to break the bonds, aren't they?" he asked, his voice tight as he took slow, controlled breaths.

"Yes," Caius answered. "We need to hurry." He glanced at the tablet Quinn had shoved into his hands on their way out the door, but it was still showing Signal Lost. Max had his phone with him, but the tracking app was being blocked. Thankfully, familiar bonds couldn't be blocked so easily.

"Right." Quinn sucked in a deep breath and got them back on the road.

Aradia chirped and flicked her tail, guiding Quinn to take the off-ramp. Then they drove a few miles into a rundown neighborhood, where Aradia started barking.

"Stop here," Caius said. He didn't like this. They didn't have the benefit of the dark to hide their approach. It was barely past noon, and whoever Kostas had brought with him would pick up their scents before they got close enough to break in. And they were missing Lukas, who arguably had the best tactical mind between the three of them.

He studied Aradia, at how she was staring intently to the east, at a house behind the one across from them. "Next street over?" he asked, and received an affirmative chirp.

"What's the plan?"

"Don't die. Kill my uncle. Get Max." Finding the Order and anyone else responsible for this could come later, after they found Lukas.

"Great plan. How do you suggest we actually accomplish that?"

Caius grimaced. "Still working on that."

Aradia lifted into the air with a gentle swirl of wind magic, landed on the power button for the window to roll it down, and promptly flew out of it.

So much for coming up with a plan.

He shared a quick look with Quinn before they got out, grabbing weapons from their hidden stash in the spare tire compartment. Their guns wouldn't do much against shifters since they didn't carry aconite bullets, but they did have several custom-made blades with aconite coating tucked into durable sheaths. Tactical blades he'd invested in shortly after Kostas took over the pack, in case his uncle sent someone after him to ensure Caius wouldn't challenge him later. Black steel, a smooth, sharp edge, and a finger ring on the end for added stability and security.

They each took two and secured one each to their inside wrist and thigh, then rushed after Aradia.

There were enough trees, bushes, and abandoned gardens filled with overgrown weeds to at least offer a little cover as they slipped through one of the yards and over a broken privacy fence.

The moment Caius hit the ground on the other side, several scents hit him at once. His uncle and several members of his pack. Max. Blood and fear sweat. And a few scents he recognized from his meeting with Savino, trace smells he'd picked up while in Max's home.

A soft, low growl built in his chest as he stalked forward.

Only one wolf was guarding the door, an older man who'd always worshipped Kostas and helped him take over the pack.

Caius saw the moment of recognition in his eyes, but before the guard could call out a warning, Caius rushed him, slamming him into the side of the house. He took a fist to the gut, grunting through it as he drove a dagger into the man's neck. He shifted his weight, clamping his left hand over the man's mouth, gritting his teeth against the pain in his shoulder and the sound of hissing as aconite burned through shifter blood.

It didn't take long for the blood loss and aconite poisoning to do their job, and Caius let the lifeless body slump to the ground. He glanced back, but Quinn had already found his own way in. Likely to find the breaker or another way to cause chaos.

The door was unlocked, and he let himself inside, flexing his hand until claws appeared and using the enhanced strength to twist the handle. That should slow down anyone trying to get in or out.

He turned and found five of Kostas' pack in the living room. Three were on their feet, finally noticing something was wrong. He adjusted his dagger and readied himself, but they all froze, their eyes widening with recognition.

"Where is he?" Caius demanded, not bothering to clarify who. He'd take either Kostas or Max right then.

Movement behind him made him spin and raise his dagger against an attack that wasn't there. At least not physically. A wall of water slammed into him. The force was enough that he skidded across the living room. Hands grabbed his arms, and he twisted the dagger around, feeling it sink into flesh even as the water coalesced around his head to drown him.

Like hell he was dying here. He wasn't going to let his uncle get away with this, and he sure as hell wasn't abandoning Max.

The water heated quickly, and he knew if he didn't drown, he'd die of shock from severe burns soon. He forced his eyes open despite the burning pain and yanked his dagger free. There was a shadow of a figure in front of him, and he prayed it was the mage as he followed through with the momentum and threw the dagger.

Water surged in front of her and hardened to ice, but not fast enough. The dagger sliced through without slowing until it came to a stop in her chest.

The bubble around Caius' head exploded outward, and he gasped for air, turning to the wolf still gripping his left arm. He didn't bother pulling his other dagger free. Instead, he twisted enough to slam his head into the other man's face, then punched him in the throat when he stumbled back.

"Kostas!" he yelled, kicking the man's knee and hearing it snap before turning to the others.

Two were still sitting with shocked expressions, the third who'd stood lifting his hands up in surrender.

Caius hesitated as he got a decent look at them. They were young. Far too young to be caught up in this. He didn't recall any of them from before he left for the Marines over twenty years ago, but he doubted they would have even been born then.

None of them made a move to attack, and he was grateful for it; he hated killing kids.

"Where?" he snarled, but he didn't need a response. He caught his uncle's scent and spun around, moving to the other side of the room as he listened to the deliberately slow footsteps echoing down the hall.

He glanced at the mage where she'd fallen to the floor. Her eyes were unfocused, but she was still breathing, her chest spasming with short, sharp gasps. She clutched at the knife with one hand, where barely any blood was soaking her shirt. If she managed to use her magic to keep herself alive, they could use her to find those in the Order responsible for this, but he turned his attention to his uncle as he stepped into the room.

If he'd been younger, the blatantly disappointed look might have chastised him. Now it only pissed him off. "You took a member of my pack."

"He's mine now. You should have protected him better."

Caius startled as the words punched through his chest, not only because they were true, but because they were an echo of what Kostas said to his father when his mother died. "Fucking bastard," he hissed.

With a quick, fluid motion, he pulled the second dagger free and hurled it at Kostas. He didn't expect it to find its mark; he only needed the few seconds of distraction. The sharp hiss as the blade at least cut flesh was satisfying enough.

His shirt ripped in his haste to toss it aside, and he kicked his pants away as he shifted. It'd been a year since he'd last let his wolf free. A year since the injury that resulted in his medical discharge. The silver-blue veins of aconite poisoning were bad enough in his human form, limiting his arm's range of motion. He had no idea how badly it would hamper his movements as a wolf, but the added speed, agility, and strength would surely make up for it.

The world readjusted as he landed on four paws, and he breathed deep. The three younger wolves were still petrified behind him, their fear turning the air sour. He knew that fear wasn't because of him. They were likely terrified of the punishment Kostas was sure to deal out for them not dying with the others.

The dagger clattered to the floor, and Caius focused on the wound where it had sunk into his uncle's arm. He had to fight back the instinct to attack there. Blood meant weakness, but the aconite could poison him just as easily if he came in contact with the wound.

Instead, he focused on Kostas' leg, launching himself across the room as his uncle began to shift, but it was immediately apparent how slow Kostas was. Slow enough that Caius clamped onto Kostas' thigh, his teeth sinking into the mostly human flesh. Blood filled his mouth and he snarled, shaking his head to rend muscle and do as much damage as possible before he let go. He jumped back as flesh turned to fur and Kostas finished his shift with a howl.

Already, his left foreleg ached, a mild burn flooding his senses as the aconite still in his body stabilized, but there was no searing pain. No hissing of his blood as the poison activated. The doctors had promised they'd rendered the remnants inert, but there'd always been a lingering fear of *what if.*

He may not have had much to live for a year ago, but he never reached the point of actively seeking death.

Kostas shook himself and growled as he limped around Caius.

He snarled as he moved to keep Kostas in his sight, letting his uncle's blood drip from his teeth. The sour tang of fear spiked from the three watching, and he distantly wondered if this was their first time seeing a true fight between alphas. One that could only end in death.

Kostas stumbled and Caius hunched, ready to pounce on the moment of weakness, but his battle instincts from two decades in the Marines urged him not to. Those instincts proved to be right as Kostas bared his teeth and leapt, driving Caius to the ground despite his efforts to dodge.

They rolled, claws and teeth ripping fur and flesh. Teeth sank into his bad shoulder. His claws raked across Kostas' belly. Blood spilled hot from their wounds before they broke apart.

Then he heard the distant report of a rifle firing, right before something exploded.

CHAPTER 21

WHATEVER DRUG they'd given him wore off as soon as the pain broke through it. When Max came back to his senses, it was to his back on fire and the taste of blood in his mouth.

He didn't know who they were or what their goal was, but he was no stranger to pain or torture. If his father had failed to break him for years, he refused to give in now.

The tenuous connections he had with Caius, Quinn, and Lukas flickered in his mind's eye, where he could almost see the threads of magic. Instinctively, he reached for them, holding them close so they wouldn't break. He may not be a decent mage, certainly not good enough to be claimed by a pack, but they were the best family he'd ever had.

Even if they wouldn't be able to save him, if they even tried to find him, the connections between them wouldn't break unless he was dead.

He lost track of time as the torture continued, burning, searing pain washing over his back and through his core for countless minutes. By the time the agony faded, he was left as a shivering, panting bundle of raw nerves huddled on the floor.

This couldn't be happening. It *shouldn't* be happening. His amulet should have protected him, but as he regained his senses and looked for Rían's amulet, it was gone. No. That was impossible, unless they'd burned through all the protections while he'd been unconscious. A soft whimper escaped his throat when he reached for his flames and found they were all but gone too. They simmered beyond his grasp, sluggish like they were drugged.

"Much more of this and he'll die," a woman said, the voice vaguely familiar. The mage who'd helped abduct him.

"You said you could break the bindings." That sounded like the man from the car.

"I said they could be broken if he was bound by force."

The man scoffed. "Mages don't consent to bindings."

"Why don't you put your own binding on over them? You're planning to kill your nephew anyway." That voice was worse than the others.

Max's lungs seized, and he forced his eyes open, unable to believe Maurice was there. There was no reason for him to be there. Except his sister had drugged him. Which meant his father was in on this.

Maurice noticed him staring and stepped closer with a lecherous grin.

Max tried to shrink away, but his hands were tied behind his back.

"Is that possible?" the man asked.

"Technically," the mage answered.

Max didn't pay any more attention to what they were saying, his entire focus on Maurice. One of his father's trusted men and the bane of Max's existence since he was twelve. When Maurice crouched in front of him and stroked a finger down his cheek, Max cringed, fear, anger, and disgust twisting inside him.

He focused on the anger and quickly turned his head enough to bite the offending finger. That earned him a backhand to the face, but it was worth it, especially when Maurice stood with a wary sneer.

That victory didn't last long. The other man grabbed Max's arm and hauled him to his feet, nearly ripping his shoulder out of its socket.

Max stumbled, dizziness sweeping the room at a wrong angle until his back slammed into the wall and a hand squeezed his throat.

"It needs your blood," the mage said, stepping up beside them and lifting a small bowl of dark liquid.

"No."

They both ignored him as the man let the mage cut his finger, then dripped blood into the bowl. It flared with Max's soft orange magic. Then he swiped his fingers through the liquid and pulled the neck of Max's sweater down to spread it across his throat.

There was no brush or artistic touch, and for a moment nothing happened. No pain. No magic. No chill. Nothing.

"Fuck you," Max hissed, spitting blood in the man's face. He wouldn't be bound to anyone else.

The man bared his teeth, his eyes glowing as he clamped a hand around Max's throat, pinning him against the wall again.

"Know your place."

Max bared his own teeth in a mockery of a grin. "You some 1800s villain? I'm not a fucking slave."

"You will be."

Fear skipped through his chest as the fingers tightened around his throat, cutting off his ability to breathe. He twisted his arms and wrists, but the restraints held tight, tearing his flesh and drawing blood. He thrashed and kicked, but it was like hitting granite. Desperate, he reached for his flames again.

Heat sparked and flickered around his fingers. The answering call of fire was still muted and dulled, but it answered. His lungs screamed for air. He felt when the flames caught on the ropes around his wrists, his desperation yanking it into a bigger and hotter fire.

The ropes snapped and his arms dropped, muscles aching and threatening to go out after being held in the wrong position for too long. But he pushed through the numbing agony, shoving the flames in his hands into the man's chest.

They never connected.

The binding around his throat snapped into existence with a rush of burning heat.

This was nothing like when his pack put their marks on him. That had been an overwhelming surge of power, like he could set the entire world on fire with his breath.

This was a thousand blades slicing through his neck and into the core of his magic itself.

He stumbled when the man released him, clawing at his throat, but there was nothing there. He hit the floor, screams dying in his useless throat. A bright red-orange glow filled his vision as fire circled his neck.

A moment later everything stopped, the pain nothing but a sense memory that left his entire body raw and oversensitive. The skin around his throat stung, and he'd seen enough movies to know exactly what mark had just appeared on him.

A collar.

"Fucker," he gasped, clasping a hand to his throat, but he still couldn't feel anything there aside from the faint pulse of magic. He flexed his fingers, warmth igniting between them. He stumbled to his feet, blinking against the dizziness, and threw himself at the nearest target as flames erupted in a fireball around his fist.

"Stop."

Max screamed. Lightning crackled through him and snuffed the flames. His body froze against his will and he stood, gasping for air, his muscles zinging and refusing to move.

He couldn't lift his arms. Couldn't run. Couldn't even turn.

"I'll kill you," he hissed, but he couldn't hide the tremor in his voice as terror threatened to drown him.

"You won't be doing much of anything," Maurice said with a leer.

"He's yours for now," the man said with a dismissive flick of his fingers. "Try not to kill him. I want Caius to see him suffer first."

"Sure." Maurice sauntered closer to Max. "Just order him to obey me and we'll be fine."

"Obey Maurice," the man said, sounding bored. "Do not fight. Do not resist." Then he turned and left.

Max looked for the mage, but she'd disappeared in the chaos. He was alone with Maurice. And for the first time he couldn't get away.

"You have no idea how long I've waited for this," Maurice said, grasping Max's chin and tipping his head back.

"Go fuck yourself."

Maurice hummed, not concerned in the least. And that was almost as terrifying as the fact that Max still couldn't move. "I have a better idea." He pressed his fingers into Max's jaw and forced his mouth open, before sliding his thumb inside.

Max gagged, trying to bite Maurice's finger off, but the binding magic tightened its hold and kept him still. He couldn't stifle a whimper, which only seemed to encourage Maurice.

"On your knees."

He hit the ground before he could even think to resist. His eyes watered when Maurice fisted a hand in his hair and yanked. This couldn't be happening. He wished his father had killed him if this was going to be his future. Bound against his will and forced to service his father's men.

He squeezed his eyes shut and tried to tune out the sound of a zipper. Revulsion twisted his stomach, but nothing came up, which was a shame. If anything might stop this, it would be vomiting on Maurice's shoes.

"Open your mouth."

Max whimpered again, his mouth falling open. He closed his throat, drawing sharp, shallow breaths through his nose as he braced himself against one of his worst nightmares.

Glass shattered beside him, and Maurice let out a surprised hiss, jerking Max forward as he fell.

Max yelped as he hit the floor, his eyes flying open to the sight of a bullet wound in Maurice's head, his eyes and mouth open in shock.

"Fuck. Oh fuck," he gasped. The binding magic on him fizzled and died and he was finally able to move again. He scrambled away from Maurice until his back hit a sofa. He pulled his legs up, tearing his eyes away from the blood pooling beneath Maurice to the window with a hole in it.

Maurice was dead. Someone shot him. Or had the bullet been meant for him?

A hysterical laugh bubbled out of him, quickly turning to a shriek as something exploded with enough force to rattle the windows. The already-broken pane shook loose and shattered across the floor.

He clamped a hand over his mouth and scrambled farther towards a corner. He might be free from Maurice, but he was still bound to the other man. Caius' uncle? How far would he have to run to break it? If he could find Rían, he knew he'd be safe, but as far as he knew, Rían was halfway around the world.

A soft squeak caught his attention, and he looked up in time for Aradia to fly into his face.

His manic laughs turned to sobs as he latched on to her, burying his face in silky fur. "How did you find me?"

When she chirped, he had the distinct impression she was calling him a dumbass, but he didn't care.

"Is Caius here?" he asked, hope blossoming in his chest for all of a few seconds before panic took over. "Where is he? He's gonna get killed!"

Aradia squeaked and lifted into the air, flying for the door and circling in front of it until he opened it. Then she took off down the hall, leaving him to follow.

CHAPTER 22

QUINN SLIPPED through the garage without encountering anyone. He didn't know much about Caius' old pack or their new alpha, but kidnapping a member of another pack was the kind of shit that made humans call them wild animals. Worse, he smelled more than one mage and Savino's people.

The door leading in next to the kitchen was unlocked, so he let himself inside. He caught the scents of a dozen shifters and Max, but no one was in the kitchen. He didn't see a single soul until he ran into one coming out of the bathroom.

"Jesus fuck," he hissed, pulling his arm up short of stabbing the kid in the neck. "How old are you?"

The kid threw his arms up, his eyes wide enough Quinn was sure he would have pissed himself if he hadn't already emptied his bladder. "S-sixteen."

"Great. Who the fuck brings kids to an abduction?" he muttered. He shoved his dagger into its sheath. "Sorry, but I'm going to choke you out now. You'll wake up in a few minutes, promise." The whimper nearly killed him, but he didn't have time to spare to soothe feelings.

He grabbed the kid before he could try to run, spun him, and put him into a choke hold. "Stay hidden until someone comes looking for you," he said before squeezing. He counted to twenty before letting go and carefully dragging the limp body into the bedroom across the hall. Once the kid was on the bed, he pulled the door shut and went back to the bathroom.

He ignored the mold or mildew on the walls as he dug through the cabinets and under the cracked sink until he found a bottle of hydrogen peroxide and a bottle of nail polish remover. That would do for a distraction.

Back in the kitchen, he grabbed a bowl, set it in the microwave, and filled it almost completely with hydrogen peroxide before adding a generous amount of acetone. Then he struggled to close the broken door, set the timer for five minutes on the highest setting, and ducked into the garage as it started counting down.

He crouched on the other side of an old, battered Volkswagen and couldn't help but wonder whose house this was since he was about to destroy their kitchen.

As planned, the microwave blew up with a resounding bang. He couldn't stop the grin and wished he could have watched it, but there were more important things to focus on. Like finding Max.

He slipped back inside.

Two more kids were arguing near the kitchen over who blew up the microwave, and he left them to it, moving deeper into the house and following his nose down a long hallway. He didn't get far before Aradia narrowly avoided flying into his face, and then Max crashed into his chest.

"Fuck," he breathed, pulling Max closer with a rush of relief. Then he pushed him back to look him over. "You're okay? Are you hurt?"

Max fisted Quinn's shirt with both hands. "I'm fine. Where's Caius?" He didn't smell fine, but he wasn't bleeding out.

"Starting fights, most likely," Quinn said, glancing past Max to make sure there were no threats before focusing on Aradia. "Why do you smell like Lukas?"

She chirped and Max startled, spinning to look behind him before staring at Quinn with a look and scent of shock. "I think he was the one who killed Maurice."

"Okay." He wasn't one to check a miracle pup for fleas, so he urged Max away from the room with the apparent dead guy. "Let's go find the Cap."

"Colonel," Max murmured.

"Yeah, yeah. Stay behind me," he said, reaching the end of the hall and putting himself in front of Max. There was still arguing from the kitchen, so he followed the sound of wolves fighting from the den.

A mage was sprawled near the entrance, a knife protruding from her chest. Max's scent was on her, and he bit back a growl, nudging Max to his other side to keep her out of Max's line of sight.

He needn't have worried. As soon as the den came into view, so did the source of the growls and snarls and crunching of furniture.

Three more kids were pressed against the back wall, but he dismissed them as a non-threat for the moment.

Two large white wolves circled the room like sharks. Blood oozed from dozens of wounds, splattered across carpet and walls alike. The wolves looked nearly identical, except for the scars visible on the left shoulder and foreleg of one. Which made the older one with gray around his muzzle Kostas. They were both limping, their fur matted with blood. Caius had a nasty gash on his face that was bleeding into his eye.

"No," Max hissed, rushing forward, but Quinn managed to catch him and drag him back before he got himself killed.

Both wolves paused when they noticed their new audience.

Kostas snarled before tipping his head back with a short howl. A call to attack.

Quinn drew his dagger and checked the hall before focusing on the kids, but they showed no sign of responding. He wasn't sure where the new threat was until Max grunted and hunched forward, flames licking the air around him. His magic smelled bitter beneath the usual smoky warmth of his fire.

"Fucking hell." He shoved the dagger back into its sheath. "Max, stop," he hissed, but Max showed no sign of hearing him.

The flames grew brighter and hotter until Quinn finally realized what smelled wrong about him. Kostas had bound Max.

He didn't have long to fix this. Already the flames were coalescing around Max's hand into a deadly fireball. When Max lifted his hand and aimed at Caius, Quinn did the only thing he thought might work.

"Cap! Arty!" he yelled. He didn't have time to make sure Caius understood. He grabbed Max from behind with one arm and clamped his other hand on the wrist with the fireball.

"Don't fight me," he snarled, pushing his will into the bond despite how much he hated to.

Max sagged against him and Quinn took full advantage, steadying Max's palm. Caius was crouched as he faced off against Kostas, and Quinn desperately hoped this would work. He covered Max's eyes with one hand, gave a quick pull with the other, and yelled, "Fire!"

He squinted against the heat and light as the fireball erupted from Max's hand. The whoosh of the tiny inferno drowned out everything but a pained howl. The fire swirled around the wolf, filling nearly the entire room with flames and smoke. The fire alarm went off, but the flames eating their way across the ceiling and into the hall killed it, the beeps dying out in a pitiful screech.

"Max! Get rid of the fire before we all die!"

Max jerked against him and crashed to his knees. He threw an arm towards the large bay window and the flames howled, shattering the glass as they spiraled through the window and out of the house.

Silence fell in their wake.

Quinn coughed, grimacing at the smell of burning fur and flesh. When he cracked his eyes open, he saw a charred and crispy wolf writhing on the floor. Caius stood nearby, his head low and his sides heaving.

"Caius," Max keened.

"He's okay." Quinn dropped his hands to Max's shoulders and pressed his face into Max's hair. "Good job." When Caius let out a low growl, he lifted his head in time to see Caius rip Kostas' throat out.

Max shuddered against him, and Quinn breathed a sigh of relief as the stench of Kostas' bond vanished. Max pulled away and stumbled to Caius before dropping to his knees beside him. "Caius," he whispered, lifting his hands to Caius' bloody muzzle.

Caius leaned into the touch for a moment before shifting. His human flesh was as bloodied as his fur, but the worst of the injuries seemed to be healing.

Quinn turned away as something slammed into the front door, drawing both his daggers as the wood splintered.

The door flew open, and Lukas stalked inside.

Quinn didn't hesitate before launching himself at Lukas, hooking both arms around his neck and pulling him down for a desperate kiss. "Fucker," he growled between kisses. "What the hell happened?"

"Long story," Lukas muttered, burying both hands in Quinn's hair and holding him close.

He could definitely get used to that. He wanted nothing more than to drag Lukas into the nearest unoccupied bedroom, but the clatter of metal hitting the floor behind them reminded him there was a clusterfuck to clean up before anyone was getting any.

He reluctantly pulled away and turned to see the mage sitting up, a hand pressed to her ribs. "Impressive," he said. "That would have killed most mages."

"I'm not most mages," she replied with a bland look. "And I have no agenda against any of you. This was one of my last missions for the Order before I get my freedom."

"Your mission was to abduct Max?"

"Not exactly." She pushed herself up further before slumping against the wall. "Savino hired the Order to help get his son back and suggested it would be easier if your pack was dealt with at the same time. They contacted Kostas, who was eager to help."

"Of course he was," Caius growled, still kneeling on the floor with Max.

The three kids at the back of the room were still standing there as if afraid to breathe. They reeked of fear and relief, which was curious and reassuring.

"There's at least half a dozen kids here," Quinn said quietly. "What's the plan?"

Caius turned towards the kids with a deep sigh. "Where's Leon?" he asked as he stood. He picked up his clothes, which looked mostly intact, aside from some charred spots and a rip in the shirt.

The kids shared looks before one of them was nudged forward as their leader. "Leon was exiled with the other traitors," he said.

"Can you contact him?"

They all shared looks again before shaking their heads, but a girl poked her head out of the kitchen. "I can," she offered.

Quinn nodded at her. "Do it," he said, holding out a hand to stop her before she reached the entrance. She didn't look any older than the others, and no kid needed to see their alpha dead on the floor. Even if he was a bastard who deserved it.

She pulled her phone out and put it on speaker. When Leon answered, he sounded frantic.

"What happened?"

Before she could answer, Caius approached and tugged the phone free. "Leon."

"Caius?"

"Kostas is dead. How fast can you be in Denver?"

"Dead…. What?"

"Leon," Caius said firmly, using his no-nonsense colonel voice.

"We're in Denver," Leon replied faintly.

"Quinn is going to give you an address," he said before handing the phone over.

THE NEXT half hour was spent rounding up the kids and corralling them in the dining room. The one he'd choked out was apparently Kostas' son, which was a surprise to Caius, who hadn't known he had any cousins. It was apparently as surprising as learning the girl, Eva, was Leon's daughter.

Quinn tried to ignore the itch of unease between his shoulders as Caius took command of the kids as if he were their alpha. He didn't mind growing their pack, he'd love to have a decent-sized pack again, but if Caius took his old pack over, that would mean moving to Wyoming. Which he didn't really mind, but he preferred the big city. And taking over a pack full of traumatized teens seemed like the absolute worst idea.

He expected the cops to show up in force, but when he peeked outside, the rest of the neighborhood looked as dilapidated as the house they were in. A cop car finally pulled up with a detached officer who took a statement from Quinn and Lukas, called it in as pack business, and left them to it.

When Leon finally arrived, it was with two dozen other men and women who'd been exiled as traitors. From the sound of it, after Kostas took over, the pack fractured until he'd kicked out over half of the adults. Obviously, he kept the kids to brainwash and mold into his own perfect little cult.

Once Leon learned what Kostas was planning, he gathered the others and followed Kostas and the kids to Denver.

Quinn left Caius and the others to discuss next moves and sank onto the only slightly broken and charred couch in the den. Someone had gotten rid of Kostas' body at some point, but his stench and the splatters of blood remained.

He zoned out as he stared at a large red stain, fighting the post-battle crash. He closed his eyes for a moment and found himself slumped against Lukas when he opened them again. With a soft groan, he wiggled closer and pressed his nose into Lukas' neck, breathing in his warm, rain-soaked scent.

Before he could wake enough to demand Lukas tell him where he'd disappeared to, a car revved as it raced down the street. There was a crunch of metal and wood as it drove into the mailbox and into the front yard.

Quinn and Lukas were both on their feet before a car door slammed shut, standing side by side in front of the broken front door.

A young woman with blood-matted blue hair and a shattered arm stalked towards them.

"Fuck," Lukas hissed. "How did you find me?"

"Tracker." The woman sneered and shoved past them, stepping into the house. "You didn't kill him. Both my dolls died because of your incompetence," she spat, standing in the hall and dripping blood like a Carrie reject. "Now the bitch has disappeared, likely to her lover, and you're going to help me find her."

"Why the hell would we do that?" Quinn asked, stepping between her and Lukas.

She gave a good impression of a wolf baring its teeth as she leaned into his personal space. "Because her lover is your little mage's father, and I have it on good authority that he wants you all dead. So help me, or I'll take him your heads and see if that's payment enough for what I want."

Fuck.

Quinn shared a quick look with Lukas before yelling into the house. "Cap, you better come out here."

If he concentrated hard enough, he could sense the structure of the house through the flames. The walls and floors and the heat of bodies inside. No one would escape.

Caius gripped Max's shoulder and squeezed, bringing him back to himself. "We have a plan."

"This would be easier," he muttered, but he coaxed the flames into sticking to the outside wall. Gunshots echoed from inside as he nudged the flames higher to cover the second-story windows, followed by yells, more shots, and snarling howls.

Ghost jerked as if hit, stalking towards the door and swearing loudly in German.

"Go," Max said, bringing his hands together to join both walls of fire at the back of the house. His heart stuck in his throat when Caius drew his gun and rushed inside, Lukas at his back.

Quinn stepped closer and pressed their shoulders together, but before he could say anything, magic flared nearby. A shimmering, translucent door appeared in front of them. Quinn's snarl echoed Max's own as the guy who'd attacked them in the parking lot stepped through.

"Motherfucker," Quinn hissed, pushing Max behind him. Even Aradia let out an angry bark and lifted into the air in front of Max.

He'd known this was too easy. There was no way his father would still be here if he wasn't overconfident in his safety.

The man said nothing as he drew magic around himself. Lots of magic. It reminded Max of Rían, but with far less finesse. A massive ball of swirling flames and smoke formed between his hands before he launched it at Quinn.

Max shoved Quinn to the side, but it didn't help. As if the spell had been locked onto Quinn, the fireball tracked him and exploded when it reached him, flames raining down and erupting into a containment circle around him.

Quinn yelled and dropped to the ground, where he rolled and writhed as he tried to put out the flames spreading over his clothes.

"Quinn!" Not again. His pack kept getting hurt because of him. Because he'd Sparked and now some assholes thought they had the right to dictate his life.

Fuck that.

Max reached for the flames covering Quinn. They weren't his, and they fought against his control, but he wasn't taking no for an answer.

Not anymore. Quinn belonged to him, and he wasn't letting anyone fuck with his pack and family again. He wrapped his will around the magic and snuffed it out, but before he could focus on the circle trapping Quinn, the flames around the house escaped his hold, roaring brighter and hotter.

"Fuck!" He didn't get a chance to rein them back in before a concussive force slammed into him, throwing him off his feet. He hit the ground with a pained grunt and rolled, coughing to get his lungs functioning again. He really could have used Rían's amulet right then, but no one had been able to find it even when they'd searched the mage who'd abducted him.

A window exploded from the rampaging, out-of-control fire. He felt the rush of fresh oxygen into the flames. The way they caught on the wood and curtains around the window. If he didn't call them back, everyone inside would die.

Max crawled to his knees in time to see the mage stalking towards him, a syringe in his hand. Terror got him the rest of the way to his feet, his heart finally getting through the shock and painfully attempting to beat its way out of his chest. Fire erupted around his hand, and he launched it at the man's face, only for it to be snuffed out with a flick of a hand.

Aradia swooped in with an angry bark, scratching the man's face before dodging his slap and flitting away.

Before Max could try another attack, the man rushed him. They hit the ground, and Max lashed out with every ounce of panic-driven violence and flames he could summon. His nails scraped flesh, and he valiantly tried to twist his body to get his knees anywhere sensitive, but a hand still closed around his throat, cutting off his air. When the needle came for his neck, he did the only thing he could think to do. He twisted into the grip and sank his teeth into the man's hand hard enough to taste blood, but the man hardly flinched.

A moment later, a giant wolf leapt out of the circle of flames. With a snarl, Quinn slammed into the mage's back and ripped him off Max before pinning him to the ground. The needle of the syringe glinted orange as they struggled. Max twisted enough to kick it out of the mage's hand before he could jab it into Quinn's side. When Quinn finally got his large, sharp teeth into the back of the man's neck, he finally stopped struggling, lying still as he panted with exertion.

Max groaned and pushed onto his hands and knees as he sucked in gulps of air. "Fuck. Don't kill him." He wanted answers, but now wasn't the time.

The garage exploded, flames billowing out several feet with the acrid stench and thick smoke of burning gasoline.

Fuck. *Fuck.* Someone outside of the jamming signal definitely would have heard that.

He could hardly focus on anything beyond the stinging ache in his lungs and intense heat in the air, but Caius and Lukas trusted him to keep the fire under control.

Reaching a hand towards the house, he willed the flames to pull back. They refused, eagerly eating through every surface they could reach. He tried again, but they still wouldn't listen. A small part of him didn't want them to listen, having imagined burning this house down since he was a kid, but his pack was still inside, and like fuck would he be responsible for their deaths. Another few minutes and the entire house would be a raging inferno.

With a snarl, Max swayed to his feet and stumbled towards the house. "*My* flames," he hissed, refusing to let the fear overtake him. He could freak out later. He focused on the anger instead, pushing it into insulted outrage. "How dare you not listen to me!" He shoved his hands into the flames, imagined gathering them all into his grip, and yanked as if throwing the fire into the ground.

The heat and flames vanished with an audible whoosh.

Max slumped against the charred brick, counting to twenty before staggering back and turning to check on Quinn. He blinked when he found Quinn back in his human form, sitting naked on top of the mage with a knee jammed into his back and a hand on his neck. He glared at the circle of flames still burning strong and wrenched them into a puff of smoke before snatching up Quinn's clothes and tossing them over. Then he stood where he could stare down at the mage and resisted the urge to kick his face. "What's it going to take for the Order to fuck off?"

There was no response.

Quinn tilted his head with a frown. "I think someone is controlling him. He smells like you did when that bastard forced a binding on you."

Max grimaced and swallowed against the nausea at the reminder. He wouldn't wish that on anyone, except maybe his father.

"Try to break it."

"Are you insane?" He didn't know the first thing about breaking bonds. What if it blew up in their faces, literally?

Quinn ignored him as he adjusted his hold and leaned down, sniffing at the mage before flexing his fingers into claws. With a quick swipe, he ripped away the back of the man's shirt, revealing a circular tattoo on his shoulder.

Max nearly recoiled from the amount of power in the mark. "No way."

"Max. Just try, yeah?"

With a hiss, Max dropped to his knees. "If I end up killing him, I'm gonna be really pissed at you." He eyed the mark and swallowed a soft whimper before hovering his hands over it. The pulse of magic was strong. Far stronger than he felt in his own bond with the three of them. Thanks to what little Rían had managed to teach him, he knew how to find the edges of spells and elements. Finding the boundary of the binding mark was the easy part. Removing it without causing damage to the mage or the core of his magic was the impossible part.

"You can do it," Quinn said.

Aradia landed on Max's shoulder with an encouraging chirp, the bond between them coming into sharper focus as she offered her help.

Max blew out a breath and reached for the magic like he had the flames, imagining his fist closing around the mark.

Immediately, the mage started fighting again, thrashing against Quinn's hold before Quinn shoved his face into the ground.

"Keep still!" Quinn snarled, his claws digging into flesh and drawing blood.

Max gripped the binding magic, but he didn't know what to do with it. If he tried to yank it out by force, he was sure it would cause damage. He wasn't patient or skilled enough to cut it out even if he knew how. The only thing he knew how to do was burn, and he shuddered at how painful that was sure to be. He remembered the mage trying to rip out his own bindings and the agony he'd felt through his entire being.

"Sorry," he said, before setting the bindings on fire. The mage screamed, and Max gagged at the stench of burning flesh. He closed his eyes and adjusted the magic, willing it to burn only the magic of the bindings and not the tattoo. It didn't help the screams or the smell.

The bindings twisted, trying to wriggle out of his grip and away from his flames like eels. "No you don't," Max snarled, gritting his teeth as he coaxed his flames as hot and bright as they would go. There was a bright flash of blue-white light before the bindings disintegrated, reduced to the magical equivalent of ash. As they vanished, so did the tattoo, leaving behind a small patch of blistered flesh.

The mage groaned and went limp beneath Quinn as if he'd passed out.

Quinn sniffed a few times before carefully easing off the man and smiling at Max. "Knew you could do it."

Max squirmed from the strange warmth wriggling in his gut and tossed Quinn's shirt in his face. "Get dressed."

Aradia chirped, clearly unimpressed by Quinn's nakedness, and crawled into her pouch.

With a laugh, Quinn pulled his clothes back on and popped his earpiece back into place. He tilted his head as he listened before looking at Max. "Sounds like they need me. You okay to go in?"

"No, but like hell I'm staying out here." Especially when he could hear sirens in the distance. He got to his feet with a groan, every nerve in his body protesting, and watched Quinn toss the mage over his shoulder in a fireman's carry like he weighed nothing. He ignored the way his stomach flipped with interest and followed Quinn inside.

The fire damage was most severe on the ground floor near the front and the side with the garage. Most of the walls and ceilings were black, but the stairs were intact, and the second floor seemed to be mostly smoke damage.

They found Caius and Lukas in the master bedroom, where Quinn dumped the unconscious mage unceremoniously onto the bed.

Caius grabbed Max with a growl and pulled him closer, tipping Max's head back before pressing gentle fingers to his tender throat. "What happened?"

"Order made him attack," Max said, clasping Caius' wrist. "I'll be fine." Not like it was anywhere close to the worst he'd ever suffered.

Caius didn't look convinced, but he turned his attention to Quinn. "Safe room. Control panel is in the closet."

Quinn's eyes lit up, and he cracked his knuckles on his way across the room.

When Max tried to pull away to enter the code, Caius growled and dragged him back. "I'm *fine*," he said with a huff, even as he tucked himself against Caius' chest. He called the code out to Quinn instead, only for it to fail.

Quinn wasn't bothered. He pulled out his phone and a short cord, hooked it up to the control panel, and started tapping away on his phone.

Lukas glowered at the mage on the bed and nudged the man's foot with his gun. "Stop pretending to be asleep."

Caius growled, tightening his grip on Max.

Max rolled his eyes and dug his elbow into Caius' stomach. "Don't hurt him. The Order was controlling him, but I broke the binding."

Lukas and Caius both stared at him, while Quinn cackled from the closet.

Max ignored them all as he looked at the mage, who was slowly sitting up with the look of someone expecting to be executed. "What do I have to do to make the Order back off?"

The man let out a humorless laugh. "Other than submit or die?" He rubbed his face with a shaky breath. "They'll be after us both now."

"Sorry," Max said, but the mage waved him off and pushed to his feet.

"I don't know if they'll give up or not, but no one has broken one of their bindings in a long time, so thanks for that." He glanced at the door, then at Caius. "They never tell us much of anything aside from handing out missions. Where to go, what we need to do. Shit like this, they use the bindings to make sure the job gets done. They're pissed at you, but you have enough clout with the military that they're wary. That's all I know. Are you going to torture me for more information, or can I leave?"

Caius was silent for a moment before sighing. "Do you have somewhere safe you can go?"

That was unexpected, judging by the look of surprise. "Not really. I'll figure something out, though."

Caius turned towards the door with a shouted, "Leon!"

A few moments later, Leon poked his head in, a few smudges of black soot on his face. "Yeah?"

"Can you keep him safe from retaliation from the Order?" Caius asked, motioning to the mage.

Leon's eyebrows went up, but he nodded. "Sure."

Max shrugged when the mage looked at him as if expecting an explanation. He didn't know Leon, but he seemed nice enough, and Caius trusted him. "That was nice of you," he said once they were gone.

"I'm hoping he'll be an ally if we need him later."

From the closet, Quinn let out a triumphant cry as the safe room door slid open, and Lukas reached inside to drag Max's father out.

Max pressed back into Caius, his fingers aching where they were digging into Caius' arm. He hardly noticed when Quinn stepped up beside him and wrapped an arm around him, too busy staring at where Lukas forced his father to his knees.

Quinn tugged, and Max followed without resistance as Quinn led him out of the room. "There a computer anywhere?"

It felt like forever before those words processed. When they did, Max nodded and headed down the hall to his room. He stopped outside the doorway, unable to stomach going in.

Quinn squeezed his shoulder before retrieving the laptop off the desk, then pulled Max back down the hall to an office.

Max flinched at the sharp retort of a gunshot followed by his sister's scream, his heart hammering in his chest. When Quinn pulled him down to sit on his lap, Max slumped into him without protest. Quinn's familiar, warm cinnamon scent soothed some of his nerves as he told himself his father wasn't worth the guilt trying to drag him under.

His father was dead.

Finally, he was free.

CHAPTER 24

CAIUS TURNED away from Savino's body and focused on the two women who had been in the safe room with him. One was Max's sister, Angelica, and the other looked like Rena Schurz. He was tempted to take them both out after hearing the part Max's own sister had played in his abduction, but before he could decide what to do, Ghost and her doll stepped into the room.

The older woman paled, her mouth going slack in shock. "No."

Ghost stepped forward with a giddy laugh. "Hello, Mother."

"Ana—"

Ghost snarled and snapped her fingers. The woman stopped speaking, her expression blanking like the doll's, and Ghost turned an interested look on Angelica. "Well, aren't you adorable. What are you doing with this one?" she asked, looking at Caius.

"Ask Max."

She made a face like that was the stupidest thing she'd ever heard. "No, I'm taking her."

The man Ghost had come in with dropped to the floor, dead, though there were no external signs of trauma or injury. Angelica's eyes went vacant, and Ghost turned for the door.

"Oh, if you have stock in Magierseele, I suggest you dump it," she said, leaving with her two new dolls following sedately behind her.

Caius tried to dredge up any remorse for letting her go without a fight, but all he found was exhaustion. He eyed Savino's cooling corpse and holstered his gun. He knew this wasn't completely over; Savino had been at the top of the food chain. As soon as word of his death got out, others would be clamoring for his place.

"So," Lukas said, "are you the new kingpin?"

Caius grimaced. "Don't even joke about that."

"No, but think about it. Most of your old pack wants you as their alpha, and we need a bigger pack if we're going to survive here after this. And we're notorious enough in the news that no one would be surprised if we took over."

Caius sighed and rubbed his eyes. He must be more exhausted than he thought, because that made more sense than he wanted it to. "I'll think about it," he muttered, just to make sure Lukas didn't try to come up with more reasons.

He headed out of the room and found Max and Quinn down the hall in an office, talking quietly as Quinn typed away on a computer. "What have you done now?"

Max looked up from Quinn's lap before standing. Then he elbowed Quinn, who spun his chair around, his legs crossed and fingers steepled beneath his chin like a cartoon villain.

Caius stifled a groan. "Do I even want to know?"

"Of course you do." Quinn waggled his eyebrows. "I transferred most of Savino's money over to Max's accounts, where I then sent it through one of my Swiss bank accounts and a few others, before spreading it out across all our pack accounts."

Caius tipped his head back and closed his eyes. "I served for over two decades, and now my pack is laundering money and taking over the underworld. What the fuck did I do to deserve this?"

"Wait, we're taking over the underworld?" Quinn asked with far too much excitement.

"Not like you can do worse than my father."

"Thank you for that ringing endorsement."

Max smiled, though it seemed forced, and slipped an arm around Caius' waist. "You'd make a very sexy mob boss."

"I hear that's the biggest qualifier to make a good one," Quinn offered with a sage nod.

"Fenrir help me," Caius breathed, pulling Max closer.

Lukas snorted and perched on the arm of Quinn's chair. "I don't think any god can help you now."

Caius ignored him in favor of burying his nose against Max's neck and breathing in his scent. He didn't like the thick, dark scent overpowering the usual citrus, but there was little to be done about that while standing in Max's old home. They would have to deal with the cops he could hear gathering on the streets before they could leave.

He straightened with a look at Lukas. "You and Quinn head back to the kids. Get them checked into some hotel rooms."

Lukas grimaced but nodded. "I need to check in with Adams too."

"Hold off on that," Caius said. If the official story was still that Lukas was MIA or dead, he didn't want that narrative to change just yet. News of them killing both Kostas and Savino would make it to the brass by morning, but they didn't need to show their entire hand.

He turned to Max as Lukas and Quinn slipped out, tempted to send him with them, but as the rogue mage causing havoc in the news, they needed to get their own story out there. There was sure to be plenty of press to talk to once they were done with the police. "Ready?"

Max made a face and blew out a breath. "Not really, but I've been dealing with nosy cops since I was a kid. This'll be easier than controlling my magic."

"We'll get you some proper training soon."

"Wouldn't mind Rían coming back."

"I doubt the Order will let him anywhere near us," Caius said, turning for the stairs.

Max slipped his fingers between Caius' as he followed. "Yeah, but he doesn't have long until he's free of them. Then he wants to open a magic tattoo parlor."

Caius glanced at Max from the corner of his eye, not sure he liked how completely in awe of Rían he sounded. Not that Caius could blame him. Rían did have one of the best reputations as a mage and could be charming as sin. But as willing as he was to share Max with Quinn and Lukas, anyone else was a step too far.

"And now you look like you want to murder him," Max said, stopping at the bottom of the stairs to look up at him.

He opened his mouth to deny it, but Max jabbed a finger into his chest before he could say anything.

"I like Rían. I don't want to sleep with him. Is that good enough?"

Caius let out a slow breath and nodded. Strangely enough, it was.

"Good," Max said, rubbing Aradia's head as she settled on his shoulder. "Let's get this over with so you can take me home. I want to sleep for a week."

CHAPTER 25

GETTING HALF a dozen teens taken care of and settled into hotel rooms took hours, especially when one of them kept disappearing. The kid's scent was a complicated jumble of grief, relief, anger, and fear, and Lukas had no idea what to do with him other than keep his senses open for danger. Thankfully, Eva seemed to realize her packmate needed someone and kept near to him.

By the time the adults started returning and he and Quinn could leave, it was late in the afternoon.

Lukas settled in the passenger seat in a borderline coma. He hadn't slept in two days. Or was it three now? Four? Everything that happened since Quinn was shot was a fuzzy haze, and he wished he could wake up to find most of it had been a PTSD-fueled nightmare.

They trudged into the house together, and Quinn caught his wrist when he started to peel away towards his own room. "Hey, hungry?"

Lukas' stomach woke up to inform them both that he hadn't eaten in almost the same time he hadn't slept. "Starving."

"Grilled cheese?"

He snorted. "Sure."

"You don't like my grilled cheese?"

"It's not really grilled cheese."

Quinn narrowed his eyes. "It's an *adult* grilled cheese."

He shook his head with a soft laugh. "Okay."

Quinn rolled his eyes and stretched on his way to the kitchen. "Go shower, you stink."

"Yessir," Lukas drawled, before shuffling into his room and tossing his clothes in the general direction of the hamper. He stood under the hot spray of water for several long minutes, fighting against falling asleep on his feet. He finally scraped together enough energy to wash up, letting out a soft, pleased sigh when he pulled on clean clothes after.

When he reached the kitchen, Quinn was finishing up at the stove, his hair damp and dripping down his bare back. Loose sweats hung low on his hips.

Lukas stopped at the island where a plate with a double grilled cheese was waiting, but he hardly noticed it. He was too busy staring at Quinn's ass and imagining following the path of water droplets with his tongue.

Quinn glanced over his shoulder, smile turning smug when he noticed Lukas' stare. "Like what you see?" he asked with a shimmy of his hips.

"Always," he murmured, far too tired for his filter to work properly. But the deepening twist of cinnamon in Quinn's pleased scent more than made up for his indiscretion. He forced his eyes off Quinn's ass and sat.

As soon as he took a bite, the entire world narrowed to the sandwich in his hands. He vaguely remembered Quinn sitting beside him, and then walking downstairs, but he was fading before he was even off his feet.

The next thing he knew, he was waking from a nightmare of being shot, mages hurling lightning at him like fucking Darth Sidious wannabes.

He rolled over and sat up with a groan, belatedly surprised he hadn't jammed his toe against his nightstand. Then his nose started working again and he breathed deep, sinking into Quinn's sweet-and-spice scent. "Sorry," he murmured, scrubbing his hands against his face.

Quinn pressed closer behind him but didn't touch. "Take your time," he said, sounding half-asleep. "Anything I can do?"

Lukas exhaled sharply and shook his head. This was usually the point he would call it quits on sleeping and go for a run, but a glance at the clock told him he'd only been out for three hours. That might have been enough a few days ago, but he didn't have the energy to get up, so he leaned into Quinn, letting him tuck them both back into bed.

Quinn hooked an arm and leg over Lukas and kissed his shoulder. "This okay?"

"Mmhmm." He wrapped his fingers around Quinn's wrist, burying his face in red hair as he drifted back to sleep.

He woke briefly when the front door opened and Caius and Max headed upstairs, immediately slipping under again when there was no sign of a threat.

His internal clock finally forced him out of bed late in the afternoon, and he hoped he'd only lost one day and not two. He stole Quinn's bathroom for a quick shower, rolling his eyes at the special shower heads with a dozen different pressure options. Then he found an oversized pair of Quinn's sweats that were borderline indecent on him and dragged himself upstairs.

He froze at the sight of Leon in the kitchen with Quinn. On the table were several plates of scrambled eggs, bacon, sausage, and pancakes that were all but demolished, like an army had already picked over everything.

"Morning, Sleeping Beauty," Quinn said with a grin, looking far too perky even if it wasn't morning.

Lukas grunted and sank into a chair at the island, letting his head thunk against the cool granite. A moment later, Quinn set dishes beside him. He lifted his head as he sucked in a lungful of the hot black coffee aroma. "Bless you," he muttered and drained half the cup. It didn't help him want to speak yet, but it helped with the wanting to stab people for being near him.

"Pack meeting as soon as you eat," Quinn said, moving to stand next to Lukas as Leon slipped out the back.

He caught the sound of teenagers yelling and pelting each other with snowballs before the door slid shut. He devoured the still-warm food Quinn had apparently saved for him, leaning into the fingers smoothing out his hair. "Thanks," he murmured as he finished, then drained the rest of his coffee and went for a refill.

He'd need another three cups before he was ready to deal with two dozen strange wolves, but he didn't get a chance for more than another sip before the door opened again.

Caius and Max led the procession. They both looked exhausted, but Max smiled as he moved towards Lukas and wrapped him up in a hug. "I never got to thank you," Max whispered. "And I'm glad you're not dead."

Lukas snorted and squeezed Max tight. "Me too."

Max kissed his cheek before pulling away, groping Quinn's ass on his way by before taking his spot at Caius' side again.

He couldn't deny they looked good together, and as they started the meeting, he could see how well they worked together now too. He wasn't sure what had changed to push Max out of the shell he'd been hiding in, but it was obvious Max was lighter. Like a weight had lifted off him.

Lukas expected the meeting to be a formality, letting them know Caius was taking over his old pack and they were moving to Wyoming. But apparently a lot of work had been done while he was sleeping. Not only were they not moving, but Caius was taking over the pack in name only.

Wyoming would become a branch pack, and Leon would assume leadership as an alpha who technically reported to Caius. They'd reevaluate in six months to see how well the change took and if it would survive with Leon assuming full control. Caius had Quinn set up a few accounts and transferred in money taken from Savino for Leon to use for the pack. Then they piled into their cars and headed back home, taking the mage Max had freed with them.

Lukas helped Quinn clean up the mess from breakfast as Caius and Max collapsed on the sofa. "So we're not taking in any new wolves?" he asked, scraping rubbery egg remnants into the trash.

Caius let out a long sigh. "No, not right now. I'd rather not uproot any of them. My family has held that territory for centuries."

"You sure you don't want to go back?" Max asked.

Caius lifted his head where he'd let it fall against the back of the couch and looked at Quinn and Lukas. "Both of you wanted to try to reestablish a pack presence here."

Lukas nodded, then shrugged. "I prefer being in a city over a big forest."

"Same," Quinn agreed. "We have plenty of space here. The lack of other shifters around is weird, but I prefer that over dozens of packs fighting over a fire hydrant," he added with a visible shudder.

"New York?" he guessed.

"Ugh. Yes. Absolute worst territory."

"Chicago is a nightmare too," Lukas said, before turning to Max. "What about you?"

Max looked at him in surprise. "Me?"

"You're pack too. Do you want to stay here after everything?"

"I don't mind staying, but...." He trailed off, staring across the room. "Christmas is next week. Can we get a tree soon?"

Quinn groaned. "Fuck. I haven't gotten any gifts."

"Me neither," Lukas said with a grimace. He'd never bought presents before, but he'd also never had a pack he truly belonged to before.

Max brightened. "We should go shopping."

Caius let out a long groan and rubbed his face. "Now?"

"No. I want more sleep," Max said, slumping against Caius. "Let's go in the morning."

"Oh, good, I have plans for tonight," Quinn said, dumping the last plate in the dishwasher.

Lukas raised an eyebrow at him. "You do?"

With a smirk, Quinn grabbed his hand and tugged him to the stairs. "Yeah, you."

He nearly tripped down the stairs, ignoring Max's laughter as he stumbled after Quinn. Nerves exploded in his gut as Quinn pulled him into the bedroom. He might have already crossed the threshold with the blowjobs, but he didn't have the excuse of a lost bet or Max as a buffer this time.

Quinn reached the bed and turned to him, tilting his head as he nudged Lukas to sit. "Is this…. Fuck, did you mean for that to be a one-time thing?"

Lukas snatched Quinn's hand when he started to let go. "No," he said firmly. "I definitely wanted this to be a long-term thing."

"Good." Quinn buried his free hand in Lukas' hair and tugged. "'Cause I really want to mark you."

"Yeah?" Lukas breathed, heat flooding him and going straight to his groin. "Please." A sharp groan escaped his throat when the fingers tightened in his hair and forced his head back, tingles of pleasure racing down his spine.

Quinn leaned in, brushing their lips together in a teasing touch. "Tell me what you like."

He shivered and pulled against the grip on his hair, trying to get a proper kiss. "I don't know. Never actually done this before." He blinked when Quinn pulled away, wondering what he'd said. Then his brain caught up with his mouth. Oh shit. He swallowed hard and sat back, bracing himself for judgment or mockery, but Quinn cupped his face with both hands.

"You've really never been with anyone before?"

"No. Never wanted to either, until I got to know you."

"I've been flirting with you for *years*."

Lukas felt his face get hot. "Really?"

Quinn groaned, but it ended on a laugh. "Fuck. I thought you hated me all this time."

"I never hated you." He grabbed Quinn's hips and pulled until he was standing between Lukas' legs. "Always just thought you were way too good for me."

Quinn shook his head, pressing his face into Lukas' hair. "Okay, then we're doing this right. What's your biggest fantasy?"

His face burned hotter as he nuzzled against Quinn's neck. "Being completely at your mercy."

"Fuck." Quinn straightened, stroking his thumbs against Lukas' cheeks before stepping back and going to the closet. He pulled a box out from the back and rummaged for a moment before standing with a pair of handcuffs with fuzzy purple padding. He spun them on a finger and held them up as if in offering. "Something like this?"

"That'll work," he managed to get out, gripping the sheets.

Quinn tilted his head, a grin slowly spreading on his face. "Can I blindfold you too?"

Lukas swallowed a strangled moan and nodded, his nerves returning with a vengeance as Quinn turned back to the box and pulled out a long strip of black cloth. "Do I want to know why you have those?"

"I don't know, do you?" Quinn raised an eyebrow and planted a hand on Lukas' chest, pushing him onto his back.

"Maybe later," he decided, pulling himself further on the bed and settling against the pillows. His breathing stuttered as Quinn fastened a handcuff on one wrist before threading it through one of the holes in the headboard. He obediently offered his other hand, heat flooding him as the handcuff clicked into place.

Quinn leaned over him, grasping both wrists with a grin and leaning down to brush their lips together. "Good boy," he purred.

Lukas shivered, tension melting out of him. His eyes slipped closed as Quinn pressed slow kisses against his lips, hands inching down Lukas' arms before delving his tongue inside. Too soon, he pulled away, lifting the blindfold and waiting for Lukas to nod before securing it around his eyes.

"Okay?"

Lukas licked his lips and forced out a slow breath. He flexed his fingers and wrists, tugging against the handcuffs before nodding.

Quinn hummed and dragged his fingertips down Lukas' chest, which was suddenly far more sensitive than it should have been.

His skin erupted in goose bumps, and he squirmed, dread and excitement both flaring in his chest when Quinn laughed.

"Oh, this'll be fun." His fingers continued their path down, hooking in the waistband of the borrowed sweats and tugging them off.

Warm hands pressed against his thighs, nudging them apart. The puff of hot breath was his only warning before Quinn took him into his mouth. He arched off the bed with a sharp gasp, the handcuffs rattling as he instinctively tried to reach for Quinn. To touch him or bury his hands in soft hair.

Whose bright idea was it to restrain him? Why did he think this would be fun?

A strong grip pinned his hips down when he tried to thrust, and he hissed in frustration. Then Quinn's mouth vanished. He opened his mouth to protest, but it died in his throat when teeth sank into his thigh hard enough to sting.

"Be good," Quinn ordered.

Lukas went limp like a light switch he hadn't even known existed had been flipped.

"Better." Quinn soothed a hand over Lukas' side, kissing across his stomach before making his way down again. This time he didn't take Lukas into his mouth, but pressed wet kisses up one side of his cock and down the other.

Lukas cursed under his breath, tossing his head back with a pleading moan. Quinn seemed intent on tormenting him, licking him from balls to tip, swirling his tongue around his head. Then repeating. Over and over, until he was sure he'd combust.

Then Quinn pulled away, sliding his hand from Lukas' thigh to his shoulder as he moved around the bed. A drawer opened and shut before the bed shifted as Quinn climbed up beside him. A bottle cap flicked open, then snapped shut a moment later.

He shuddered in anticipation, turning into Quinn's heat as much as possible when he pressed closer. He parted his lips and eagerly slid his tongue against Quinn's, sucking away the taste of himself. He braced his heels against the bed and groaned as slick fingers pushed into him. When they pressed deeper, he broke the kiss and dropped his head to the pillow.

Then they shifted and flexed and hit a spot that made sparks explode behind the blindfold, pleasure igniting his nerves.

"Fuck," he gasped, turning his head when he felt Quinn's smile against his shoulder.

Quinn leaned over him, nipping his lower lip as he flexed his fingers again.

That was apparently all that was needed for Lukas to beg. "Please. Quinn, please. Need you inside me."

"I know," Quinn murmured, pulling his hand away for more lube, then pressing another finger in. That one burned a little, but it wasn't unpleasant.

"I can take it."

"I know," he said again, somehow sounding completely unaffected.

"Fuck you," Lukas hissed, then yelped when Quinn pressed a warning thumb against his balls.

"Don't make me gag you."

Lukas swallowed the urge to dare Quinn to do exactly that. As willing as he was to explore those urges, he could only handle so many new things at a time.

Quinn waited a moment for a response, then hummed and returned to his task, driving Lukas insane as he worked his fingers in deeper while kissing Lukas' neck, teeth scraping against sensitive flesh in mockery of a claim.

Lukas shuddered with need, flexing his wrists against the handcuffs until he felt the cheap metal threaten to snap. "*Quinn.*"

"Fine, fine." Quinn pressed a quick kiss to Lukas' lips and pulled his fingers out. "So much for being completely at my mercy," he said with a soft laugh.

"You're a sadist."

"Only a little." The bed shifted as Quinn settled between Lukas' legs, his warmth a phantom presence as he leaned closer, before a hot, wet tongue slid from Lukas' navel up to his nipple.

Lukas arched beneath Quinn as hands groped his ass and lifted, hissing an eager "Yes" when Quinn finally pushed into him. He was bigger than Lukas remembered from when he'd had his mouth on him, but he wasn't complaining. As many times as he'd imagined this, none of them came close to being as good as the real thing.

He clamped his legs around Quinn's hips, digging heels into his ass to urge him on.

"Fuck, you feel so good." Quinn dragged his teeth against Lukas' neck again as he slammed his hips forward, finally giving him what he wanted.

"Fuck me like you mean it," he gasped. "Wanna feel it tomorrow."

"You're gonna feel it for days," Quinn growled, digging his fingers into Lukas' ass hard enough to bruise.

"Yeah? You think you can fuck me that good?" he taunted, a thrill going through him when hot breath rushed against his ear.

"Yeah, I do," Quinn murmured, before doing just that.

Lukas lost track of everything except the places Quinn touched him. The alternating feathery light kisses and sharp bites on his neck. The hands sliding up his back, down his sides, and back up his chest. The fingers pinching his nipples or pressing past his lips to stroke his tongue. The thick, hard cock driving into him over and over and over as his own cock was left aching and neglected.

"Quinn please," he gasped, on the verge of sobbing.

"Yeah," Quinn grunted, gripping Lukas' hair and pulling his head to the side.

"*Yes.*" Lukas eagerly bared his neck, the feel of Quinn's teeth sinking into his flesh everything he'd ever fantasized. His entire body clenched from the sharp pain and deep twist of magic as Quinn claimed him. The pleasure that followed was so intense that his vision went white and he came untouched, his muscles aching as he shuddered through the longest orgasm of his life.

"That was hot," Quinn murmured, tugging the blindfold off before fumbling with the release on the handcuffs.

Lukas grunted when his arms hit the bed, too dazed and focused on steadying his breathing to bother moving yet.

"Mark me," Quinn ordered.

It took a moment for his brain to register that. "Really?"

"You don't want to?"

"Of course I want to." Lukas slid his hands into Quinn's hair and tugged. "Didn't think you'd really want me to."

Quinn huffed and braced his hand next to Lukas' head before bumping their noses together. "Years, Lukas. Fucking *years*. Not letting you get away that easy. Now mark me."

"So bossy," he murmured, nuzzling his way down Quinn's neck and breathing in his scent, the sweetness of it muted with arousal. He twisted his fingers tighter in the soft hair and held Quinn steady as he bit down.

Quinn jerked against him with a strangled shout, his hips slamming forward to bury himself deep in Lukas' ass as he came.

Lukas slumped against the pillows again with a grunt of satisfaction and a breathless laugh when Quinn collapsed on top of him. He carded his fingers through Quinn's hair as they both fell silent, their breaths slowing into a matching rhythm.

Eventually, Quinn stirred, tilting his head to nuzzle and kiss at the mark he'd left. "Good?" he asked softly.

"Great. You?"

Quinn smiled. "Yeah, same." He sighed and shifted enough to pull out before grabbing the covers and settling in.

"We need to clean up."

"Don't give a shit," Quinn muttered, yawning and throwing an arm and a leg over Lukas. "We'll shower later."

Lukas wrinkled his nose, already itching for said shower, but he was too comfortable and worn out to move. Despite sleeping so long already, he yawned and closed his eyes. "What're you getting Max for Christmas?"

"Fuuuck, I have no idea."

"Yeah, me neither."

CHAPTER 26

SHOPPING FOUR days before Christmas was a special kind of chaos, and Max absolutely loved it. He focused on every aspect of the holiday he could with a deliberateness that was probably unhealthy. He knew he should have been more concerned with and upset about his father's death and sister's disappearance, and he was, but he wasn't going to let it ruin the first Christmas he'd ever been able to celebrate with people he cared for. Honestly, he figured Angelica was better off with Ghost, if only because she might murder a foster family.

The grief and mourning and guilt could have their moment later. There was too much to celebrate now.

Like the fact the news had already forgotten about the rogue mage and feral pack living in the city. The brutal murder of one of the most prominent businessmen had taken over briefly, also to be forgotten when an anonymous source provided details on said businessman's multiple crimes and the fact that he was the head of Denver's mob.

Apparently Max had a few admirers within the police force for his numerous attempts to escape his father, who were willing to help out. One of them had even dropped by with Max's motorcycle the day before. Now all the news could talk about was the scandal and decline of Magierseele.

Rena held a live press conference two days ago where she admitted to being Helga Fuchs. Thanks to decades of magical genetic experimentation, she'd turned back the clock on aging, assumed a new name, and pretended to be her own granddaughter. She admitted to killing thousands as a result of failed experiments in her quest to profit off of magical luxuries. She disappeared shortly after, and her company stock plummeted in the face of a federal investigation.

It was obvious Ghost still had Rena under some kind of control, but Max couldn't find any fucks to give about it.

He found it rather hard to give a fuck about absolutely anything with two large mugs of warm hard apple cider in his system.

He let his head loll to the side where he was propped up against Caius' chest, surveying the living room. He may have gone overboard with the tree. All he could think was that it was big and bright and sparkly. The green was hardly visible beneath all the tinsel and decorations, and it was starting to tip precariously to the side thanks to the large stuffed wolf they'd tied to the top in lieu of a star. But it was real and made the room smell like pine, which was worlds better than the fake pre-decorated tree his family had always used, and Aradia had spent the last hour climbing and leaping from the branches.

Between that, the fresh snow falling outside, the crackle of the logs in the fireplace, and the quiet music filtering from the speakers, Max couldn't have asked for a more perfect Christmas.

He wiggled against Caius' chest with a long hum, inhaling the cinnamony apple scent of his cider as he focused on Quinn and Lukas sprawled on the other end of the couch, mirroring him and Caius, their legs tangled in the middle. Quinn's thumb had slipped into Max's sock and absently rubbed his ankle, while Caius' hand had found its way under the layers of his sweater and the oversized hoodie Lukas and Quinn had gifted Max for Christmas. It had *sarcasm is my love language* written on the front, and Max had immediately fallen in love with it, pulling it on over his sweater despite the bulk.

"This is a very large and comfy couch," he said, draining the last of his cider. The mild burn was pleasant, nothing like the time he'd downed half of a bottle of tequila with some painkillers to ensure he blacked out for a while. He'd never been buzzed before. It was nice.

Except Lukas had both his hands curled against Quinn's wrist where it rested on his chest. Come to think of it, Lukas hadn't put a mark on him like Caius and Quinn. That! That was unacceptable. They'd all three put their blood tattoo bindings on him. He deserved a claiming mark from them all too!

"Hey," he said, more sharply than he meant to, but nothing to do about that now. He sat up and passed his empty mug behind him to Caius as he narrowed his eyes at Lukas, jabbing a toe against his thigh. "Why you no bite me?"

Lukas blinked at him, a touch of pink spreading across his cheeks. He licked his lips, glancing at Caius before focusing on Max again. "I wasn't sure you wanted me to."

"You're not as scary as you thought I were," Max replied, wrinkling his nose and wondering why that sounded wrong as he crawled forward. Didn't matter. He grumbled as he worked to get Quinn's legs out of the way, finally resorting to pinching him. He ignored the yelp and quiet cursing as he straddled Lukas' lap with a grin.

"You're lucky I like you," Quinn muttered.

Max stuck his tongue out and draped his arms over Lukas' shoulders, tweaking one of Quinn's nipples since it was within range and snickering when Quinn squeaked.

"Cap, get your mate under control!"

Caius snorted. "I don't want to be suffocated with a pillow in my sleep."

Max nodded like that was the most sage advice he'd ever heard. "Smart man."

"You're drunk," Lukas said, resting his hands on Max's waist.

"Noooo." He was not drunk. He'd hardly had anything to drink. His thinky was very clear. Two drinks was not enough to affect his thinky. "I can still cossent…. Constant. Co—you know what I mean!"

Lukas raised an eyebrow and didn't look convinced, which was as unacceptable as him not doing the biting and claiming thing.

Max rocked his hips forward with a soft growl. "You bit Quinn." He'd seen the marks on both their necks. He'd have to find a way to mark Caius. Maybe he could use the magic-blood-ink tattoo trick, but he could figure that out later. "Now bite me," he said, tilting his head to the side, baring the mark Quinn had left on him. That felt right. Quinn's and Lukas' marks should be next to each other.

Lukas flexed his fingers, gripping Max's hips tighter.

He watched in fascination as a soft glow lit Lukas' eyes and his face shifted. Not full-wolf, but enough for a few of his teeth to sharpen. He'd missed what this looked like since Quinn and Caius had both been fucking him from behind when they bit him. If he'd seen this the first time, he might have freaked out a bit, but he'd seen all of them as wolves now, and he knew none of them would intentionally hurt him.

Max dragged his thumb across Lukas' lip and the tip of his sharp canine, anticipation burning hotter than the cider in his gut. "Do it," he whispered.

A soft rumble of a growl vibrated in Lukas' chest as he gripped Max's hair and pulled him close.

His breaths stuttered as Lukas licked his neck and Quinn's mark. He tangled his hands in Lukas' hair at the first scrape of teeth on his flesh, a sharp cry tearing out of his throat when they pierced skin. The pain was more intense than he remembered, but this time he felt the initial twist of magic that coiled around the mark. A warm burst of sensation that seemed to whisper *home* and *belonging* and *family*.

The pain faded almost immediately, and he slumped into Lukas with a low groan. He nuzzled against Lukas' neck, trailing a line of slow kisses to his ear. He dragged his teeth against flesh and bit down over Quinn's mark on Lukas' neck, grinning when that earned a hiss.

"Unless you're going to put on a show, you need to get a room," Quinn said.

Max lifted his head with a curious hum. Putting on a show sounded fun. He opened his mouth to say exactly that, but Lukas beat him with a low, throaty growl and lurched to his feet. Max yelped and dissolved into tipsy giggles as he clung to Lukas like a monkey, waving to Quinn and Caius as he was carried off like a princess about to be ravaged.

Except he wasn't the one about to be ravaged. Oh no. He remembered all too well how Lukas melted between him and Quinn. How readily he submitted.

Max laughed as he hit the bed and bounced, squirming out of his hoodie and sweater when he was suddenly far too hot. He grumbled as he got tangled up in the bulky material and too large sleeves, flopping back to the bed in defeat when he couldn't escape the knitted death trap. "Help."

Lukas snickered, walking his fingers up Max's chest and making him squirm, before tugging the sweater away with a soft crackle of static in his hair.

"My hero." Max yanked Lukas forward with both hands in his shirt, grinning when Lukas caught himself before their faces smashed together. "Hi."

"You are so drunk," Lukas said with a soft laugh.

"Nope. Just happy." When was the last time he'd been able to say that? No worrying about that now. Life was sure to be worlds better without his family trying to kill him.

Max tugged at Lukas' shirt and managed far better at getting it off and tossing it across the room. "Pants. Off. Now." Lukas looked about to protest, so Max pressed a finger to his lips and leaned closer. "Good boys do as they're told."

Hot breath rushed against his skin, and even in the low light, Max saw the faint flush spreading across Lukas' cheeks. He pressed the advantage, dragging his nose across Lukas' cheek to his ear and flicking his tongue against the shell. "Are you a good boy?"

Lukas whimpered, parting his lips and licking Max's fingertip. "Yeah," he breathed.

Max hummed approval and nipped Lukas' ear. "Good. Then get naked." He flopped back on the bed with an expectant look.

There was only a moment of hesitation before Lukas stripped out of his own clothes. When Max lifted his hips, Lukas snorted and stripped the rest of Max's as well.

"Lube."

Lukas raised an eyebrow, but he leaned over Max to the nightstand. "When did you get so bossy? You're picking up Quinn's bad traits."

Max sucked in an exaggerated gasp. "I'm telling," he sang, plastering his hands against Lukas' chest. He bit his lip with a hum as he dragged his fingers over warm flesh, tracing the definition of muscles with a soft sigh of bliss.

Caius and Quinn were both in good shape, but it was obvious that Lukas still worked out regularly. Max might have been jealous, but he was allergic to exercise. He was just thankful for his genes and metabolism keeping him slim.

When Lukas planted a hand by Max's head and reached behind himself with the other, Max slid his hands to Lukas' hips, biting back a giggle.

"You're gonna be in sooo much trouble," he continued, dragging out the last syllable.

Lukas narrowed his eyes, but the twitch of his cock gave him away.

Max grinned. "He might even spank you," he said in a scandalized whisper.

"Fucking hell," Lukas laughed. "Do you talk to Caius like this?"

He looked up with wide eyes. "Of course not. I call him my pirate Daddy and beg him to plunder my booty," he said, cackling as Lukas toppled off him, clutching his sides and wheezing. Max snickered as he fished for the dropped lube and coated his fingers before rolling into Lukas and wiggling his hand between the wolf's legs.

Lukas was still gasping for air, but his laugh turned into a deep groan when Max pushed two fingers inside. He went pliant a moment later, his hands twisted in the covers as he pushed into the intrusion. "Yeah," he gasped.

Max bit his lip, transfixed by the sight of Lukas curled up beside him, eyes shut and lips parted on soft moans, dark hair sticking to his face. He was gorgeous. And he belonged to Max, just like Caius and Quinn.

Somehow these three shifters had found him and claimed him as theirs. Called him pack. Made him family. And they were his. He really needed to figure out a way to put his mark on them. Ooh, maybe Rían would help him tattoo them. He'd have to ask.

He pushed Lukas onto his back and crawled between his legs, fumbling the lube as he tried to get more to coat himself. He wasn't sure if it was the alcohol or pure desire, but he needed inside Lukas. Now.

Once he pressed inside, he couldn't stop. "Sorry," he gasped, clutching at Lukas' hips as he buried himself with a few quick thrusts.

Lukas arched beneath him with a sharp grunt, tearing the sheets with clawed fingers.

Max shivered and dropped his forehead to Lukas' chest, rocking his hips with short, shallow thrusts. "Feel so good." He rarely imagined how good it might feel on the other side; he was content being pinned and taken. But this was so much better than his imagination. Even better than jerking off.

He dragged his hands across Lukas' hips and stomach, smearing lube as he groped for the wolf's cock. Once he found it, he latched on and started stroking.

Lukas bucked beneath him with a shout, the glow of his eyes visible beneath his lashes. "Max."

"Yeah." He felt over-hot, like his flames were pressing up beneath his skin. He may not have found Rían's amulet, but practicing with the trainer every day ensured he no longer felt on the brink of turning everything to ash.

He bit and kissed his way across Lukas' chest until he found a nipple to sink his teeth into. Then he bit the other when Lukas thrashed beneath him with a throaty growl.

Tiny sparks flickered around his fingers as he continued stroking, and Lukas gasped, his eyes and mouth flying open with a look of shock, before his eyes rolled back and his body shuddered with his release.

Max groaned as Lukas tightened around him, giving a few last spastic thrusts before his orgasm slammed through him. He collapsed on top of the wolf with a breathless laugh, nuzzling against Quinn's mark on Lukas' neck.

"Fuck," Lukas groaned, his chest heaving. "You can fuck me whenever you want."

Max grinned and made himself comfortable, ignoring Lukas' protests of needing to shower as he let sleep claim him.

MAX STARTLED awake when his pillow abruptly vanished. He sat up in alarm, squinting at the unfamiliar shadows and swallowing against the faint threat of nausea. Then he heard a ragged breath and focused on Lukas on the other side of the bed.

"Wh's wrong?"

Lukas blew out a loud breath. "Nothing. Sorry I woke you."

Max crawled closer and settled on his knees behind Lukas. He knew better than to touch, thanks to Caius waking like this sometimes. "Should I get Quinn?" When Lukas didn't respond, he crawled to the edge of the bed and held his hand out. "Or we could go down to him together." He wiggled his fingers when Lukas remained silent.

Finally, chilled fingers gripped his own and he tugged Lukas to his feet, only realizing halfway down the hall that they were both naked. Oh well.

Bright moonlight reflected off the snow out back, illuminating the house with silver.

Max led the way to the stairs to Quinn's lair, the moonlight vanishing a few steps down. Thankfully, Quinn's several computers lit the room up enough he didn't stub his toes.

When they reached the bedroom, he knocked lightly on the door. "Quinn," he called.

Covers shifted as Quinn stirred. "Yeah?" he replied, his voice rough with sleep.

"We're coming in." Max tugged Lukas to the bed and nudged him in first, then stretched out on the other side as Lukas curled into Quinn. He closed his eyes with a yawn and a murmured, "He needs a spanking in the morning." He grinned and drifted back to sleep to the sound of Quinn's soft laugh.

WHEN MAX woke again, it was to the sharp sound of flesh slapping flesh. He rolled over with a groan, cracking his eyes open to see Lukas bent over Quinn's lap as Quinn spanked him.

He pushed himself up with a startled laugh, crawling on his knees to Quinn and draping himself against the shifter's back. "Knew he'd like that," he said, settling in to watch for a few moments before kissing Quinn's cheek and mussing Lukas' hair.

He hopped off the bed and into the bathroom for a quick shower, then headed upstairs with a towel wrapped around his waist. He stopped in Lukas' room long enough to grab his hoodie before heading to his own room for clean boxers and sweats. Then he found Caius in his office and slipped inside.

"No, of course not," Caius said into his phone, swiveling his chair towards Max with a tired smile.

They really needed to get away for a few days. Between the attacks from the Order and his father and struggling to control his magic, Max felt like he'd been on high alert for months. He made a note to find a way to block the Order from tracking them later and straddled Caius' lap with a sigh of content.

"I didn't forget. We can meet soon," Caius said.

Max tilted his head before leaning in to nuzzle Caius' neck, grinning when Caius tipped his head to the side with a soft groan. He dragged his tongue against the warm column of flesh before sinking his teeth into Caius' earlobe. He smothered his laugh into the wolf's shoulder when Caius jerked with a sharp hiss.

"I'm not," Caius said, voice tight, and Max heard the sound of laughter on the other end of the line. "You're dead to me," he continued, the laughter growing louder.

When Max lifted his head, Caius glared at him before sighing into the phone.

"Yes, fine, tomorrow. See you then."

"What's tomorrow?" Max asked, wrapping his arms around Caius' neck and threading his fingers through the salt-and-pepper hair.

Caius hesitated, settling his hands on Max's hips before answering. "My ex wants a double date."

It took a few moments for that to sink in. Max sat back enough to eye Caius. "With me?"

"I'm not dating anyone else," he replied dryly.

Max grinned. "We're dating?" He laughed when Caius narrowed his eyes with a growl, relishing the warm pulse of pleasure at hearing this wasn't just a fling between them. "Will I get to hear embarrassing stories about you?" he asked, and Caius' pained groan was more than enough reason to agree before attacking his neck again.

Caius leaned back in his chair with a throaty moan, his hands sliding down to grope Max's ass. "What's this about me plundering your booty?"

He collapsed into helpless laughter. "You weren't supposed to hear that!"

"No? Am I not allowed to plunder?" Caius groped Max's ass before lifting him as he stood.

Max yelped and latched on like an octopus. "You all like to carry me around way too much."

"Should we stop?"

"Don't you dare."

Caius laughed, a deep, throaty rumble in his chest.

Max marveled at the sound of it. At the fact that he'd caused it.

His life might still be teetering on the edge of a clusterfuck, but at least he had three shifters to call his own.

And he was a mage who could summon fireballs. What wasn't to love about that?

Keep reading for an exclusive excerpt from
If You Let Me
by Saria Bryant!

CHAPTER ONE

SPRING BREAKS had never been more than a week of Jasper locking himself in his room and keeping quiet. How enjoyable the week was always inversely correlated to the number of times he saw his father, which meant spring breaks were usually shit.

This year was different. Now that he'd moved in with his cousin Amber, her fiancé, and their three housemates, he no longer had to sneak around his own home to avoid verbal or physical blows. This year, Jasper intended to enjoy himself. Which was how he ended up standing inside a kink club on Saturday night.

He scrubbed his palms against his slacks—a bit too small, since they were borrowed from Matt, one of the housemates—for the fifth time since getting out of the car and looked around. The club was far classier than other clubs he'd been to, but then, none of them had catered to anything more than dancing and drinking. The bar was well-stocked with every kind of non-alcoholic drink imaginable, and there was a sitting area with posh leather sofas and dark-wood, live-edge coffee tables. Black-and-white photos were interspersed along the walls, but he was too far away to make out anything more than the shapes of bodies.

Amber and the others had already vanished into the play area, and while he was curious what it looked like, he wasn't ready to cross that threshold yet. Despite the fetish videos and his curiosity about being tied up, seeing all this up close and personal was something else entirely. Especially when Amber had invited him along only a few hours ago.

Instead, he went to the bar and ordered a soda, wishing he was a few months older and could have downed some liquid courage. Then again, Amber would probably kill him if he got drunk just to try something new with a stranger. He wasn't *that* stupid, thanks.

He took his drink to a comfy-looking armchair and settled in to people-watch, ignoring the little voice in his head piping up with a *You're stalling.* Maybe he'd get lucky enough to catch someone's eye while lingering in the sitting area. He sipped his drink with a soft snort. *Yeah, right.*

People weren't wearing as much leather as he'd expected. Most were in casual clothes, but there were a few who looked the part: leather pants, corsets, fishnet. He caught sight of a man wearing a collar with a leash attached. A shiny silver collar that glinted against his dark skin.

Jasper watched him as his partner led him into the dungeon, absently touching his own throat before slumping further into his chair. No way was he going to get anyone's attention sitting in the corner like this, but the thought of going in there alone made him feel like puking. He wasn't entirely sure if that was the excitement or the nerves, or both. With a sigh he pulled his phone out, finding a game to keep himself occupied until his cousin was done.

At least he'd gotten out of the house for a bit. He could even call it experiencing something new if he ignored the heat of self-loathing in his gut for getting all the way here and chickening out.

He'd only finished half his soda when someone sat in the chair next to him. From the corner of his eye, he caught what looked like an expensive suit. Someone way out of his league. Probably waiting on someone. Probably *straight*. Such a travesty.

"Seeking pain or pleasure?" a quiet voice asked, and it took Jasper a moment to realize Mr. Suit was talking to *him*.

Jasper looked up, choking on his soda and nearly shooting it out his nose. Dark hair, hazel eyes, and a face that belonged on a *Forbes* issue about the hottest entrepreneurs of the decade. "Uh, what?" he asked, pinching his stinging nose, his eyes watering. *Real smooth, dumbass.*

Mr. Suit raised an eyebrow, and Jasper kissed his chances of making a good impression goodbye. "Are you here to play?" he asked, glancing at the white band on Jasper's wrist. The band had a red line through the center that marked him as a guest, new to the scene, and "vanilla." Because Amber was a bitch.

Jasper sat up, nerves fluttering in his stomach. "Maybe? Are—" He cut himself off, looking Mr. Suit over again. Definitely out of his league. "Are you offering?"

"Depends." Mr. Suit tilted his head before offering his hand. "I'm Vincent."

"Jasper," he replied, shaking Vincent's hand. "And pleasure. Definitely pleasure."

Vincent smiled briefly and let go. "In that case, why don't we talk?" He stood before motioning to a set of doors near the bar.

"Sure," Jasper said, hating how he was suddenly breathless. No way was he this lucky. "Holy shit, he's hot," he whispered as he stood and followed Vincent into another lounge, this one empty aside from chairs and tables.

This was fine. Have a talk with the gorgeous guy who hopefully wanted to play with him.

He totally had this.

CHAPTER TWO

VINCENT MOTIONED to a chair at one of the smaller tables before sitting across from Jasper. Once they were settled, he sat back and crossed his legs. "What kind of pleasure are you looking for?"

Jasper wrapped both hands around his glass, looking like he was trying hard not to fidget. "What do you mean?"

Well, that partly answered the question of how new to the scene Jasper was. The white band had caught his eye on his way out, and the way Jasper had been absorbed in his phone was not an image he liked to see in his club. He wasn't sure who'd brought Jasper in—few of the members even had guest access—but maybe he should rescind that completely if this was the result. He didn't mind members bringing in their friends, but abandoning them was a dick move.

"Some people enjoy being tickled," Vincent said. "Or having hot wax dripped over their bodies. Others are more interested in sexual release." He tilted his head when Jasper shifted in his chair. "What is it that brought you to my club rather than a seedy strip joint?"

Jasper cleared his throat. "I-I kinda want to know what being tied up is like."

"Kinda? Is that a 'I like thinking about it, but don't really want to experience it' kinda, or a 'please tie me up and torment me' kinda?" Vincent asked, holding back a chuckle when Jasper squirmed.

"I've never done any of this before." Jasper glanced up, his blue eyes bright in the low light. "But I want to. I'd like to try. With you."

Vincent couldn't exactly say no in the face of that eagerness. Especially since he didn't like the idea of someone so inexperienced getting in over their head. He did everything he could to keep his club a safe space, though there were more than a few hard players among the members.

"All right." He clasped his hands in his lap, tapping his thumbs together. "Do you have a safeword?" he asked. When Jasper shook his head, he continued, "Are you familiar with the stoplight system?"

"Yes.... Sir."

smiled. "Good," he said, glad when Jasper smiled back and finally seemed to relax. "So tell me how you'd like tonight to go."

"Besides being tied up?"

"Once you're tied up. Do you want to be naked? Touched, kissed, fingered?"

Jasper licked his lips. "Y-yeah. All that."

"Anywhere you don't want to be touched? Anything you don't want done?"

"Tickled."

Vincent chuckled. "No tickling. How about aftercare?"

Jasper shrugged. "I don't think I really need it?"

"Is that a question?"

"No. I think I'm good without it." He glanced towards the door with a grimace. "Do we have to use the dungeon?"

Vincent followed Jasper's gaze as he considered. The rooms upstairs were for select members, and there were no rules about guests not being allowed, though maybe that had been an oversight. Not that he had any reason not to trust those he'd screened, but then, few as green as Jasper ever made it to his club. At least not alone. "No," he said. "If you'd prefer a private room, we can go upstairs."

"Yeah." Jasper drained the last of his soda. "That sounds good."

"This way, then."

Vincent stopped by the security room on the second floor, ignoring the look of surprise from Ian, one of tonight's security guards. Vincent had said he was going home an hour ago, and technically this was supposed to have been his day off to begin with. "I'll be in room two."

Ian saluted and didn't bother to hide his grin when he caught sight of Jasper. "Yessirrr," he drawled.

Vincent stifled a sigh and counted himself lucky that Ian didn't wink. He turned and continued down the hall.

Room two was one of their tamer rooms by far. There was a bed near the far corner, a sofa, a low table long and wide enough to tie someone down, and a large wingback chair with a cushion in front of it. Next to the bed was a small chest with basic necessities and toys, and a mini fridge stocked with water. A door in the adjacent corner led to a bathroom.

Vincent closed the door behind Jasper before shrugging out of his jacket. He draped it over the end of the bed before turning. "So. Just so we're clear, you'll be tied up. Naked. I can touch you, kiss you, and finger you. No tickling. And at the end, you'd prefer to get off, yes or no?"

"Yes. Definitely yes." Jasper let out an unsteady breath where he still lingered by the door. He took a step forward and stopped. "What is it you want in return?"

Vincent raised an eyebrow. "Tonight is about you. I'll show you a good time and hopefully bring your fantasy to life."

"That's it?"

"Were you expecting me to only do this if you gave me a blowjob?" he asked, frowning when Jasper shrugged. "That's not how this works, Jasper. I'll only do what you've given me permission to do, and if you decide you don't like it, just give me the word. No sex or sexual favors in return. Understood?"

When Jasper nodded, Vincent turned the chair and sat facing him. "Let's get started, then. When you're ready, strip."

CHAPTER THREE

JASPER FLEXED his fingers and stared as Vincent sat and looked at him. "Strip," he repeated.

Vincent really expected him to strip in front of a stranger. Just like that. Even if he'd agreed to it, he'd expected *something* before taking his clothes off. Like making out, maybe. Or at least being naked *together*. Not to be watched like he was a stripper, though that could be kinda hot too.

"You do know how to undress yourself, don't you?" Vincent asked, sounding amused.

Jasper glared, a brief flare of indignation stamping out his nerves. "Fucker," he grumbled, swallowing hard when Vincent raised an eyebrow. That might have been all he did, but somehow that conveyed a warning all on its own.

He cleared his throat, toeing off his shoes and socks before stepping closer to the chair. He was hyperaware of Vincent's eyes on him as he toyed with the bottom button of his shirt.

"Changing your mind?"

Jasper took a breath and shook his head. "No."

"No, what?"

"No, Sir."

"Good boy," Vincent purred, and *damn* if that didn't do pleasant things to Jasper's stomach. "When you're ready, then."

Jasper resisted the urge to roll his eyes and shrugged his shirt off, tossing it in Vincent's face before kicking his pants aside. His boxers followed his shirt, and he smirked as Vincent dropped them to the floor with narrowed eyes.

Now that he'd committed to this, he sure as hell was going to have fun. It was either that or let the nerves paralyze him.

He let out a slow breath as he was left standing there. Naked. While Vincent sat and looked at him.

He refused to fidget. This was some kind of test, he knew. He'd been around his cousin and housemates long enough to at least know that much. He may not understand all the finer subtleties of the whole kink thing, but hopefully he knew enough not to make a fool of himself.

Vincent finally let out a soft hum that sounded like approval and stood. He moved across the room to the chest and pulled out a long strip of black silk. "Hands behind your back."

Jasper clasped his hands behind him. He glanced back as Vincent adjusted his arms until they were bent at the elbows, his hands clasping his forearms instead. The feel of the cloth winding around his arms set off a spike of panic in his chest, but he breathed through it. When Vincent finished, Jasper found he couldn't budge his arms an inch, and the panic intensified enough that he squeezed his eyes shut.

Shit. This was such a bad idea. He didn't even know this guy!

Vincent gripped Jasper's biceps and pulled until Vincent was pressed flush against Jasper's back. "If you say Red, I untie you, you get dressed and can go back downstairs," he murmured into Jasper's ear. "Understand?"

Jasper licked his lips and forced in a deep breath. And then another. He could do this. He could get free whenever he wanted, right? That was how this was supposed to work, at least according to Amber. "Yes," he whispered.

"Good. Then give me a color."

Jasper swallowed, surprised when Vincent didn't move at all until he said "Green." He shivered as Vincent hummed again and finally moved his hands, sliding them down Jasper's arms and over his chest.

That felt nice. For some reason, he'd expected a rougher touch. To be manhandled and pushed around, and he couldn't stop the hitch in his breath when Vincent merely skimmed his palms over Jasper's skin.

"You said you didn't want pain," Vincent said. "Does that mean you don't like things rough either?"

"I don't mind," Jasper murmured, cracking his eyes open to watch Vincent's hands. "I just don't see how pain can be pleasurable."

Vincent chuckled. "I see." He moved a hand up to Jasper's nipple, circling a finger around it. "Maybe I'll show you sometime," he said, rubbing the nipple between his fingers before squeezing.

Jasper bit back a groan as his head dropped to Vincent's shoulder, sure he'd fall over if Vincent weren't standing there. Why was it so hard to keep his balance with his arms trapped behind him? "You assume there'll be a next time." He tried to sound taunting, but the words came out breathless.

"Not enjoying this?" Before Jasper could think of a smartass response, Vincent found both his nipples and tugged.

Jasper whimpered, his knees threatening to give out on him. The low, rich sound of Vincent's laugh in his ear didn't help in the least. "Fucker," he moaned.

Vincent *tsk*ed and pulled his hands away. He tangled his fingers in Jasper's hair instead and gave a sharp tug. "You have a strange way of showing your appreciation. Don't tell me you don't know at least basic etiquette."

Jasper shivered, surprised at the intensity of the arousal that shot through him and pooled in his gut from the tug. "Yes," he said, moaning at the pointed jerk Vincent gave his hair. "Yes, Sir."

"Good boy," Vincent said, releasing him. He dragged blunt nails down Jasper's back and stepped around him, glancing down with a smirk. "You sure look like you're enjoying yourself."

"Fuck you, Sir," Jasper replied lightly, because he could.

Vincent snorted and looked up, grasped Jasper's chin, and tipped his head back. "I should have known you'd need a gag," he said, pressing two fingers past Jasper's lips. "For now this will do."

Jasper's eyes widened, and he let out a muffled curse around Vincent's fingers. What the hell? He tried to pull away, but Vincent held his chin in a firm grip, moving his fingers in and out in quick thrusts. When he finally pulled them away, they were slick with saliva. Jasper hardly had time to tell Vincent off for putting his *fingers* in Jasper's *mouth* before those same fingers were rubbing against his entrance.

"Oh fuck," he gasped. He arched into Vincent with a strangled whimper as a single finger pressed into him.

"I would have enjoyed playing with you more, but you obviously have no desire for foreplay," Vincent said, as if he were commenting on the weather. "I might have even sucked you off, but if all you want is a quickie, I'll give you what you want."

Jasper squirmed as Vincent nudged his finger deeper, his hips jerking forward at the thought of Vincent's mouth on him. No way would

Vincent really do that. Would he? "No. Wait," he groaned, trying to get away from the finger and only managing to rub against Vincent. "Please."

Vincent stilled with a soft hum. "Please what?"

Jasper squirmed as embarrassment crawled through his veins, dropping his forehead to Vincent's shoulder. Bastard. Of course he was the perfect few inches taller. "Please.... Foreplay."

Vincent hummed again as if considering it before pulling his hand away. "I don't think you've earned it."

Jasper swallowed, a strange warmth spreading through him. He wanted Vincent to tell him he'd earned it. He wanted—he very much wanted to earn it.

He turned his head, carefully nuzzling against Vincent's neck. "How can I?" he asked, momentarily distracted by how good Vincent smelled. Sandalwood and citrus. "Sir."

Vincent's fingers slid into Jasper's hair and tugged. Not hard, disappointingly, but tight enough that Jasper swallowed a groan. Intense hazel eyes studied him for a moment before Vincent loosened his grip. "Ask nicely for what you want."

Heat crept into Jasper's face as he imagined all the things he could ask for. He never thought he'd ever be in this kind of situation in real life. Standing in a private room in a fetish club. With an actual Dom. If there was anyone on the planet he could actually ask to indulge any of his fantasies—

But he was already tied up. Kinda. He wasn't sure he could handle adding blindfolds or gags tonight.

His attention flicked to Vincent's lips before he tipped his head back. "Will you kiss me?"

"With pleasure." Vincent's fingers caught Jasper's chin, holding him steady as he closed the distance between them.

And *fuck*, Vincent could kiss. He kissed Jasper with intention. Like kissing was his sole purpose of existence. Maybe it was all part of being a Dom, but Jasper could get used to it *far* too easily. No one had ever kissed him like it was a luxury rather than a means to an end. By the time Vincent's lips ghosted across Jasper's jaw and moved to his neck, his apprehension at being bound and helpless faded. Forming in its place was something else he was all too familiar with.

Infatuation.

at the ceiling and fought the sudden urge to laugh. _wrong_ with him? He'd sworn off anything close to relationships after the last one ended in a dumpster fire. Like hell he was going to even _think_ about getting involved with Vincent. As if it were even possible. This was a one-time deal. A bit of fun before the next semester started.

"Planning on kissing me all night?" he asked, his voice hitching as Vincent's teeth grazed his neck. "Thought you were going to make my fantasy come to life?" Taunting the guy who had him tied up was probably a worse idea than letting a stranger tie him up in the first place, but at least it helped him keep his feet under him, instead of throwing himself at said stranger like a dumbass.

Vincent chuckled and lifted his head from Jasper's neck. "Your mouth ever get you into trouble?"

Jasper grinned, his smartass response cut off by Vincent claiming his lips again. At least Vincent seemed to have a good sense of humor. And _gods_, he was such a good kisser. To the point that Jasper chased after Vincent when he pulled away.

"In the chair," Vincent said, his voice a bit rougher.

Goose bumps broke out on Jasper's arms; Vincent sounded as wrecked as Jasper felt. He barely even considered protesting before moving to the chair to sit.

Vincent stood in front of him and let out a slow breath. "Good boy."

Jasper shivered at the warmth that traveled through him from the praise. He looked up as Vincent touched his cheek and leaned into his palm, still surprised by the gentle touches.

Vincent's fingertips pushed against Jasper's chest, guiding him back against the chair before tracing his thumb along Jasper's lower lip. "Relax," he said. He hooked a hand under Jasper's knee, lifting it up and over the arm of the chair before leaning down.

Jasper squirmed at the awkward position, his eyes widening as he felt Vincent secure something around his leg, just above his knee. He let out a strangled sound as he tried to pull his knees back together, only to have his leg kept in place by the restraint.

"Shh," Vincent soothed, running his fingers through Jasper's hair. "I thought you wanted foreplay?" He pinched Jasper's nipple before securing his other leg to the opposite arm.

Jasper whimpered as Vincent stepped back, feeling Vincent's intense gaze move over every inch of him. He was utterly exposed and helpless and… fuck. He liked it. Something not quite panic and more intense than excitement coursed through him, settling in his gut. Whatever it was, he relaxed into it as easily as a warm bath.

It was liberating. This…. This was what he'd been wanting without really knowing how to get it.

Vincent ran his fingers through Jasper's hair again with an approving hum. "That's it. Now the real fun can start."

Jasper shivered and had a momentary thought that maybe he should be worried before deciding to hell with it.

He had a safeword for a reason.

CHAPTER FOUR

VINCENT RETURNED to the chest for lube and a condom, eyeing the numerous clamps and gags. The clamps were tempting, but he decided not to risk overwhelming Jasper his first time in a scene.

He closed the chest, grabbed a latex-free glove from the wall dispenser, and deposited everything on the table. Then he stepped behind Jasper's chair and tipped it back, biting back a laugh as Jasper gave an undignified yelp. He gripped both sides of the chair and dragged it towards the table and sofa, turning it before setting it on all fours again.

He sat on the edge of the table, raising an eyebrow at Jasper's glare. "Problem, brat?"

Jasper raised an eyebrow in return before rolling his eyes and shifting against his restraints. "No," he replied. "Sir."

"Good." Vincent pulled the glove on and popped the lube open before coating his fingers, aware of Jasper's eager stare. He tilted his head, waiting to see if he had anything to say. When Jasper remained silent, Vincent leaned forward, braced his ungloved hand on the chair, and sealed his lips around Jasper's nipple without preamble.

Jasper arched with a groan. It turned into a hissed curse when Vincent bit into the sensitive flesh, and he regretted not grabbing the clamps.

Vincent hummed, tugging at the nipple with his teeth and rubbing his fingers against Jasper's entrance at the same time.

The sound Jasper made was somewhere between a whimper and a sob, and he alternated between fighting against his restraints and slumping in defeat.

Vincent moved his lips to the other nipple, circling it with his tongue until it hardened. When he sucked it into his mouth, he pressed a finger into Jasper, enjoying the drawn-out groan as it rumbled through his chest. He sank his teeth into Jasper's nipple again, hard enough to make Jasper's entire body jerk, before letting go and sitting back.

Vincent moved his hand from the chair to Jasper's thigh, taking in the sight of him—flushed, exposed, and panting. "How's it feel?" he asked, pushing his finger in until his knuckles settled against Jasper's ass.

Jasper struggled against the restraints again before looking away. "Get on with it," he murmured, his ears pink.

Vincent *tsk*ed and curled his finger a bit. "That wasn't an answer."

Jasper whined and managed a weak glare, though it looked more like he was trying to cover a pout. "Would feel better if you got on with it."

"I know it would." Vincent pulled his finger out and absently fondled Jasper's balls instead. "But I can do this all night without breaking a sweat. Keep being a brat and I will."

Jasper grumbled something that sounded like "Fucker" as he looked away again. He licked his lips and let out a slow breath. "Feels good."

Vincent hummed in approval. He added more lube and a second finger when he pressed in again. "How long's it been since you were taken care of?" he asked. Surely Jasper had a boyfriend or girlfriend somewhere. He'd been almost infuriatingly responsive so far. In the way that made Vincent want to seek out every single one of Jasper's buttons and push them until he begged for mercy.

"None of your business," Jasper said through clenched teeth. "Sir." He looked like he was trying hard to keep quiet.

"Fair enough," Vincent replied, flexing his fingers.

Jasper turned his head with a soft whimper, trying and failing to hide his face against the chair.

Vincent contented himself with working his fingers into Jasper. Stretching him. Avoiding his prostate and the pleasure it would bring. With his other hand, he explored Jasper's body, sliding over a straining thigh and the taut muscles of his stomach.

He brushed his palm over the swollen, leaking head of Jasper's arousal, just enough to draw a shuddering gasp out of Jasper before moving away. Up his chest. Curling lightly around his throat and feeling the quick pulse beneath.

"Are you enjoying this?" he asked, tracing his thumb over Jasper's lip.

"You call this foreplay?" Jasper asked, his voice coming out remarkably steady, considering. "Sir?"

Vincent snorted softly at the pointed delays in the "Sirs." Jasper's future Dom was going to have their hands full breaking him in. "You're tied up, naked, and completely at my mercy. What would you call it?" he asked. "Pet?"

He noticed Jasper's expression shift, but didn't give the brat time to figure out if he liked the pet name or not. He pressed his fingers deeper, finding the spot he'd been avoiding.

The response was instant and glorious: Jasper's eyes widened as his body arched as much as the restraints allowed, his mouth open on a gasp that didn't quite escape his throat.

Vincent hummed, ignoring the way his pants felt tighter. He drew his fingers out, let Jasper take a single, shuddering breath, then pushed them back in to hit the same spot.

This time Jasper choked on a groan, shifting his hips to try and drive Vincent's fingers in deeper. His eyes squeezed shut as Vincent continued moving his fingers. Drawing out slowly, then shoving back in with a quick thrust, ensuring he pressed nice and hard, and repeating.

Over. And over. And over.

Vincent didn't stop until Jasper let out a choked sob, tears of frustration in the corners of his eyes.

"Please," Jasper gasped.

Vincent let his fingers go still inside Jasper. "Please what, pet?" he asked, cupping Jasper's cheek with his other hand. He pressed his thumb against Jasper's lower lip, swollen from where Jasper had bitten down on it.

"Please let me."

"Let you what?" Vincent asked. "I'm not stopping you from doing anything." He raked his eyes over Jasper, thoroughly enjoying the sight: a warm, healthy flush in his limbs, neglected erection hard and steadily leaking, precum smeared against his stomach.

Jasper whimpered again, breaths hot and quick against Vincent's thumb. "You can fuck me. Please, just—"

Vincent pressed his thumb against Jasper's lips to stop him. "I didn't ask to fuck you, so that's off the table," he said firmly. Christ, this brat was worse than any overeager sub he'd ever met. He refused to think how much trouble Jasper could end up in by playing with the wrong people.

He pulled both his hands away from Jasper and sat back, ignoring the frustrated whimper. "Now that you're sufficiently aroused," he said dryly, chuckling at the lovely flush that spread across Jasper's nose, "why don't you tell me what you want? And I suggest you be specific."

Jasper remained silent for a moment, finally licking his lips and glancing up at Vincent. "You said you would suck me off."

Vincent raised an eyebrow, keeping his expression neutral. "Did I?"

Jasper pressed his lips together with a frown. "You said you might."

"I did say that," Vincent agreed, enjoying the way Jasper squirmed when the silence stretched between them.

"Will you?"

"Will I what?"

"You know what," Jasper snapped.

"Do I?" Vincent couldn't help but rile Jasper up, especially since he was such a brat. He was quite a sight when flustered and aroused. And completely helpless to do anything about it.

SCAN THE QR CODE
BELOW TO PREORDER!

SARIA BRYANT has been an avid reader since childhood and a fan fiction writer since middle school. They enjoy traveling and exploring, and learning about other cultures and languages.

They are constantly dreaming up new ways to torment their characters, playing servant to their cat, or feeding a caffeine addiction.

Their favorite stories are M/M/+ relationships with a healthy dose of angst and drama with a HEA. When not reading or writing, they can usually be found watching anime or playing video games.

Saria can be found on Twitter / Instagram / Tumblr @sariabryant.

Follow me on BookBub

SHADOW'S WOUND

ELEMENTAL THRONES
BOOK 1

SARIA BRYANT

Elemental Thrones: Book One

With the realm teetering on the brink of magical annihilation, Callith Ratearynn, the reluctant heir to the Sun Throne, is thrust into power centuries too soon. With his father dead and corruption tearing the kingdom apart at the seams, Cal must battle rising racial tensions and unravel a dark conspiracy. Justice, a manipulative human official, has stirred hatred between humans and the magical community, using enslavement collars and control over the Black Sun—an elite group of soldiers loyal to the Shadow Throne.

Just as civil war seems inevitable, Cal's Fate string—a magical bond tying him to his soulmate—leads him to a grim prison where he finds Haru, his bonded, broken and tortured. But Fate has more in store. Cal discovers he is bound not to one, but two: Rashi, a fox shifter, and Haru, a fierce dragon warrior. Together, this reluctant triad must face cult attacks, dark rituals, and the creeping Wound, a void threatening to consume their realm.

Cal's new reality is one of impossible choices—between duty and heart, loyalty and passion. As war looms, the only hope lies in Cal's ability to trust in his newfound soulmates and uncover the depths of the corruption before it's too late.

SCAN THE QR CODE
BELOW TO ORDER!

Oathsworn

Can love set a
mage free?

Sebastian Black

CharmD
Saga

CharmD Saga: Book One

Former chef Jasper Wight has been magically ensnared in his apartment for over three months. Cabin fever doesn't begin to cover it. All he can do to pass the time is indulge in his hobby—painting portraits of his neighbors. But once a handsome new man moves into a swanky nearby penthouse, Jasper is no longer content merely to watch. Following his gut, he reaches out through astral projection....

Finn Anderson is the CEO of a food app funded by his parents, but he struggles to believe in the dream. When a mysterious someone starts leaving messages on his mirror, he learns the world holds more possibilities than he ever imagined.

When a chance encounter brings Finn to Jasper's door, the pair are soon as enamored with each other as Finn is of the magic he's just discovering. But navigating a relationship that spans two worlds is only the tip of the iceberg. They still have to figure out how to free Jasper from his apartment, how to make Finn's business into a success, and whether an outsider can be trusted with the secrets of the magical world.

SCAN THE QR CODE
BELOW TO ORDER!

DREAMSPUN
BEYOND

KISSING
FROGS

Terry Wylis

All he needs is a kiss.
And to escape that damn vacuum.

Modern-day American "prince" Ellis Faraday has a problem: he's been a frog for a year, his time before hibernation is ending, and he's afraid there will be nothing left of him come spring. The castle-house up the hill seems like a promising place to start looking for a cure… if he can convince a human to take him seriously. A conversation—and maybe a kiss—with the pretty man who owns the koi pond might do the trick.

On a Friday night, Galen Townsend just wants to curl up and read in the backyard of the house he shares with his brothers, but the frog addressing him from the wall of the koi pond has him questioning his sanity. Moreso when he gives the frog a peck on the nose—just to be nice—and the frog becomes a handsome, precious man.

Unfortunately, Galen's "cure" proves temporary. After a few hours, Ellis is back to hopping and croaking, but at least he has an ally and a warm place to stay. Now they just have to keep Galen's brothers from discovering a frog in the house while they work out how to break the spell. How many kisses can it possibly take?

SCAN THE QR CODE
BELOW TO ORDER!

AMY LANE

Sometimes the
best magic is just
a little luck...

THE RISING TIDE

THE LUCK MECHANICS 🐎 BOOK ONE

The tidal archipelago of Spinner's Drift is a refuge for misfits. Can the island's magic help a pie-in-the-sky dreamer and a wounded soul find a home in each other?

In a flash of light and a clap of thunder, Scout Quintero is banished from his home. Once he's sneaked his sister out too, he's happy, but their power-hungry father is after them, and they need a place to lie low. The thriving resort business on Spinner's Drift provides the perfect way to blend in.

They aren't the only ones who think so.

Six months ago Lucky left his life behind and went on the run from mobsters. Spinner's Drift brings solace to his battered soul, but one look at Scout and he's suddenly terrified of having one more thing to lose.

Lucky tries to keep his distance, but Scout is charming, and the island isn't that big. When they finally connect, all kinds of things come to light, including supernatural mysteries that have been buried for years. But while Scout and Lucky grow closer working on the secret, pissed-off mobsters, supernatural entities, and Scout's father are getting closer to them. Can they hold tight to each other and weather the rising tide together?

SCAN THE QR CODE
BELOW TO ORDER!

A GROWL, A ROAR, AND A PURR

K.C. WELLS

Lions & Tigers & Bears: Book One

In the human world, shifters are a myth.

In the shifter world, mates are a myth too. So how can tiger shifter Dellan Carson have two of them?

Dellan has been trapped in his shifted form for so long, he's almost forgotten how it feels to walk on two legs. Then photojournalist Rael Parton comes to interview the big-pharma CEO who holds Dellan captive in a glass-fronted cage in his office, and Dellan's world is rocked to its core.

When lion shifter Rael finds his newfound mate locked in shifted form, he's shocked but determined to free him from his prison... and that means he needs help.

Enter ex-military consultant and bear shifter Horvan Kojik. Horvan is the perfect guy to rescue Dellan. But mates? He's never imagined settling down with one guy, let alone two.

Rescuing Dellan and helping him to regain his humanity is only the start. The three lovers have dark secrets to uncover and even darker forces to overcome....

SCAN THE QR CODE
BELOW TO ORDER!